Introduction

After the Harvest by Lynn A. Coleman

Handsome and well built, Rylan Gaines turns Judith Timmons's head, but the man's carrying a pack of frustration on his back. Rylan, smarting from his fiancée's rejection, has a farmstead he's invested three long, hard years into and an empty house. Judith's berry tea quenches his thirst at the county fair but also stirs up another hunger. Judith wants to return to the civilized East, but will Rylan make an offer she can't refuse?

A Test of Faith by Freda Chrisman

Before the Prairie County Fair of 1905, Anita Gaines's life is redefined when her father, a widower, marries a new wife with a sixteen-year-old daughter. That her new relatives are not saved causes further anguish. Anita is flattered when the town's most eligible bachelor, Dr. Clifford West, a Christian, is attracted to her. Will Anita trust God to guide her in matters of the heart and home?

Goodie Goodie by Tamela Hancock Murray

Willa Johnston meets Garrison Gaines when the caterer judges the 1946 county fair cookoff. Willa thinks he is a dreamboat and is thrilled by the offer to become his business assistant. But when Willa's old flame, Dirk, appears at her catering debut, her worst nightmares materialize as her dessert flops and Dirk's wife causes a scene. Will the disaster cause Willa to lose Garrison—and true love?

A Change of Heart by Christine Lynxwiler

Since his wife's relentless ambition caused her death two and a half years ago, Zachary Gaines has refused to relinquish control of his family to anyone, even God. For the sake of his children, he's determined not to become involved with another career-driven woman. But, when his secret high school crush, Beth Whitrock, breezes back into town just in time for the county fair, his resolve is tested. Will the busy auburn-haired beauty be able to break through his emotional barriers and cause him to have a change of heart?

Prairie County Fair

Love Takes the Blue Ribbon in Four Novellas

Lynn A. Coleman
Freda Chrisman
Tamela Hancock Murray
Christine Lynxwiler

BARBOUR BOOKS
An Imprint of Barbour Publishing, Inc.

Illustrations by Mari Goering

ISBN 0-7394-3088-2

All Scripture quotations, unless otherwise noted, are taken from the King James Version of the Bible.

Published by Barbour Books, an imprint of Barbour Publishing, Inc., P.O. Box 719, Uhrichsville, Ohio 44683

ecpa Member of the Evangelical Christian Publishers Association

Printed in the United States of America.

Prairie County Fair

After the Harvest

by Lynn A. Coleman

Dedication

To my granddaughter, Leanna.
May you grow up to be strong in the faith
of our Lord, Jesus.
All my love, Grandma.

Chapter 1

September 1857

A gentle breeze stirred the white tips of rye and barley stalks. Rylan's face creased with a satisfied grin. The bountiful harvest testified of God's good grace.

Tall stalks continued to dance and play like carefree children. Children! The next step in Rylan's plan—a wife and a pack of children. He shifted his weight on his chestnut sorrel, the creak of the leather protesting the sudden change.

Months had passed since his last letter to Margaret. Three years he'd worked to develop the land enough to support her and the children they would have one day. Five months and not a word.

Truth be told, he hadn't had an encouraging word from Margaret in more than a year. The first year he'd come and settled on his land in Kansas and received regular letters. The second, they came less and less. But he refused to believe her love for him had dwindled. No, theirs was a strong one, a divine one. God had placed her in his life. Their love would withstand the hardship of separation. Yet her constant praise of Jackson Pearle, his best friend, made Rylan wonder. . . .

Rylan reached down and pulled the grain from a stalk. The seed rolled in his palm. A farmer with land to work. What could be more exciting than that?

Margaret's fine features glowed in his memory. "Ah, yes, Lord, she is a fine one."

Tomorrow the harvesting would begin. Today he would go to town and hire a few extra hands for the harvest. Rylan shifted in his saddle and nudged the horse forward. Perhaps Margaret's letter had arrived, telling him when to expect her and her family. A man could hope.

He rode toward the dozen or so buildings that made up Prairie Center, the seat of Prairie County. This new territory of Kansas represented the hope and future of overpopulated Massachusetts and the rest of the North. Rylan had come and staked his claim, yielding to the enticement of free land. Margaret had agreed to postpone their wedding for a couple years to allow him to get the farm established. The fact that it had taken him a third year to build a suitable house and raise the funds for her ticket shouldn't have been a problem.

Admittedly, her letters came less frequently after he wrote her of the need for yet another year of separation. Rylan shook his head. No, he wasn't going to entertain those dark thoughts again. She was coming; he could feel it in his bones. It was just the knot in his stomach that didn't seem to share the same conviction.

Rylan hitched his horse outside the general store and ambled inside. "Hello, Pete."

"Afternoon, Rylan." Pete Anderson stood behind a counter with a white apron spread across his broad belly.

"Know of anyone needing a couple days' work?"

"Crops ready?" Pete placed a pencil down on the counter.

"Yup, and it's a good one."

"Glad to hear it. How many men do you need?"

Rylan removed his hat and wiped the inside brim with his red handkerchief. "Six is a good start, but I'll go as high as a dozen if there're enough men looking for work."

"Usually are. A day or two's work before a man continues west isn't bad to line his pockets a tad bit more."

Rylan grinned. Hiring extra men at harvest time wasn't difficult in Prairie County. Keeping men to stay and work the season. . .that was another matter. "Spread the word. Tell 'em to be at my place by sunup, and we'll work 'til sundown."

Pete picked up his pencil. "Can I get you anything else today?"

Rylan didn't want to ask if he had a letter. He'd been asking every time he'd come to town for the past two months. "Think I'll just browse and see what's new."

"There are some newspapers from back East, Boston, in fact. Didn't you tell me you came from there?"

"Yup."

"Set and read a spell."

"Thanks, don't mind if I do." Newspapers were like gold, and once in awhile someone would leave a previously read paper at the store, with a little prompting from Pete, of course. Occasionally Pete would pull them out of the trash and save them.

Beside the front window of the store, Pete had set a table and a couple of chairs. A man could grab a cup of coffee and read to his heart's content. Rylan searched through the papers and found the one from Boston. He placed his hat on the table and sat down in the chair, spreading open the paper. Pete brought over a mug of coffee. Old names, familiar streets. . . Rylan journeyed back to Boston, to his family home, to a life he'd left behind.

An hour passed before he turned the final page. His heart stopped. He jumped up. The half-full mug of coffee toppled over. The table wobbled. "No!" he moaned.

Randolph and Wilma Cousins are proud to announce the betrothal of their daughter, Margaret Elizabeth to Jackson Pearle. . . .

Rylan couldn't believe his eyes. He blinked and read the malicious lines again and again. Why? All the work. . .all the planning. . .for what?

❊

Judith leaped out of the way as a man barreled out of Pete Anderson's store. She brushed the skirt of her dress to remove any vestiges of the dust and dirt he kicked up. "How rude," she mumbled under her breath.

Singularly focused and driven were the best ways to describe the human train pushing his way out of the store and to his horse. She opened the basket carrying the few tomatoes she hoped Pete could sell. They weren't much, but they were something to help ease the burden of her father's debt.

Her father wasn't a farmer. He should have stayed in Worcester. Coming to Kansas to start over again seemed impossible. And having looked over the fields her father had planted in the spring compared to the other farmers in the area, it was painfully obvious he should have stayed back East.

"Hi, Pete. Who was that?"

Pete's generous smile warmed his full face. "Rylan Gaines owns the spread west of your father's."

"Oh." The farmer whose fields shouted her father's ineptitude. "I brought some tomatoes. I'm hoping you can sell them and put the money towards my father's debt."

"Sure," Pete said, reaching for the bundle of tomatoes. "Fine-looking vegetables. They'll sell."

Judith smiled. She didn't know if Pete was being truthful or simply generous. It didn't matter. What her father owed for seed, a few tomatoes wouldn't make a dent in.

"There's a paper from Boston over there." Pete pointed to the small wooden table and chairs. Over the summer it had been her only hiatus in this horrible place her parents now called home. They had let her stay in Worcester the first year while they settled.

Judith examined the soiled newspaper, an overturned cup, and a wet brown substance she assumed was coffee. The newsprint bled. The paper bubbled. "Pete, do you have anything to clean up this mess?" she called out.

"What mess?"

"Appears to be coffee."

"Well, I'll be. Something must have rattled Rylan." Pete sauntered over with a dry rag.

Judith scanned what she could of the obituaries, birth announcements, and wedding announcements. "Perhaps someone he knew passed away."

"Always possible. Rylan was one of the first to arrive. He came in fifty-four. Far as I can tell, he hasn't been back East since." Pete sopped up the coffee the paper hadn't. His hand paused in midair.

"What?"

"Uhh, nothing." Pete finished his work and hurried back behind the counter.

Whatever bothered Rylan Gaines had hit Pete with nearly as much force. Judith scanned the paper again. No one named Gaines had passed away, married, or had a baby. Of course, she had no idea who his maternal grandparents were. It was always possible one of these names represented someone from that side of his family. But if someone had died, wouldn't Pete have said?

Pete wasn't a true gossip, but the man openly shared the comings and goings of most folks. He was Prairie County's newspaper. No, it was something worse than death—and something more personal, she assessed. Mind your concerns, Judith, she heard her mother's voice chide her. Ever since childhood Judith had felt the urge to butt in and know why so-and-so did this and so-and-so did that. Gossip was the hardest sin she fought. Her natural curiosity craved finding out information. Truly this wasn't her concern. If so, Pete would have said what was wrong. But he hadn't, and she needed to leave it at that.

Judith tore the damp page from the rest of the paper and placed it over the other chair to dry. She settled down and read about life back East, the life she'd left behind. The life she desperately wanted to return to.

"Excuse me, Judith," Pete called over to her.

Judith popped her head up over the edge of the newspaper. She'd been reading nonstop.

"Are you aware of the county fair coming up?"

"County fair?"

"Yeah, we hold it once a year. The farmers bring their crops, and the women—what few we have—bake pies. There are horse pulls, judging contests. . .it's a lot of fun."

"No, I guess I hadn't heard about it." Even if she had, she knew her father wouldn't be bringing his crops to show off.

"Reason I mention it is there's some prize money for the best foods, and I thought you and your mother might like to enter." Pete continued to count his stock.

Prize money. Could she and her mom possibly win?

"There's a flyer hanging in my window. You know, on your father's land there's the best batch of wild black raspberries. They'd make some mighty fine jam."

"If one had the sugar," she mumbled.

"They're so sweet, hardly need to add sugar."

Had he heard her? She really did need to stop mumbling to herself.

"So you hold this fair every year?"

"It's a grand time. Helps bring the folks in the county together. We're spread so far apart."

She'd seen enough of the county to know how true a statement that was. Eighty acres were given to each man and woman who set up their claim, but they needed to stay on the land for five years before the property actually became theirs.

Five years. She closed her eyes as if to shut out the knowledge of how much time stretched out before her until her parents would own their claim. Why did it bother her so much to be here? Nothing remained of the family home or her father's bank back East. Her parents were here. Folks seemed friendly enough. She hadn't left an admirer behind, so why her discontent?

"Where did you say these berries were?"

Pete rubbed his well-shaved chin. "I'd say on the hill behind where they built the house. There's a line of trees that forms a 'V' and points right to it. You can't miss 'em."

"Thanks. Don't know if I'll be making any jam, but the berries would be a nice treat for the folks." Judith headed toward the door.

"Don't have to make jam—that was just a suggestion. You can make anything and enter it," Pete encouraged.

Judith turned and waved. "Thanks, Pete."

Something for Momma's sweet tooth to get her through the winter would be worth the effort to find those berries. She hadn't searched the land much. She'd been so busy tending the garden and livestock, who had time for exploring?

On the other hand, the money would be a blessing if she should win. Who was she kidding? She held her own in the kitchen, but she was certain she couldn't compete with the other ladies who lived in this territory.

Of course, there weren't all that many women living in the county. Judith's father had had more offers for her hand in marriage since she'd arrived in Prairie Center than during her entire eighteen years in Worcester. Some men who hadn't even seen her came proposing. She climbed up on the buckboard and headed home.

"Howdy, Miss Timmons, may I escort you home?" Brian Flannery tipped his hat and rode proud in his saddle. He wasn't an unhandsome man, but the lack of a front tooth gave him a less-than-intelligent appearance.

"Thank you, Mr. Flannery, but it isn't necessary."

"Nonsense. A pretty woman like you shouldn't be alone."

Alone? How could she be? If Brian hadn't shown up, there was a list of at least a dozen other men who would. She'd never made a trip back from town without an escort.

"Thank you," she said with a smile. Inwardly she sighed, praying just once an opportunity would arise for her to go home in peaceful solitude.

❋

Rylan stormed home, pushing Max as fast as the workhorse could run. Back in the barn, he brushed the animal down with care. The poor beast wasn't the problem. Margaret and Jackson, they were his problem. How long had they been seeing each other behind his back? The newspaper was nearly a month old, and he'd not even received a sorry-but-I-fell-in-love-with-another-man letter.

"Nothing. Not one single word," he huffed. "Why, Lord?" He threw the brush against the shelf and left Max with a bag of oats in payment for the hard ride home.

He'd trusted her. He'd worked himself weary preparing this place for her and their children. He looked over the barn. A barn, a house, and a root cellar. How much more did a woman need? And what was so great about Jackson?

Rylan didn't consider himself a vain man, but he beat Jackson hands down in the looks department. Jackson barely had a chin to speak of. The poor guy was all neck.

"Jackson, thanks—friend." The bile in his stomach boiled. He kicked a small stone with his boot.

He looked up at the house built for Margaret, a labor of love, now an empty tomb of disappointment and despair. "Why, Margaret? Didn't I give you everything I promised I would? And why Jackson?"

Rylan turned his back to the house. He couldn't sleep in there tonight. Not tonight. He needed to get a handle on his emotions. The temptation to tear the place apart board by board burned at him. Thankfully, something held him back. Perhaps it was all the hours he'd put into it, or hopefully it was God's grace giving him some good common sense.

Every instinct he had urged him to storm home to Massachusetts and demand some answers. His head throbbed from the war being fought within. He needed time. Time to absorb. And time to decide what to do with his future.

He pulled a wool blanket from the barn, tucked a knife in his boot, and grabbed his rifle. Tonight he would camp in the small woods bordering his land and Oscar Timmons's. Oscar wasn't much of a farmer, but you only had to farm ten acres of the eighty to earn your land. The fact that he still lived in a dugout only proved how poorly the man was doing. Oscar once had told Rylan he was a banker. But his bank went bust when some investments he'd made hadn't panned out. In the end, he ended up selling all he had to pay off the debts the bank had accumulated before he sold it off for pennies on the dollar.

Whatever Oscar's ability with numbers, he certainly didn't have a hand for growing.

The brisk pace Rylan took as he headed toward the woods raised a sweat. A refreshing swim in the small pond on his property would help chill his burning temper. Most days it took Rylan quite a bit to lose his temper. Today was not most days.

He stripped to the waist and dove in. His long frame sluiced through the water as he swam deeper and deeper under the surface. No sound penetrated under the water. His lungs burned for oxygen. How long did he dare stay below the surface?

Rylan scanned the murky bottom and spun around, looking toward the sky. The water was so clear above him. Below him it was dark, murky, full of decaying leaves and matter. Above, the pure, clean water fed by a small stream.

He pushed his arms upward and kicked his legs with all his strength. He was a man brought to this earth by God for a purpose. He needed to look up to find his direction in life, not down in the pit of darkness and despair. Another strong kick and pull with his arms and Rylan's head broke the surface, his lungs sucking in the precious oxygen that gave him life. "Lord, show me what to do," he gasped.

Chapter 2

Judith stretched her back, placing the heavily laden baskets of fruit on the rustic wooden table.

"Goodness, Dear, where did you get these?" Her mother's pale blue eyes widened.

"Pete Anderson told me there were some wild berries on our land. And, Mother, you won't believe how thick those bushes are. I hardly made a dent."

"Mercy, what are we going to do with all these?" Judith's mother, Riaxa, wiped her hands on a small hand towel.

"Enter the Prairie County Fair. Pete said you can win prize money for the best—"

"Judith, sit down," her mother interrupted. Her once-thin frame now seemed to be more rugged and definitely wider in the hips. Back home, she never would have allowed those extra pounds to take over.

Judith obediently sat down. Her mother sat across from her at the small, pine kitchen table.

"The fair is a lot of fun but hardly the place to make a lot of money. Yes, there is a contest, and some prize money is handed out, but it's not much. Mostly, it is a place for everyone to gather together and have a good time. The farmers discuss farming, tools, seed, everything under the sun. The women talk about quilting, canning, children, and how to make do with what you have."

"But—"

"Honey, I know you're having a rough adjustment, and yes, money is tight, but we will survive. We may not have the wealth we had back in New England but. . ."

"Don't you miss it?" Judith couldn't believe her mother didn't miss her silk dresses, fancy evening apparel, and the rest. They used to dine out three or four times a week.

"Actually, not too much. Oh sure, I wouldn't mind having servants take care of all the housework, but your father and I have rediscovered ourselves, our relationship to each other, and to God."

"You both do seem happier." Judith realized there had been a change in her parents' behavior. They seemed closer. They talked more often to each other. Many times back home they seemed to simply exist in the same house, each with their own life to live. Here, well, here things were definitely different.

"We are, Dear. Extremely," she added, leaning slightly toward Judith.

"I'm happy for you. But we are in need of money. The seed bill alone will bury us. What's Father going to do when it comes time for planting next year if he hasn't paid off this year's debt?"

Her mother's shoulders slumped.

"Don't you see? We need to at least try to win. Even if we don't, perhaps we can sell some of the jam to those heading West."

Raixa Timmons had once reigned as a paragon of proper posture and manners in Worcester. That woman and the woman before Judith now were scarcely the same. Her once finely manicured eyebrows had grown thick. "I suppose you're right. It couldn't hurt to at least try."

Judith jumped up and embraced her mother. Perhaps they could earn enough to return to Worcester. She let that thought exit her head as fast as it entered. A few berries and a few pies wouldn't provide one so much as the cost of meals on the return trip.

"I'll go pick some more. I think there's enough time before sunset."

The older woman chuckled. "Be careful of those briars."

"Yes, Mother."

Judith lit through the door with renewed purpose. Her heart hadn't felt this gay since leaving Worcester.

Bending over in the bushes, Judith realized the only thing she and her mother could make at this point would be jam. The pies and tarts would spoil. She'd have to pick again in a few days. Her picking done, she headed for home. In the distance she spied a man heading toward the grove of trees that ran along their property and her neighbor's. Rylan Gaines. If she didn't know better, she'd guess he was still in an ugly disposition. Perhaps he always walked around with a chip on his shoulder. "Curious," she mumbled.

Back at the house after dinner was served, she asked, "Mother, have you ever met our neighbor?"

"Rylan?"

"Yes."

"Sweet young man." Judith's mother crushed another handful of berries. "Why do you ask, Dear?"

"He nearly plowed me over in town today. He didn't seem the friendly sort."

"That is odd. I've never known Rylan to be anything less than a perfect gentleman." She paused in her crushing of the berries and looked toward Rylan's home.

"I think he read something in a paper from Boston," Judith persisted. "I couldn't figure out who died or what bothered him. His surname wasn't listed in the paper."

Her mother turned her gaze back to Judith with a look that was all too familiar. "There you go again, Daughter. You must stop this unbridled curiosity of yours. Every man is entitled to some privacy."

"I know, I know, but—"

"Judith Joy."

Her mother had scolded her on more than one occasion in that tone. "Sorry," she replied sheepishly and looked down at her berries. What was it with this place? Everyone seemed to be overly sensitive about knowing what was going on with others. *I was just being curious, trying to relate in some small way. . . . Stop lying to yourself, Judith, you know you're just curious about why he was so upset. A mystery you haven't been unable to unlock.* She sighed.

Her mother laughed. Judith could hear her father snicker in the other room.

❊

The next morning, Rylan fought the demons that had kept him awake all night. Sleeping in the woods hadn't helped.

Nightmares of seeing Margaret and Jackson arm and arm. . . He tossed a pitchfork into the wagon.

"Whoa, you trying to kill someone?" Ed Randolph asked as he walked up to the wagon.

"Guess I wasn't thinking," Rylan mumbled. If he wanted the men to work for him, he'd better rein in his emotions. He'd need the money from harvesting the rye and barley in order to pay for his trip back to Massachusetts. He'd decided he'd have to go back and confront them. Even just for his own peace of mind.

"Pete says you could use some help." Ed's thin frame hid the man's strength. He didn't bulge in the muscle department, but he held his own. Enough so that Rylan wouldn't want to cross him.

"Sure could. Hoped more would be coming, though."

"Ah, not to worry. I saw some headed here. I cut across Timmons's place. That man can't farm for anything. The ground is so rich here all you have to do is drop the seed, but. . ."

"Now don't go pickin' on the man. Seems to me I had to show you a thing or two." Rylan winked.

"Yeah, yeah. But even at my worst, I wasn't as bad as Timmons."

"He's not a farmer."

"What ever gave you that idea?" Ed asked in a sarcastic tone.

"Told me he's a banker."

"Why ain't he being a banker then?"

"That's for him to say, not me. But he has his reasons."

"He couldn't have robbed the bank. He wouldn't have ended up here if he had."

"No, he didn't rob the bank."

"Who robbed the bank?" George Steadman sneezed into his handkerchief and deposited the folded cloth into the back pocket of his overalls.

"No one. You guys are worse than women," Rylan teased.

"No worse than anyone else." George set his hands on his hips. "Didn't know if you'd need my wagon, so I have the youngin' bringing it over later, after the missus uses it to buy her supplies."

"Thanks, George. Of course we'll use it."

George nodded.

Half a dozen others showed up, and Rylan put them all to work. The sweat beaded on his back. It felt good to work. Healthy, even. Perhaps a trip to Boston isn't worth the effort. The damage is done; they're married. What could I do anyway?

By nightfall they'd cleared a good third of the fields. Rylan paid each man and encouraged him to bring others the next day. As the workers departed, he finished bagging the grain that a couple of the men had threshed. He sewed up each fifty-pound burlap sack after filling it. Dried, the stalks would be used to feed his horses through the winter.

Stretching his back, he realized he'd sleep tonight. He smelled worse than the pigs after a fresh roll in the mud. Pumping out some fresh water, he stripped and bathed in the yard.

"Hello," a male voice called from the darkness.

Rylan grabbed his trousers and pulled them on. "Who's there?" he called. A light swayed in the distance.

"Oscar Timmons."

"What brings you out so late?"

"I need a favor." Oscar's shadowed image came into view.

"What can I do for you?"

The pencil-thin man with his freshly tanned face seemed much older this year than last.

"I need your honest opinion."

Rylan leaned against a fence rail. "I'll be as honest as I can. What's up?"

"Me, I'm no farmer. The second season is in, and I've barely anything to harvest."

"True, but do you have enough to feed your family?"

"I imagine so, if we're careful. Judith has tried to help. She has more of a green thumb than either her mother or I, but—"

"Say no more. Look, the deal with the New England Emigrant Aid Society that helped us get out here is that we live on the land for five years. There's no conditional clause about us having to make a profit. The thing you need to worry about the most is feeding your family. That's all. If you can do that, in three more years the land is yours, free and clear."

A slight grin rose on his cheek. "Thank you for the reminder."

"Don't fuss about it. I might be needing your encouragement soon."

"What's the trouble? I heard you barreled out of town yesterday."

How'd he know that? Of course, everyone knew everything about everybody. But this tidbit was his. No one else needed to know his shame. "Just in a hurry."

"Oh."

Oscar wouldn't ask. Rylan knew he wasn't that kind of a man. Being a banker, he was used to keeping other men's secrets.

If Rylan could confide in anyone, it would be Oscar.

"Are you entering the fair?" A change in subject was necessary.

Oscar laughed. "Are you serious? Is there a category for the smallest tomatoes?"

Rylan chuckled. "I'm entering the team pull. My team seemed to finally get their act together this year."

"I don't have a team. I have a single mule that's more stubborn than Judith." Oscar's smile slipped.

The man certainly had his problems.

"Don't think they have a 'most stubborn mule' category, but if I hear of one, I'll let you know."

Oscar chuckled. "Good night, Rylan, and thanks again."

"Good night." Rylan watched the light grow dim as Oscar headed across the fields. If Oscar could stick it out, he'd be happy to purchase some of the land from him. He'd even considered farming a section of Oscar's land on a rental basis but hadn't checked the agreement to see if that was allowable or not.

Inside the house, he fought the memories of Margaret's promises. He'd made the furnishings for her. Even the house had been for her. He'd be just as comfortable in the barn. Well, perhaps not as comfortable as the feather bed he'd put together. "Lord, why? Why'd she do it? Why Jackson?" He fell to his knees, covering his anguished face with his rough hands. Tears fell for the first time. The only time. He was a man. He couldn't allow this. He sniffed and straightened himself up. No, with God's grace, he'd get through this, just like every other bad moment of his life.

He wiped the tears from his face with his red handkerchief. *I'll place an ad in a New York paper for a wife. Any woman* would do now, since his one true love had deceived him so. Yes, I'll place an ad tomorrow. Tonight, I'll sleep outdoors again. The air is fresher, he reasoned. He lied. He knew it.

❋

Thursday, the day before the fair, Judith marched out to the berry patch early. The sun rose slowly over the hills as she worked her way toward the plentiful harvest. Getting an early start would allow time for possible failures. The jam she and her mother had made had turned out extremely well. Little sugar had been used. Instead, because of the bounty of the berries, they were able to thicken it with the fruit. The family had tried it last evening on warm bread fresh from the oven. Judith had never tasted anything better.

In the distance she saw a man heading toward Rylan Gaines's place. *All right, Lord, I know I'm not supposed to be so curious, but even You have to admit this is very strange behavior. The man has a huge house. Two stories, clapboard, with a wide front porch. Why on earth is he spending the nights in the woods?*

A bird cawed. The world seemed to be waking up. Was it possible that Rylan Gaines had been hunting? Judith squinted her eyes for a better glance. He didn't appear to be carrying a rifle. But he was carrying something. "Humph." She wouldn't be finding out today what her strange neighbor was up to. Everyone seemed to think rather highly of him, yet there was something about him, something Judith couldn't put her finger on, something she knew wasn't right. Perhaps she was here in Prairie County to discover the truth about a certain Rylan Gaines. *Perhaps he has a secret past no one knows about. Eww, could he be running from the law?* It wasn't unheard of for criminals to head west hoping to get lost in the crowds. No laws existed. The lands were uncharted. A shiver rolled down Judith's back. She'd given herself enough reasons to stay away and watch him like a hawk. After all, her parents thought the world of him. Yes, she had a purpose for coming to Prairie County. Once that purpose had been fulfilled, she could encourage her parents to move back home.

Judith bent down and picked with renewed vigor. Today she'd discovered the real reason God had seen fit to send her to this godforsaken land.

"Hello."

Judith shrieked.

Chapter 3

Rylan stepped back.

"Get away from me," Judith screamed.

Rylan raised his hands. "Sorry, I didn't mean to scare you. I saw you over here and assumed you were Oscar Timmons's daughter, Judith. I'm Rylan Gaines, your neighbor."

She patted her heart. He squelched a chuckle, seeing her berry-stained hand leave its indelible mark on the white bib of her dress.

"Yes, I'm Judith."

"I won't intrude any longer. I just thought I'd come by and say hello. Good day, Miss Timmons." He nodded and headed home. Rylan searched his memory. He couldn't remember a single time he'd scared someone so badly in all his life. Not even the time he scared his six-year-old sister when she'd been sneaking a pickle out of the pickle barrel. She'd jumped, knocked the barrel over, and sent pickles flying everywhere. The cellar reeked of vinegar for years.

"Pickles, nice big sour ones." His stomach grumbled. Yes, a wife would be a good thing. Pete had thought it foolish to advertise for a wife. Pete being Pete, he only said, "You're wasting your money." Then silently he wrote out the ad to be wired to New York later in the day.

Rylan shot back a glance at the berry-stained woman with a set of lungs that could deafen a man. . . . *It's all your fault, Pete.* Rylan stuffed his hands in his trousers and headed back toward his farm.

If Pete hadn't gone on and on about how pretty the Timmons's daughter was, Rylan wouldn't have taken the time to say hello. Granted, Pete was right. The woman was a real looker. But she seemed. . .what? More afraid than scared of me? *Maybe I just scare women off, Lord.*

With the rye and barley shipped off to market, Rylan began work for the winter. The seeds needed to be dried and bagged. The hay needed to be bundled for the livestock. And wood needed to be split for the cold winter months. The harvesting might be over, but there was plenty of work to be done. Plus, he'd be helping his neighbors pull in their harvests. Rylan's crop choices were rye and wheat. But he'd planted a couple acres of corn too. It made for variety over the winter months.

Most of the area farmers planted corn. Many had trouble with the lack of rainfall for their crops during the summer. Having come to this land earlier, Rylan had been blessed with prime property. Two streams ran through the land, a river to his south, and the pond northeast that abutted the Timmons's property.

His mind drifted back to Judith Timmons and the blackberry stains on her white apron. Rylan chuckled. "She's an odd one, Lord."

❋

The next day he found himself at the Prairie County Fair. This year the number of people seemed double over the previous. The place buzzed with activity. Children ran from one event to another. The women huddled near their wares, and the men gathered around their livestock.

"Morning, George." Rylan held back his team.

"You entering in the pull?" asked a man Rylan didn't recognize.

"Yes, Sir. My team's ready this year."

"Take a look at McCoy over there. He's really been working his team. Seems mighty impressive," George added.

Rylan watched for a few moments. No question about it, McCoy would offer serious competition. "Just means we'll be putting on a better show."

The men roared and continued to talk about their harvests. Several of the farmers who were raising corn had had a bad go of it.

"I'm hoping some of your wives will trade some of their canned vegetables for some of my rye," Rylan offered.

"Hazel should be willing. She's rather fond of rye bread."

"Wonderful. You're wife packs away some of the finest vegetables I've ever had. Afraid most of my summer vegetable crop will go to feed the pigs. I don't know how to can. Not that I have the time to do it."

Ralph Davis scratched his chest. "Seems to me you might be able to bring some of your vegetables to some of the women folk, and they might can some for you."

"I couldn't impose. Besides, they're a might busy taking

care of their own."

"Hey, there," Josh Williams called, striding over with a bushel basket of apples. "Look at these fine apples. Hard to believe I got such a fine crop from those wee trees this year."

Everyone admired the beautiful apples Josh brought over. A row of apple trees would be nice around the house, Rylan thought. But his thoughts darkened. When would he have time to care for them? Perhaps a single tree was all he could handle. *A wife, I definitely need a wife.* "Excuse me, gentlemen, I need to take care of my team."

He brought his team over to the corral and noticed Judith Timmons sitting at a table. "Blackberries," he murmured, chuckling, then brought the horses into the corral.

❊

Judith couldn't ignore Rylan Gaines. He stood tall, and he smiled, a warm genuine smile. Perhaps she'd been wrong in thinking he was a criminal, she reflected as she watched him work. He walked his team of horses into the corral. The way he treated his animals spoke volumes of the man's character. He placed some feedbags on their snouts and brushed them down.

Judith scanned the fairgrounds. So many people she didn't know. Yet they all knew her. At least, they all knew who she was. She hadn't seen her father this proud in all his life, introducing her to everyone he met. Men were plentiful. They came over to her table in a steady stream. Everyone bought something, whether a piece of pie, a tart, or some jam, it didn't matter. They were there not to purchase goods but to try and purchase her, she supposed. Three marriage proposals this morning alone. And ages varied from a young boy of sixteen to an old man of sixty. She certainly had plenty to pick from. But if she picked one, she wouldn't be returning to Worcester, and Worcester was the only place she wanted to be. Not that she was looking for a husband.

"Good morning." Rylan's distinguished voice drew her from her musings. "I see you've made good use of those berries." His smile was disarming.

A capricious smile rose up her cheeks. "Yes, Mother and I worked hard."

"It shows. How do you like Kansas?"

"Not much." She snapped her mouth shut and placed her hand over it. "I'm sorry," she mumbled.

Rylan's rich laughter eased her troubled state. A woman of society would not have spoken her mind so. "It's quite all right. Nothing wrong with being honest."

His eyelids closed over the most vibrant brown eyes she'd ever seen. Brown eyes never appealed to her. They seemed to just be dark orbs that blended into the background of one's soul. Blue eyes, now those were eyes that attracted her. So why was she so taken in by Rylan Gaines's brown eyes?

He opened them slowly; his posture stiffened. "Truth comes in short supply these days. Good day, Miss Timmons, and keep being honest."

He left as silently as he'd appeared. Was the man half fox? Another gentleman appeared in front of her table. "May I help you?"

"That ya can, Lass. I'm looking for a wife. . . ."

Here we go again. Judith put on her pleasant "but I don't want to be here" smile. When would these men get the message?

"I'm sorry. I'm not available."

"Oh, I apologize, Lass. I heard ya were single."

She had to admit she loved his Irish accent. "I am single, so you didn't hear wrong. However, I'm not available."

He knitted his red eyebrows, then released them. "Many pardons, Lass. You'd best tell your husband-to-be to put a ring on your finger, and do it soon, or they'll be no end to the proposals."

Judith chuckled.

The poor man's face reddened even more.

"I'm sorry," she replied.

He scurried off before she could explain. Perhaps she shouldn't clarify the issue. Perhaps it would be best to let the entire town think she was engaged to be married. Of course, Mother and Father won't appreciate the deception. But what's a poor girl to do in a county where men outnumber the women twenty to one?

The day continued with plenty of sales and far fewer proposals. They had actually stopped. Word must have gotten around. Her mother was working the table, which gave Judith her first real opportunity to peruse the fairgrounds. A crowd gathered at the corral; cheers and whistles filled the air. Judith came up and worked her way toward the front. Inside the corral she saw Rylan working his team. "Oh my," she gasped.

"They're a pretty sight, aren't they, Miss?" a man next to her observed.

Pretty wasn't exactly the word she had in mind. Muscles bulged on the horses. . .and on Rylan. They worked in unison, pulling the heavy load.

"What are they doing?" she asked the stranger.

"The goal is to have your team pull in unison as heavy a load as possible and work them around those posts without losing your load."

"Oh my."

"Rylan did well last year, but I think he's going to beat McCoy this year. He's got a fine team. They were just too young last year."

Rylan's broad shoulders were straining the seams of his perspiration-soaked shirt. Was it that hard to keep a team working? Shouldn't the team work with ease? "Why is he working so hard?"

"His team wants to move faster than Rylan is allowing them to, but he knows they can't make the turn if they move faster. It's the difference between man and beast. The animal has learned how to haul but doesn't have the wisdom to analyze. On the other hand, in the wild these animals wouldn't be hauling this amount of weight, either."

Judith clenched the rail as Rylan worked his team around the first post. The crowd roared with excitement. Her informative new companion whispered, "This is where he lost his load last year."

Lord, help him, she silently prayed. Why was she so concerned about Rylan Gaines? It didn't make sense, but something deep inside of her wanted, no, needed him to succeed.

The horses pulled together. The load wobbled but stayed on the flat. They strained forward and twisted around the second post. Sweat beaded down Rylan's forehead. His grin was infectious. "Excellent job, Rylan!" she heard herself scream. He turned toward the crowd.

The crowd turned their attention on Judith. She felt her cheeks flame.

Rylan nodded.

Judith escaped from the probing eyes of the crowd. She heard murmurings but didn't care to listen. The safest place for her was back behind the table.

As Judith approached their stand, her mother asked, "Did you have fun, Dear?"

"I found it quite interesting, Mother."

Her mother stood and straightened the skirt of her dress. "I'm glad. We've just about sold out. The raspberry tea is chilled, and your father insists we simply give it out as a gesture of friendship to our neighbors."

"Yes, Mother."

"They're about to judge the jams. Do you want to watch?"

"No, thank you." Judith sat down behind the table.

Her mother took two steps back toward her. "Is everything all right, Dear?" she whispered.

Judith startled back to her senses. "Just fine, Mother. I think I'll have some of that tea myself."

"Great. Don't forget there's a sandwich in the basket also. Oh, and your father had me make one for Rylan if he should ever come around."

Judith swallowed and waved her mother off. The mere thought of meeting up with Rylan after such an outburst. . .

Her cheeks heated up again. *Lord, what's happening to me? I've been here for all of four months, and I'm forgetting all the social graces I've learned. Why?*

She poured herself a tall glass of tea and grabbed the smaller sandwich in the basket. Why had her father asked her mother to make a sandwich for Rylan?

"Congratulations, Miss Timmons." Pete waved as he walked past.

"Congratulations? What for?" she mumbled. Had they won the contest? Her spirit brightened. The sales and the prize money would make a good dent on the debt with Pete's store. But Mother just left to go to the judging. Could it be over that quickly?

❇

"Congratulations, Rylan, excellent job."

"Thanks, Jim." Rylan took McCoy's hand and pumped it.

Jim smiled. "I'll have to see what I can do to beat you next year."

Rylan chuckled. "Good idea. I worked hard on my team this past year."

"It shows. Excellent job, just excellent. By the way, when'd you have time to get yourself engaged to Judith Timmons?"

"What?"

"Everyone's talking about it. I didn't even know you were courting her. I thought you had a gal back East."

"I thought I did too. I don't know about being engaged to Miss Timmons, though. When did this happen?"

Jim McCoy chuckled. "Well, if you're not the reason she's unavailable, who is?"

"I wouldn't have a clue. I've barely spoken with the gal. Who told you I was engaged?"

"Everyone. . .and no one in particular. Seems Michael O'Hara asked her earlier, and she told him she was unavailable. Seems he wasn't the only one asking, either. Anyway, when she burst out at the pull, I guess everyone assumed you were her beau."

"Hmm, don't suppose it occurred to anyone that we're just neighbors."

Jim chuckled. "What would be the fun in gossiping about that?"

Rylan wagged his head. "None, I suppose. I'm hunting for a wife, but I want one who wants to live here, not back East."

"Oscar said she wasn't too fond of the area." Jim leaned against a rail.

"He said the same to me. They gave up a lot to live out here." Rylan continued to brush down his horses.

"Can't understand why society folks would come back to the land. Wouldn't it be easier to hire folks to work your land instead?"

"If Oscar could afford that, I'm sure he would."

"I heard he ran into some financial troubles back East. Guess we all came for various reasons. But free land is free land and worth the work."

"Amen," Rylan added. He finished brushing down the horses after allowing them to walk off the heavy labor from moments before.

"Well, I won't be keeping you. Just wanted to congratulate you. And warn ya that I'll be winning next year." Jim smiled.

"If you can." Rylan winked.

As Jim took off, Rylan turned to his team. "Engaged! Can you imagine?" he muttered.

"I heard it too," Pete said with a wink as he walked over. "Congratulations."

"Don't tell me the entire town?" Rylan asked.

"Just about. Probably the entire county will have heard by the end of the day."

"Wonderful," Rylan moaned.

Pete took a step closer. "You mean, it's not true?"

"Not in the slightest."

"Oh, but I thought. . ." Pete rubbed his chin with his right hand.

"I have no idea why she cheered me on, but we are just neighbors."

"True, she doesn't know many."

"No, I can't imagine that she does. I've barely seen her all summer."

"That explains how she didn't know you when you nearly toppled her over a few days ago."

"What are you talking about?"

Pete reached over, placing his hand on Rylan's shoulder. "I read the announcement in the paper. I'm sorry."

"Thanks, but what does that have to do with me practically running over Miss Timmons?"

"Oh, well the day you read the announcement, she came into the store as you were departing."

"I wasn't in a good mood."

"No, I suspect not. She asked who you were, seemed to recognize your name, but I gathered she hadn't met you."

"No, I've been too busy working on the house in the evening after a full day of working the farm. I suppose I should have introduced myself to my neighbor sooner, but I was preoccupied."

"Doesn't matter. I'll start letting folks know it's not true."

Pete took a step back.

"Thanks, Pete."

"No trouble at all. I don't mind being the man in the know." He wiggled his eyebrows.

Rylan chuckled. Then his mind sobered. Perhaps others would be congratulating Miss Timmons as well. He worked his way to her table. *She's a pretty thing, Lord,* he realized as the distance between them disappeared.

"Good afternoon, Miss Timmons," he said with a smile.

"Mr. Gaines, I–I. . ."

"Shh, I thank you for your praise."

She teased golden hair back and forth. Her yellowish brown eyes captivated him. "I'm so flustered. It's not right for a lady to speak so openly."

"Is it wrong for a woman to speak such to her fiancé?" he teased.

"What?"

Chapter 4

What on earth are you talking about?" She planted her hands on her hips. These backwoods yokels weren't going to mess up her reputation.

Rylan grinned. The dimple on his right cheek eased her tension. He reached for her hand. The warmth of his fingers made her breath catch in her throat. "Rumors have us engaged."

"How?. . .When?. . .Why?"

"Apparently you told Michael O'Hara you were unavailable."

"Michael?"

"Red-headed Irishman."

"Oh." *Lord, what have I done?* she silently petitioned.

"And when you spoke up after the pull. . ." His grin broadened.

"Oh, no."

"Oh, yes. When shall we set the date for our marriage?"

"You can't be serious," she hissed. Only a fool would propose something so preposterous on the basis of rumors and gossip.

Rylan released a deep barrel laugh. "No, Miss Timmons, I'm not serious, but the reaction on your face was worth the trouble."

"Oh, you! What is it with folks around here? Don't they have an ounce of proper manners and respect?"

Rylan's gaze narrowed. "Look, we may not be fancy here like Boston. And we don't have the high society balls, but we are honest folk. Which is more than I can say about your high society. Here, if a man gives his word, it is his word. He doesn't change his mind and back down."

"Huh?"

"Sorry, that has nothing to do with you. Or perhaps in some small way it does. Oscar never said you were engaged."

"I never said I was. I simply said I was unavailable. And I am. I have no interest in courting anyone." She held back her tongue, not wanting to anger the man any further. "What has you all fired up about high society?"

"You wouldn't understand." Rylan's shoulders slumped, and he looked down at his feet.

"Try me."

"All right, Miss Timmons. Here's the situation. If you pledged yourself to a man, and he went off to build your future together, would you wait for him?"

"Of course. That is what making a pledge is all about."

"Well, some don't."

Her curious nature piqued, she reached for the cask of black raspberry iced tea and poured him a glass. "Here, drink this. Tell me what happened."

"Maybe some other time." Rylan gulped down the tea. "Excellent tea."

"Thank you. I have a good ear, if you decide you need to talk with someone."

Rylan chuckled. "I lived in the East, Judith. I know how society women gossip."

"I don't. . .all right maybe I do, sometimes. But who do I know here to gossip to? Besides, I never said a word to anyone that someone shared confidentially. I do have my morals."

Rylan leaned toward her, his gaze so beguiling she rapidly blinked, trying to break the connection she felt. "I do need a wife. Perhaps, we should get engaged."

"Did you fall off your horse?" Judith stepped back. She needed air. For a fleeting moment she actually considered his absurd proposal.

"No, I'm just being practical. I need a wife; you need a husband. I've got a good farm, a house; I can provide nicely. Why not?"

"If you didn't just fall off your horse, he must have stomped on your pretty little head."

"You think I'm pretty?" he asked with a wink.

She was dying here. What kind of a man could be so forward and so intoxicating at the same time? "It's just not done that way!"

"In Boston, perhaps. But you're in the wilds now, remember?"

"Don't even get me started on that. I'm not available for the same reasons I told the young Irishman earlier, because I'm moving back East. I don't want to live here. I wouldn't make anyone a good wife. Not here."

"Perhaps, Miss Timmons. On the other hand, a woman with as much spirit as you possess is born for life in the untamed country of this land. Think about it."

Rylan placed his hat on his head and worked his way back into the crowd.

Judith collapsed in the chair behind her.

"Judith." Her mother came running. "I just heard the news. Honey, I'm so happy for you. I didn't even know you and Mr. Gaines had met each other."

Judith groaned and buried her face in her hands.

❋

"Stupid, stupid, stupid, Gaines. Why'd you do something so foolish?" he chided himself and headed back to the corral. The safest place was home. He'd gather his horses and be gone. The sooner, the better.

"Rylan!" Oscar called.

Rylan took a deep breath and eased it out slowly. "I'm sorry."

"What are you sorry for?" Oscar's face filled with complete puzzlement.

Perhaps he didn't know. "Rumors have your daughter and I engaged. There's no truth to the rumor, but I found myself teasing your daughter, and I probably went too far."

"Oh. Well, she needs a good shaking. The girl's got her mind so muddled with what she thinks life is all about, she's forgotten what matters most."

"Money?"

"That and social standing. It's all rubbish, you know. Once you're in trouble, your so-called friends leave you faster than a hot coal cools in water."

"It was pretty rough, huh?"

"We had our moments. We sheltered Judith from the worst of it, and that quite possibly was a tragic mistake. She doesn't understand the difference living out here makes on a person's soul. You know?"

"Yeah, I know. My fiancée married another. She won't be coming. Guess I was feeling the sting when I teased your daughter."

"What did you do?" Oscar's voice lowered.

"I told her we ought to get married anyway. I needed a wife, she needs a husband. . . ."

Oscar roared. "And you're still standing?" Oscar slapped him on the back. "My boy, you just might be what the good Lord has in mind to tame that one."

Rylan guffawed. "The good Lord better not."

Oscar sobered. "The reason I came over to see you was, I'm. . .I'm. . ."

"What's the matter, Oscar?"

"My bills, I don't know if I'm going to meet them. The women gave it a good-hearted try, and they raised some funds, but it won't meet my debt at Pete's store for the seed I ordered last year. Do you have any ideas how I can raise some cash and still live on the land?"

Rylan scratched the day's growth on his chin. "Not at the moment, but I'm certain the Lord will help us out here. You know the men made a suggestion to me earlier. I have vegetables that need canning, and I have no wife to can them. I don't have the time to do it, either. I'd hate to see the food spoil. Do you think your wife and daughter might come over and do some canning for me?"

"I'm sure they'd lend a hand, but how's that going to help with my debt?"

"It won't, really. However, whatever they harvest and can that I don't need, you and your family can have for payment.

You might not have any cash, but your bellies will be full."

"I'll speak to Raixa. Thank you."

"My pleasure. I've tasted your wife's cooking. Having her put up vegetables for the winter will be a blessing for me."

After exchanging a brief handshake and good-byes, Rylan gathered his horses. The sassy smile of Judith Timmons shot back into his mind's eye. *Lord, she is beautiful. And what's with those eyes? Yellow and brown. . . I've never seen anything like them. I could possibly find myself. . . Nope, I won't go there. Sorry I teased her, Lord.*

He guided his buckboard out of the fairgrounds. A woman with slumped shoulders walked by the side of the road. "Whoa, boys, who's that?"

He paused before asking hesitantly, "Judith?"

She turned, her eyes damp. His heart sank. "Judith, I'm sorry. Please forgive me."

"You don't understand. My mother heard the rumors. She thinks it's just wonderful. She didn't believe me when I told her it wasn't true."

"What? I spoke with your father. He knows I was just teasing you."

"Father knows?" She nibbled her lower lip.

"Yes." He leaned over the edge of the wagon. "Judith, are you heading home?"

She nodded.

"May I give you a lift?"

"But it isn't. . ."

"Proper, I know. But everyone thinks we're engaged anyway. You can end our engagement tomorrow, and no one will think the worse of you. Of course, you'll have to contend with the others who are standing in line to propose to you."

She audibly sighed.

"Please, let me make amends for teasing you."

She looked to her left and to her right. Rylan fought the desire to check if others were watching him too.

"All right."

She placed her slender hand in his. How can a woman's hand be so small? Shifting, he made room for her on the seat of his buckboard.

He sucked in the hot afternoon air, making the clicking sound that told his team to move forward.

"I was fascinated with how well you worked your team," Judith said. "I've never seen anything like that before."

"I've been practicing all year. I lost to Jim McCoy last time, and I was determined not to lose to him this year. Consequently, Jim is determined to beat me next year."

"Healthy competition?"

"But of course, Miss. A man has few things to compete with."

Judith giggled. The purr of her laughter set his insides doing flip-flops. What was it about this woman? He stared into her eyes.

"What? Do I have dirt on my face?"

"No, a little dust maybe. I'm just fascinated with your eyes. I've never seen any others quite like them."

She smiled. "They're rare, but I'm told they are a family trait. My grandmother on my mother's side is said to have had them, as well as my mother's great-aunt Ruth."

"Interesting."

"When I was young I was teased by the other children. But when boys started noticing girls, things changed. Some were attracted because they were so different; others were afraid of them. One boy said they reminded him of tigers' eyes. Not that the boy ever saw a real live tiger, but that's how he described them."

"Fascinating. Truthfully, I think they are beautiful. They remind me of golden wheat when the sun is setting on the grains at harvest time."

Judith blinked and turned her head, looking to their right.

"I'm sorry, did I offend you again?" Rylan sighed.

She placed her hand on his forearm. "Who hurt you?"

"Her name is Margaret. She married my best friend. They didn't have the decency to tell me they'd married. I read it in the newspaper the other day."

"I'm so sorry. No wonder you were in such a bad mood that afternoon."

"Pete said I nearly knocked you down. I'm sorry. I didn't even know I banged into anyone."

"All is forgiven. You had reason to be upset."

"I reckon I did, but it doesn't excuse my rude behavior to you. I guess I was feeling pretty sorry for myself. I've spent the last three years building up the farm, building the barn and house, all for Margaret, and now she's not coming."

"I guess I've been feeling rather sorry for myself too. I don't want to be here. I want to be back home with my friends. Mother and Father are happier here, but I miss the evening socials."

"Is there a gentleman waiting for you?"

"No. I have a bit of a sharp tongue, as you have seen."

Rylan chuckled. "But it comes with such a pretty face. Those men in Worcester must be fools."

"I thank you for saying so, but I've been hard on them. Especially when they'd talk about Daddy and the bank. So many lies were being said."

Her face whitened. "Oh, no!" She cupped her hand over her mouth.

"Your father told me of his business troubles back East. I know what happened."

"Phew, I thought I'd blown it again. You're right when you pegged me for having trouble with my tongue."

"Everyone has faults, Judith. I can't imagine yours being so difficult a man couldn't look past them."

"It's like I was saying—it had more to do with Daddy's business misfortune. Once people knew I was the daughter of Oscar Timmons, the invitations ceased. I guess that's why I want to go back. To prove to everyone they were wrong."

"Why? What would it matter? I wanted to go back and see Jackson and Margaret, but then I realized it wouldn't change anything. They would still be married. They still had betrayed me. It wouldn't have made any difference, except for the possibility of me sinning with my fist."

"Ouch. Jackson better stay in Boston."

Rylan's spirit lifted. "Thanks."

He eased the buckboard to a halt at the corner of the path to her home. "You're easy to talk with, Judith. Thank you."

"You're not so bad yourself. I suppose there really isn't anything for me back East."

"Wanna reconsider my offer?"

Chapter 5

"I should probably scare the pants off you and accept your foolish invitation."

Rylan chuckled.

Just how forward should she be with this man? Judith wondered. He did fascinate her, and not just on the curiosity level. The man had genuine appeal, and she felt irresistibly drawn to him in a way she'd never before experienced. "You did say you needed a wife." She wiggled her eyebrows.

"And you need a husband."

"Why?"

His smile slipped. "Uh, uh."

"Seriously, why? Why do people think a woman needs a husband? I can cook, clean, take care of my house. I can even make an income for myself. Admittedly, it isn't as much as a man could make but. . ."

He placed his finger to her lips. "Shh. Save your passion."

Judith didn't dare move. His finger seared her lips. Her insides felt like jelly.

"I used to believe a man and woman should have a passion

for one another. I loved Margaret, but apparently it wasn't enough."

Judith cleared her throat. "Is it possible she wasn't the right one? I used to believe that God designed the perfect spouse for me, and I simply hadn't found him yet. But as time went by, that belief has dwindled. However, seeing my parents now, the love they have for each other, I've been wondering again if perhaps God may still have a perfect spouse for me."

Rylan leaned back and knitted his fingers behind his head. "I used to believe Margaret was the one. I did until a few days ago. But now, I don't know. I just don't know what to think anymore."

"Tell me, Rylan, what would you have done if Margaret came out here, saw the farm, married you, then left in less than a year? If she couldn't live without proper society, things might have turned out that way."

"I don't know. The thought never crossed my mind. I assumed she'd be happy here with me. Isn't that what true love is—to be happy when you're with the other person?"

"You're probably right. I haven't experienced it yet. And while I'm getting older by social standards back East, living here doesn't mean I'm at a loss for possible husbands."

Rylan chuckled. "No, I'd say you're the prime choice for wife this year. How many proposals have you had? Not counting mine, of course."

"Ha, you're not getting off that easy. Last count was around ten, I think. It might be closer to fifteen. It's hard to keep track."

Rylan let out a slow, lazy whistle. "Someone better knock you off your feet soon, or you might hit the world record. You could be an attraction at the county fairs—the woman with the most proposals."

"Thanks a lot," she huffed.

He held his hands up in the air. "Just teasing."

Judith stood to get down from the buckboard. "Thank you for the ride home. Our engagement is officially over."

He gave an exaggerated sigh. "This one was shorter than the last. I didn't even make it to a full three hours."

"At least you didn't have to build me a house." She jumped down.

"Ouch! You're a vexing woman. Beautiful, but vexing." Rylan smiled.

She reached up and touched his hand. "Rylan, pray about whether or not she was the right one. God will help settle it for you."

"I will. And Judith—" He paused. "Pray about your new home. Ask the Lord to show you the beauty of the area. We're good, hardworking people here. All of us are trying to make a better life for our families."

"I will. And thank you, Rylan."

He tipped his hat and snapped the reins.

"Lord, have mercy he's a handsome man," she mumbled.

"I heard that."

Judith's cheeks flamed.

❋

Rylan avoided Judith for days. Every time he saw her in the meadow, he'd steer clear of her. Every time he saw her in town, he'd cross the street and wave from a distance. The woman was not good for his system. She brought up feelings he hadn't sensed in years. Feelings he'd had for Margaret and more. He'd tried to pray about Margaret and whether or not he'd made the wrong decision three years ago. He couldn't help but wonder what life would have been like if he'd not moved west. If he'd stayed in Boston and married her. Would they have moved to New York, where his parents lived? Would they have stayed in Boston? Would he have been happy there? He felt so much pleasure working the land, digging his hands deep in the soil. Had it been best that he'd been delayed a year in bringing Margaret to Kansas? Was it what was best in the long run?

He didn't have an answer, and every time he thought about it, his head pounded.

Then memories of Judith and their conversation would flood his mind. She would be a woman to wrestle with, so forward and open, yet also sensitive. She didn't know it, but she was perfect for living in an untamed area. Her stubborn, defiant way fought well the hardships of nature. Unfortunately, those thoughts went on to suggest how perfect she'd be as his wife. He wanted a wife, needed a wife, but was he just grasping at the only available woman in the area? Or was the Lord above opening his eyes to another?

It was futile. All this thinking was going nowhere. Unable to sleep in the farmhouse, he knew it was another matter to take to the Lord in prayer. Indian summer had set in across the region. The days were uncommonly warm, and the nights pleasantly cool. Rylan stripped to the waist and dove into the pond.

The cool water washed away the day's heat. He floated on the surface and allowed the warmth of the sun to warm his face and torso.

"Caught ya."

Rylan splashed the water, rousing himself from his peaceful slumber. "What are you doing here?"

"I followed you," Judith answered.

"You followed me?" Rylan treaded water and stared at his unexpected visitor.

"I need to know why you're avoiding me."

"I'm not. . ."

She placed her hands on her hips. "You know and I know you've been avoiding me. So 'fess up. What did I do wrong?"

"Nothing."

"Then why? I thought we'd become friends after sharing such intimate conversation with one another."

With a hard kick, Rylan swam toward shore. He didn't want to hurt Judith. She turned her head and looked toward the thick forest as he stepped out of the lake. Quickly he gathered his tossed shirt and covered himself. "Judith, my avoidance had nothing to do with you."

Golden eyes searched his own. Perhaps it had everything to do with her. He squashed the thought. "I'm sorry, I didn't mean to hurt you."

"Rylan, I don't understand. You're the only friend—or almost friend—I have in these parts and—"

"Shh. I'm sorry. It has nothing to do with you, and everything to do with me and my feelings for Margaret. I need to get a handle on them."

"But what does that have to do with your avoidance of me?"

Because you are threatening my sanity, he wanted to shout. "I need time. Time to work through my hurt emotions before. . ."

He let his words trail off. Did he want to label his feelings for Judith? No, it wouldn't be right.

"Before?"

Rylan drew in a deep breath and expelled it slowly. "Come over here and sit down." He pointed to a fallen tree that made a perfect bench at the pond's edge. He combed the wet strands of his hair back with his fingers.

Rylan paced back and forth in front of the log bench, then stopped and faced Judith. "I hadn't told anyone until that day of the fair about Margaret and Jackson, and you know more than most. It's hard for a man to admit he's no good at love, and that something he's been working for, planning for, and praying about for the past three years burned up as fast as grass in a prairie fire."

"Which is why I thought we had developed a friendship."

"Yes, but it wasn't just friendship, was it?"

"Of course it was."

Rylan came to her and sat down beside her on the log. "Judith, I'm attracted to you, and you're attracted to me. We can't deny that."

"I'm not. . .well, maybe a little."

He knitted his eyebrows and locked his gaze with hers.

"All right, maybe more than a little." She looked away. A soft glow of pink rose on her cheeks.

"I can't, Judith. Not until I'm over Margaret. I can't even sleep in my own house yet."

"What?"

Judith couldn't believe her ears. The man hadn't slept in his house since the day he'd nearly run her over, the day he'd learned of Margaret's betrayal.

"The house was my wedding gift to her."

"What makes the house so specifically for Margaret?"

"You mean besides the fact that I built it for her?"

"Let's do this. Let's remove Margaret from the picture. A man builds a house for shelter for himself and his family, correct?"

"Of course, that's what I just told you."

"No, you said you built it as a wedding gift for Margaret. Are you telling me you never slept in the house before you got the news?"

"Don't be ridiculous. Of course I slept in it, ate in it; it's my house."

"Exactly. It's your house, Rylan, not Margaret's. You may have built it with her in mind, but you also built it for yourself."

He folded his hands in his lap. "True. But so much of the house is her."

"How so?" She fought the desire to reach out and touch him.

"The wallpaper in my bedroom is covered with her favorite flowers, lilacs."

"You wallpapered?" *And with my favorite flower. I wonder if he has some more?*

He jerked his head up and probed her with his glance. "Only the one bedroom. I wanted one room of the house feminine for her. Most of the house would be a working farmhouse and the children's rooms, of course."

She smiled. "How many children were you hoping for?"

"A dozen, but I'd settle for six."

"A dozen! Are you raising children or farmhands?"

Rylan grinned. "Both."

Judith couldn't resist a chuckle. "What else in the house is specifically for Margaret? Is it something that can be removed? Wouldn't that be easier for you than sleeping in the woods?"

Rylan was silent for a moment, then got up to pace again.

Judith knew her attraction to him was strong, but more than her feelings had created her desire to see Rylan through this problem. She wanted to help him work this out. He'd helped her so much with his admonition to give this wilderness a chance. She still didn't want to give up her longing to live back East, but an overall appreciation for the area and its people daily grew within her. But the idea of her and Rylan having a personal relationship deeper than friendship was one idea she buried deep. He wasn't ready, and she wasn't ready. The mere thought of being that close with this man kept her awake to the wee hours of the night.

"Rylan?" He stood there motionless, staring in the direction of the pond but not really focusing on it. "Rylan?" she called again.

"Huh? Oh, sorry, I guess I got to thinking."

"I guess," she grinned.

"I was pondering your questions. I'm not really sure what in the house is Margaret and what is me. To me it's more of a sense of her in every room, in every nail I put into the place. I probably should just take it down and build again."

"Are you a glutton for punishment?"

"No, I. . ."

She marched over to him, grabbed his forearm, and yanked. He stood firmly planted. She released her grasp. "Come on, show me this shrine. I can't believe it's as bad as you say it is."

"It's not bad. It's a beautiful home," he protested.

"I didn't mean bad in the sense that you didn't do a good job. I meant bad in the sense of the overwhelming feelings you have when you're in the place. Let's go confront this demon before it takes the last bit of common sense you have out of your head."

She yanked his arm again.

"Can I at least put my socks and shoes on?" he muttered.

"If you must." She winked. *Watch your step, Judith, or you'll be encouraging that personal relationship that neither one of you are ready for.*

They walked in silence across the field and down the pasture toward his home. Judith gasped as the wonderful structure came into view. "You built this?"

"Yes." He beamed.

"Are you sure you should be a farmer? A woodworker or carpenter seems more in order." She wagged her head. It was a real house, a grand house with a large front porch and beautifully paned windows.

"The house is built for additional rooms in the back. I did start with three children's bedrooms and one large bedroom for me—and Margaret."

"Lead on, oh master of wood. I'm impressed."

"Thank you."

He opened the front door, and the well-polished hardwood floors reflected the fading sunlight. Rylan had spared no expense on the house. It had large, nine-over-six paned windows, which Judith imagined would be hung with heavy drapes for the winter. A hearth stood between the kitchen and the living room.

"I put the fireplace here for warmth in the front parlor, as well as a working fireplace and bread oven over on the other side in the kitchen."

"It's lovely. Did you use stones from your field?" She reached up and touched the rough-hewn stones held in place with gray mortar.

His grin widened. "Yes. Growing up in the north, I have a healthy sense of being frugal."

"I don't think you were tight-fisted here. The hardwood floors, the large windows. . ."

"I purchased the glass, but the wood is lumber I cut and milled from my land. It's one of the reasons I had to delay Margaret's coming for a year."

"The house is beautiful, but we're here to have you point out what you put in for Margaret."

"Come into the kitchen."

She followed behind, looking over the tall ceilings and the mixture of wood and plaster walls. He might think he was being frugal, but she was convinced he'd spent a bundle on the place. Inside the kitchen he pointed out the cabinets for canning, the wood stove, and the sink with a pump.

"I'm sorry, Rylan. I see a functional kitchen here. Well designed, but still it's simply a kitchen. Nothing that shouts Margaret to me."

He scanned the room slowly.

Father, help me get through to him. I know he's hurting, and the loss is great, but help me show him that there's room for him and another in this house. He's too fine of a man not to have a wife, Lord, she prayed.

Rylan continued the tour. With the exception of the flowered wallpaper in the master bedroom, Judith didn't find anything that shouted Margaret. She tried to gently point this out, a real exercise in controlling her tongue. She didn't need to bait the man. He needed to allow the reality to sink home.

"You can change the wallpaper, Rylan. It's beautiful, but if it reminds you too much of Margaret. . ." She let her words trail off. She wanted to ask if he had more rolls of the paper for her own family, but she couldn't see putting wallpaper up on the dugout's walls.

"I suppose I could do that. I don't have the heart right now. I'm afraid my anger may take over, and I'd be replacing more than wallpaper. Perhaps a wall or two."

"You don't seem like the kind of man who can lose his temper."

"Normally, I'd agree with you, but this hurt went deeper than any other I've ever experienced."

"You mean more than the hurt God felt when your sins kept you from Him?"

He groaned. "You don't play fair."

"Am I supposed to?" She quirked a smile.

"Well, you should at least give me a chance."

"Never. I take all the advantages I can."

"I can tell." Rylan reached for her hand and caressed the top of it with his thumb. "Thank you, Judith. I don't know if I can sleep in here but. . ."

"Give yourself time. Sleep in one of the children's rooms. You know those aren't going to be used for awhile," she teased.

"You are vexing."

"I try," she chuckled.

"As a woman, do you approve of the house?"

"Do you have to ask? I've been drooling since I saw it in the distance. You've done a wonderful job. And that kitchen is so workable."

"Good, because I wanted to hire you and your mom to come do my canning. I have some tomatoes, corn, and squash that need to be canned soon or they'll spoil. The winter squash, turnips, carrots, potatoes, and other hard vegetables can go in the root cellar."

"Father mentioned you would like us to can. It would be a dream to work in this kitchen after working in my parents'."

"When can you start?"

"Tomorrow morning. Mother might not be able to right away, but I can."

"Thank you. You don't know how much of a blessing that will be for me."

"I can guess."

He released her hand. "Don't misunderstand me; I love my meat, but I also love vegetables."

"Guess that's a good thing for a farmer, huh?"

"Judith, I promise not to avoid you again."

She gave him a soft punch in the shoulder. "You'd better not, or I'll come after you again."

"Is that a promise?" He wiggled his thick reddish brown eyebrows. Judith's stomach fluttered.

The sun had set, and it was getting darker inside the house.

"Rylan!" A panicked cry came from outside.

Chapter 6

Father, what's the matter?" Judith ran toward her father.

"What's the trouble, Oscar? How can I help?" Oscar wrapped his arms around his daughter and pulled her close.

After a few awkward moments, Rylan cleared his throat.

"Sorry," Oscar offered. "I came running over for your help to find Judith. Her mother and I feared she'd gotten lost in the woods."

"I'm sorry, Father. I should have told you where I was off to." Crimson-stained cheeks and pleading eyes implored Rylan to explain.

"I was showing her the house and the kitchen. She's agreed to can what's left of my vegetables for the winter season."

Oscar grinned. "Wonderful. She's nearly as good a cook as her mother."

A few pleasantries exchanged, then Oscar and Judith departed for their home. Rylan gazed up at the farmhouse. He'd painted it white. No curtains hung in the windows, and bits of colored sunlight played off the glass. He'd spent a small fortune in glass to bring in the sun. He'd even positioned the house at the right direction for the breezes to blow through and cool the house during hot summer days.

Judith's words about it being his house played back in his mind. "Father God, can I start looking at this place as my house and not Margaret's?"

He fought his legs and forced himself up the porch stairs. Each step closer to the front door became more difficult. He placed his hand on the wrought-iron latch. Broken promises, betrayal, stormed his mind. He released the latch. Perhaps tomorrow he could tackle those demons. He turned to leave. At the base of the stairs, he stopped. The empty house seemed to reach out to him and envelop him in its presence.

Rylan squared his shoulders and marched back into the house. Tonight he would slay these dragons. Tonight with God's grace, he would begin to move forward with his life.

The next morning Rylan woke in one of the children's bedrooms. The cock's crow and the glorious sunrise gave him a new outlook on the day. He hadn't slept much, but when he finally did fade off, his sleep was deep.

❈

Day after day Rylan found himself getting stronger. The pain of Margaret's betrayal wore less on him. The house began to smell alive, and Judith's canning every day helped tremendously. The smell of new wood was mixed with wonderful aromas. Several evenings he even arrived to find homemade meals, thanks to Judith.

Oddly enough, he and Judith spent little time with each other. She'd leave him a message of what she'd accomplished each day and what she planned to do the following day. Only once had he managed to get home early enough from the fields to find her cleaning up.

Today would be different. He needed to see her. He needed to thank her, he continually told himself. He caught a whiff of. . .of. . .roast beef? Rylan took the front steps two at a time.

"What smells so heavenly?" He tossed his hat on the old rocker and rounded the corner into the kitchen.

"Rylan!" She jumped. "I wasn't expecting you."

"Sorry to startle you. What smells so good?"

"Beef brisket."

"Judith, you don't have to cook my meals for me. But thank you, they are most enjoyable."

She smiled. "I know, but I'm here cooking anyway. Besides, I figured it would help you feel more at home in your own house."

He pulled out a chair and sat at the table. "It does, and I'm doing better on that score. Thank you very much. You were right. There's more in this house that is a part of me than Margaret."

"Oh, Rylan, I've prayed for you every day. I'm so glad to hear the Lord is answering our prayers."

"I hope you don't run out of vegetables to can. My stomach will never forgive me if I make it go back to my own cooking."

She giggled. "Better prepare your stomach. One more day, and I'll be done."

Rylan didn't know what to say. He searched his mind for any other possible vegetables needing canning. "Did you get the vegetables out of the root cellar?"

"All that needed canning, yes. We don't need to can the potatoes, carrots, or hard squashes."

"I wouldn't want to have them spoil." He knew she'd see through this ruse but. . .

She slapped him on the shoulder. "You can hire me as your cook."

"Now that's a thought. How much?"

"Hmm." She tapped his shoulder. "How much is it worth?"

❇

Judith chuckled as she left Rylan's house. She hadn't meant to work herself into a permanent job, but it looked promising. The extra income would be helpful, and the change of scenery a blessing. The dugout, while functional, depressed her. Its dark interior didn't compare to Rylan's light-filled home. She enjoyed her time there, perhaps too much.

The next day she found Rylan in the kitchen when she arrived. "Good morning, Rylan. Are you feeling ill?"

"No, I'm fine. I've been waiting for you."

Why? Was he regretting his decision to hire her to cook his meals? She poured herself a cup of coffee, added some cream and sugar, and sat down beside him. "What's the matter?"

"Nothing." He looked down at his hands, then back at her. "Everything."

"I don't understand."

"We need to talk."

"All right." She sipped the bitter coffee and added more cream and sugar.

"I've had a response to my ad."

"What ad?" She sat down at the table with him.

"For a wife."

A wife? He advertised for a wife? Why would he do such a thing? He's a handsome, caring man. Any woman would love to have him as a husband.

"After I read the marriage announcement in the paper, I decided I had little choice. I need a wife, Judith." His gaze pierced her soul. "Do you know why I've been working late every night?"

"Avoiding me."

"Yes, but do you know why?"

What could she say? He was afraid of his feelings. She was avoiding her own as well. They had connected at the fair, a real connection. She'd been dreaming about Rylan every night. She'd been wondering if she could be happy as his wife. She knew she loved his house, but that wasn't the reason a woman should marry a man. It should be for love. Something both of them avoided, and something that each of them was too afraid to talk about.

"Judith." His voice softened. He reached for her hand. "Am I just fooling myself, or do you care about me, even a little?"

Her mouth went dry. Did she want this much honesty? Could she afford to? "I care, Rylan, but we don't know each other. Do I care only because of your house?" She slipped her hand over her mouth. She hadn't intended to be that open.

Rylan grinned, then relaxed. "I hadn't thought of that."

"I understand your desire for a wife, but I'd be lying to you if I said I was in love with you. I love your house, I love the way the light streams through the windows, and I enjoy speaking with you. But are we right for each other? Do we. . .can we have a love for one another?"

Rylan pushed himself from the table, scraping the chair across the hardwood floor. He paced for a moment, then stopped and kept his back to her, looking out the back door. "I've given up on love, Judith. I need a wife to have my children, to care for my house."

Judith's heart sank. She wouldn't marry a man without love. She understood his anger and hurt to some extent, but he hadn't seen the woman in three years. And he'd confessed Margaret hadn't written to him in well over a year, and the year before that had brought only occasional letters. Quietly Judith got up from the table and walked over to him. She placed her hand on his shoulder. Warmth radiated from the gentle contact. She cared for Rylan more than she wanted to admit. "Rylan?"

He turned and faced her. Hurt, anger, confusion swirled in his rich orbs. She wanted to tell him there was more to love than what they'd both experienced, but what could she say? She'd avoided relationships. She'd kept men at a distance, not wanting to be dragged into a life of social commitments and a house empty of love. Then reality hit. She didn't like the lifestyle she'd been raised in, she hated its false pretense, and she yearned for a real and honest relationship. One like her parents now had. One she could have with Rylan, if he could open himself to love.

She reached up and touched his cleanly shaved face.

He placed his hands on her shoulders, holding her but keeping her at a distance. "Please, don't give up on love," she whispered. "God can heal all our wounds."

His grip softened.

Words unspoken played between them for what seemed like

an eternity. Unspoken and yet heard, the language of lovers. She knew then that she loved this man, not for his house, not for his land, but because of him. Just him. It wouldn't matter if he owned nothing, if they lived in a simple dugout. She'd love him until she breathed her last breath. But should she marry him when he was still hurting?

"Judith, should I answer the letter?"

"Do you care at all for me, Rylan?"

"Yes, I care. But I can't. . ."

She placed her finger to his lips. "Don't say it. Just promise me one thing, and I'll marry you."

"What do you need me to promise?" His stance became more ridged.

"That you will continue to pray and ask God to heal the hurt Margaret has caused you."

"But. . ."

"I'm asking little, Rylan. I'm not asking you to declare your love for me. I'm not asking for anything more than a promise to allow God to do what we are all asked to do in the Scriptures. I realized something just a moment ago. I never got involved with the men back home because I didn't like the shallowness of their lives. I didn't like how people lived for recognition in society and not for one another in their homes. Marriages were unions that bettered one in business and in social standing. I didn't want that in my life."

"Why were you all set to go back?"

She moved from his arms and walked back toward the table.

"Because I didn't recognize the truth about my life back there. I also now realize that I love you for who you are and not your beautiful house. I'll accept your marriage proposal."

"But I don't love. . ."

She held back the hurt.

"I'm sorry. That is unkind. I care for you, Judith, truly I do." He came up beside her and wrapped his arms around her. "I would never do anything to hurt you intentionally. At least I will try not to do that. But. . ."

She turned in his arms. "Stop talking and kiss me," she said, wiggling her eyebrows.

❋

Rylan had not been prepared for the heat of passion that filled him when he'd kissed Judith. It pretty near stole his breath away. They decided to wait a couple days before they told anyone the news of their engagement. But Rylan couldn't wait. He'd gone straight to town and sent word for a preacher. He'd also sent off a letter to the woman who'd answered his ad, gently declining her offer.

What he didn't expect was to find Judith on his doorstep later that evening. "Judith!" Her name brought a smile to his face.

He came closer. Red eyes. . .

"Rylan, we need to talk."

"What's the matter?" He came and sat beside her.

"My parents and I are moving home by the end of this week."

"What?"

"They need me, Rylan. They can't afford to make it on their own. They can't pay the debt for the seed, which means they can't plant next year. . . ." She burst into another round of tears. He held her close to his chest. He wasn't going to lose her. There had to be a way to keep Oscar and his family in the area.

"Did you tell them we're getting married?" He stroked her head.

"No, we agreed to wait."

"But, for pity's sake, Woman. I can afford to have your parents live with us. They don't need to move."

She pushed herself from his embrace and placed her hands on her hips. "My father has some pride, Rylan. He can't accept a handout like that. Besides, I can't leave them. I don't want to leave you, but. . ."

He'd grown to appreciate Judith. *She'd make a perfect wife. But I'm not about to lose another one to the call of the East.* "I thought you said you loved me?" he challenged.

"I do, but they. . ."

"They need you, and I need you. What's it going to be, Judith, me or your parents?"

"Don't."

Why did I send that letter off to the woman who answered my ad? Rylan's anger bubbled to the surface. "Go, Go! I don't need you. I can get along just fine."

She wiped the tears from her eyes and punched him in the chest. "You stupid oaf." She stomped off and headed toward her home.

"I still have that woman's letter," he mumbled to himself. "I could write to her again." A bitter knot rose in his stomach at the very thought of someone other than Judith as his wife.

He marched into his house, a house filled with Judith's presence. She'd left a bouquet of flowers on the table and a note. His hand trembled as he reached for the paper.

Dear Rylan,

As you look at these golden mums, think of me, and know that I love you and look forward to our life together.

Love,

Judith

Rylan closed his eyes and swallowed back the bile. He'd hurt her. His chest still smarted from the solid punch she'd landed on him. "Of course you hurt her. You are an oaf," he chided himself.

He crumpled down in a chair. "And now you've lost her."

Chapter 7

Judith wiped her tears away and washed her face by the well before coming into the house. Her parents didn't need to know her heart was breaking. She'd given them months of grief, telling them how much she wanted to go back home, and now that they'd decided to go. . .

No, don't think about it. Don't even trek down the path where those foolish thoughts will lead. Who got engaged without a courtship anyway?

She'd been affected by the constant marriage proposals, forgetting her good social graces and openly discussing matters of the heart that were best left in private.

In her room, if the small section of the house could be called a room, she began packing her trunk.

"Judith," her mother called.

"I'm in my room, Mother. Packing."

"Goodness, Child, we have a few days."

She kept her back to her mother. She could still feel the swelling of her eyes.

"We aren't moving back to Worcester."

Judith turned. "We're staying?" she said a bit too brightly.

"No, what I meant to say was that we were going to Springfield, to stay with your father's cousin. But, what's going on Judith? You look like you've been crying."

"Must be the dust," she said evasively.

"The dust, my foot. Sit down, Daughter, and tell me what's going on."

"There's nothing to tell, Mother."

"Judith Joy Timmons."

Judith cringed. It didn't matter that she was twenty-two years old. She still felt as if she were five years old and had been caught doing something wrong.

"Please, Mother, don't ask."

"All right. But if someone's— No I won't finish that thought." She bit her lower lip and lines of worry etched across her forehead.

"Oh no, Mother. Nothing like that." Judith drew in a deep breath. "All right, I'll tell you. But promise me you won't tell Father."

"I'm not promising anything. 'Fess up, Child. What has happened?"

Judith filled her mother in on the details of her short-lived engagement with Rylan and his insistence for her to choose between her parents and he.

Her mother held Judith's hand. "He is right, you know. A woman needs to go with her husband."

"But he isn't my husband yet, and. . ."

"No, Daughter. If you consented to marry him, then he had the right to want you to stay and be with him."

"But you need me."

"Truthfully, Dear, we can get along quite well without another mouth to feed and body to clothe. I would miss you terribly, and I would miss seeing my grandchildren. You say he wants a dozen?"

Judith chuckled. "Yes. I do love him, Mother. And I think he loves me more than he realizes."

"Then go back to him and work this out."

"But what of you and Father? I don't want you so far away."

"Leave it in the Lord's hands, Judith. He'll work everything out. Even with you and Rylan."

Judith got up to leave. "You're sure?"

"Positive. Now shoo."

She practically ran to Rylan's, her third trip in one day. The small path between their two farms was getting well worn.

"Rylan," she called. No answer. She called again. She entered each room. Nothing. "Where are you?" She placed her hands to her hips and sighed. Then it hit her. He spent so much time in the woods, perhaps he was there.

The sun was setting by the time she made it to the edge of the tree line. She could smell a small campfire and headed toward it. "Rylan," she called.

"Judith, what are you doing out here?"

"Looking for you."

He came to her and held her to himself. "I'm sorry, Judith. I didn't mean to speak so sharply."

"I'm sorry too. I want to be your wife, but I don't want my parents to move back to Massachusetts. Mother said they would move back to Springfield and work in the mills or factories."

"There's got to be an answer." Rylan held her close. "Judith, I don't want to lose you. I–I. . ." He bent down and kissed her again. She wrapped her arms around the back of his neck and savored the sweet kiss. A lifetime of his kisses would keep her satisfied, she mused.

Rylan cleared his throat. "I sent for a preacher."

"Already? I thought we were going to wait. Oh, I did tell my mother."

Rylan chuckled. "When the preacher comes, we'll marry. He should be here by the end of the week."

"You give a girl a long time to make her wedding dress," she said with a smile. In all honesty, she didn't want to wait, either.

"Come sit by the fire. The air is starting to cool."

She looked around at the canopy the trees made. "It's beautiful in here."

"I find solace here—the gentle lull of the brook, the way the trees circle and make this an outdoor cathedral."

"It's beautiful."

"You're right, you know. I am an oaf. Just this morning I promised not to hurt you, then I did. I am sorry."

"It's. . ."

He placed his finger to her lips. "Shh, I have more to say. I found your note and flowers. Thank you. But more importantly, when I walked into the house, I couldn't imagine anyone but you as my wife. I don't want anyone else. I want you, Judith, only you."

Her smile brightened.

"I only want you for a husband, Rylan. Tell me about yourself as a boy. What do I have to look forward to when raising our sons?"

Rylan roared. "A handful. I wore my mother out. I brought home more critters in my pockets—toads, snakes. The spiders had a way of getting out long before she found them, though."

"Oh dear, maybe I ought to reconsider."

"For better or worse, you're promised to me." Rylan grinned and kissed her again.

Under the sparkle of the stars, they talked for an hour, maybe longer. "I better take you home," Rylan finally said, regret tingeing his words.

"Yes, Father will be worried."

"Do you need anything to prepare for our wedding?" To hear those three special words. She held back her tongue and decided not to push. He'd almost said he loved her when he'd said he didn't want anyone else as a wife. For now, she'd have to settle for that.

"No, I couldn't possibly sew a new dress by week's end."

He nodded and held her elbow as he escorted her out of the woods and toward her home. "Careful, there are some gopher and prairie dog holes around the area."

"Rylan, would you pray with me about my parents?"

"I have been, but sure, I'll pray with you." They stopped in the field under the black velvet sky. He took her hands. "Father, we don't know the answer here, but we're trusting you to work out the details in the Timmonses' lives. You know their financial needs, and you know where they should live. We trust them into Your care. Amen."

As they prayed together for the first time, Judith's heart warmed hearing Rylan's words. She cleared her throat. "Father, we also ask that You would help lead us in making the right decisions, and I thank You for someone as wonderful as Rylan for a husband. In Jesus' name, Amen."

"Judith, how can you pray that way? You don't know me."

"But I do. I know you by the character you've expressed to me and to others. How you care for your animals. The details you put into the house when building it. And I now know that you kept your mother hopping as a boy. I do look forward to getting to know you better, though."

He wrapped his arm around her shoulders and pulled her toward himself. "You're too good for me, Judith."

"Perhaps you don't know me all that well, either."

Rylan chuckled.

❋

What a day! Rylan pulled the covers up over his weary body. First he got engaged, then not, then engaged again, and now he was sitting here wondering why she loved him. It wasn't like he'd given her many reasons. The memory of their shared kisses brought assurance that he would be happy with this woman by his side the rest of his life. But there was still the issue of love. Could he really love her? A part of him ached to love her. Another part of him refused to open his heart.

The words of Proverbs 24:27 circled around and around in his head. For three years he'd lived by that Scripture. Every decision he'd made about the farm, the house, Margaret, and himself revolved around that verse: "Prepare thy work without, and make it fit for thyself in the field; and afterwards build thine house."

First he'd prepared the fields. Then he'd built the house. Preparing the fields had taken him the extra year. He couldn't develop the land and build the house as fast as he'd hoped. But now, with Judith, the fields were prepared and so was the house. She didn't have to wait. He didn't have to wait. They could, and would, be married by the end of the week.

But he knew she loved him, and he couldn't say the words to her. "Father, am I so hard-hearted that I can't receive the love she's giving me? I want her love in return. I crave her love. But shouldn't I be giving her that same love? Doesn't she deserve that from the man she loves? Is it really fair to her to go into a marriage when I don't know if I love her?"

Rylan rolled to his side and pulled the covers higher. The heat of Indian summer had passed. Kansas was now experiencing much cooler temperatures. He glanced out the window to the wooded area between his land and Oscar's. He'd cleared most of the trees from his land for farming. Those trees gave him the wood to build the barn, the house, and have many winters of heat from the cords of logs stored behind the barn.

"The trees!" Rylan jumped up out of bed. "That's it."

He hustled into his pants and shoes. Oscar could cut and sell the wood from the trees on his property.

Rylan stopped buckling his trousers. It was late, real late. The news could wait until morning. He reversed his actions and went back to bed. Proceeds from the sale of the trees would clear up Oscar's debt, but it wouldn't solve the problem of his needing to live on the land for three additional years. It would only be a temporary fix.

He took in a deep breath and sighed. Oscar and Raixa would still end up leaving the area. But it would help with the debt, he reasoned.

Late into the night he considered Oscar's problems. Even later into the night he thought about bringing Judith into his home as his wife. A smile crept across his face. Yes, God had blessed him. The woman with golden eyes weaved through his dreams.

❋

The next morning Rylan found himself studying his bedroom. "Should I tear down the wallpaper, Lord?"

"Only if you must," Judith whispered from behind him.

"Judith, when did you arrive?"

"A minute ago."

He reached for her and held her close. "Do you mind that the flowers are purple lilacs?"

"No, they are one of my favorite flowers too. And look here, they've put the pink and white lilacs in the design as well."

She traced the floral pattern. He'd noticed it. He thought he remembered them being there. Guess I didn't pay too close attention to them. "You don't mind?"

"No, but if it's too hard of a memory for you. . ."

"I don't believe it's a problem."

She smiled. "Great, because I think this has to be one of the prettiest rooms I've ever seen. Come here." She grabbed his hand and brought him to the bay window facing the east. "The room fills with the morning sunlight. It's wonderful."

"Do you. . .would you want to make curtains?"

"Yes, I'm thinking some light sheers under some nice thick colonial off-white. What do you think?"

"I'm thinking I don't know the first thing about curtains, as you can tell, because there isn't one in the house. Just tell me what you need, and I'll purchase it."

"You'll spoil me, Rylan. I haven't had spending money in a few years."

Rylan smiled. There were things he could do to let her know she was special. "I'm not rich, but I have some set aside for the house."

"All right then, if you don't mind, I think we should put heavy curtains up before winter sets in. I'll measure the windows and tell you what I need."

"Excellent. Now, I need to speak with your father. I think I found a way for him to pay off his debts."

"Really?" Judith jumped into his arms. "Tell me."

Everything was fitting into place, Judith decided. Rylan's news about the trees answered her parents' needs. Rylan and her father went to work on cutting the trees the next day. The goal was to cut only what was needed. The wooded cathedral area would stay intact. Her parents would try and stay another year but knew they would need help with the planting. Rylan couldn't work both farms, but he'd given his word to help them with a small section.

In the past two days, she'd seen Rylan increase in his comments of appreciation, complimenting her beauty and repeating how happy he was that she'd agreed to be his wife.

Judith searched the cleaned kitchen. Satisfaction flooded her soul. Tomorrow the preacher was due in. The house sparkled. The wedding was to be held in the house at two in the afternoon. She went to Rylan's room and made the bed and dusted. Her mother had helped her move her clothing in earlier in the day. Tomorrow she'd be spending her first night with her husband. . . . Judith trembled at the thought. "Husband," she whispered.

"Judith," Rylan called from downstairs.

"I'm upstairs." She wanted to add "in our room."

"Judith!" Panic filled his voice.

Judith ran down the stairs. She didn't know what to expect. To see him lying in a pool of blood or what? Relief washed over her when she found him sitting in the rocker with a crumpled paper in his hands. "What's the matter?"

"Margaret is arriving tomorrow."

"What?" Couldn't this woman have picked a better time to ruin this man's life again?

"Here." He handed her the paper from the telegraph office.

She plopped onto the floor.

"Does she not know you read about her marriage to Jackson?"

"I didn't tell her. But look, they're both arriving. Why?"

"I don't know, but can't you have someone meet them at the stage and tell them not to bother to get off?" She knew he still loved Margaret. Was she so afraid of Rylan seeing his first love that their marriage would end before it began?

"I thought of that, but it doesn't seem right somehow."

"And you think it's right that they should be arriving on our wedding day." Her voice rose.

He jumped up from the rocker. "Of course I don't think it's right, but what can we do? I have to see them. I have to postpone our wedding."

"No you don't."

"It's the Christian thing to do, don't you think?"

"That's not fair."

"Look." He knelt beside her. "I know this isn't fair. It's not fair to you, and it's horrible timing. But I do feel I need to speak to them. Especially when she wires that she's here to discuss our marriage. Don't you think that's a bit odd?"

"It's more than odd, it's deceitful." She could taste the bile in her words.

He knit his reddish brown eyebrows together. "I want to find out what's going on. I need to know, Judith. Can you understand that?"

"Yes and no. Oh, Rylan, I don't want to lose you."

"You won't. I'm not a foolish man. They can't deceive me."

He pushed back the strands of her hair that had fallen in her face. "I promise we'll marry."

"But. . ." The tears came. She couldn't hold them back. He'd never declared his love to her, and now on their wedding day, he was going to meet the woman he loved. It was horribly unfair and dreadfully painful.

"Oh, sweet Judith. Come here, my sweet golden eyes. I give you my word we shall marry. I promise."

"Marry me now, Rylan. Let's not wait. The parson is in town tonight. Can't we call upon him?"

She leaned forward to kiss him.

He placed his finger upon her lips. "Trust me," he whispered and left.

Left her alone, sitting on the floor of the room that moments before had held so much promise.

"Oh, God, no," she cried.

Chapter 8

Congratulations, Rylan, I'll see you at the wedding," Dick Morgan called out from across the street the next morning. Rylan had left a note on the door of the house explaining that the wedding had been postponed. He'd even filled Pete Anderson in and asked him to spread the word. Apparently it hadn't spread as quickly as he'd hoped. Thankfully, the parson understood the situation and agreed to stay another day. The town needed to hear a gospel message on Sunday, anyway, Rylan reasoned. He avoided Judith. He'd promised not to hurt her, and that's all he'd been doing.

The stage was late.

Rylan felt the pulse on his neck throb. "Get control," he reminded himself.

He released his clenched fist.

The noise of creaking leather, clinking chains, and horses working their way down Main Street indicated the stage was rounding the bend into town. Rylan placed his hat upon his head and waited.

The door of the stagecoach opened slowly.

Rylan's breath caught in his throat.

Margaret emerged from the carriage. He'd always thought her beautiful, but her looks paled in comparison to Judith's.

"Rylan!" She waved and smiled, her hands gloved in white.

He gave a slight nod.

Jackson emerged, a bit thinner than in years past. "Hello, Rylan, it's good to see you." He reached out his hand.

Rylan accepted the gesture.

"He knows," Margaret whispered.

Jackson eyed him slowly. "Yes, I believe he does. Sorry, Rylan. We'd like to talk with you, if you wouldn't mind."

"There's not much to say, is there?"

Jackson put his arm around his wife. "Actually, I believe there is. If I didn't, I wouldn't have wasted our time coming out here. I. . .we need a favor."

"You two are really something." Judith's voice rang through the air.

"Pardon me, Miss, but this is a private conversation." Jackson bowed slightly.

Rylan caught his voice and his temper. "Judith, not here. Jackson, Margaret, you can come to my home and discuss the matter. And Jackson, this does involve my future wife." He held out his hand and grasped Judith's. "You shouldn't have come," he whispered.

"I know, but I was going stir-crazy in the house."

"I'm glad you're here." He held her closer.

Rylan made arrangements for Jackson and Margaret to be transported to his home and returned with Judith in his wagon. "They're in trouble, Judith. I don't know what the problem is, but I can see it in their eyes. Something is terribly wrong."

"Why would they come to you?"

"Other than the fact that Jackson and I have been through thick and thin together as young men, I wouldn't know."

"She's in a family way," Judith offered.

"Are you sure?"

"Fairly. I'm not certain, but she looks to be."

Rylan felt his jaw tighten. "I'll. . .no, we'll need to help them. I don't know how, but. . ."

Judith reached over and took his hand. "The Lord will show us what to do." She paused then, hoping to break the tension, teasingly added, "You sure you don't want to swing by the parson's and get hitched before we go back to the house?"

Rylan chuckled. "I'd love to, but you deserve better, Judith. I'll not be a party to giving you less than you deserve on your wedding day."

"On our wedding day," she corrected.

"On our wedding day." He reached his arm around her and pulled her close. "I love you, Judith. I love you more than I've loved anyone else. I didn't want to admit it. I didn't want to admit that I'd been wrong for three years. But seeing Margaret." He paused and eased out his breath. "I know I never loved her the way I love you. What I feel for you is so much more than what I ever felt for Margaret."

"Oh, Rylan, hearing those words, I can wait as long as it takes."

Rylan grinned. "Not too long, I hope. Do you know how hard it was to sleep in that house last night, knowing your belongings are all in there and that I shouldn't have postponed the wedding?"

"We could still call on the parson." She winked.

"Come here, golden eyes."

She snuggled closer. He leaned over and kissed her. "Soon, my love. Soon."

❄

Rylan could take all the time he wanted. She'd heard the words she'd been longing for. He loved her; he truly loved her. She could wait. But she prayed it wouldn't be too long.

By the time they all gathered at Rylan's house, it was time to start cooking dinner. Rylan and Jackson went for a walk to speak privately with each other, while Margaret stood in the kitchen and observed Judith's preparations for the noon meal.

"How far along are you?" Judith asked.

Margaret paled. "Five months."

"Oh." Judith flinched. Only one interpretation could be given to Margaret's answer. The woman had been expecting before she married Jackson.

"My father is furious. He's ruined Jackson's chances of employment. We came here because. . ."

"Because you hoped Rylan could help."

Margaret nodded.

"Why didn't you write him, tell him the truth? You hurt him." Judith clamped her mouth shut.

"How do you tell a man who writes you faithfully that you've fallen for his best friend, and worse yet, how do you tell him you've, you've. . ."

"Got your point there. But still. . ."

"I should have written him. I know there's no excuse."

"Sit down, Margaret. Can I get you anything?"

"Some tea would be nice."

Judith poured boiling water into a china teapot.

"That's beautiful. Is it yours?" Margaret asked.

"Yes, it was my mother's. She gave it to me for our wedding."

"When is your wedding?"

"It's been postponed."

"Why?" Margaret's gaze met Judith's. "I'm sorry," she offered. "I didn't know."

"Your timing could use some work."

Margaret plopped her swollen feet up on the chair next to her. "You are so right. Seriously, I am sorry to have ruined your plans. Jackson says we can go west and build a home."

"Plenty of land around here." Judith clamped her mouth shut again. Why did she offer that?

"Jackson is hoping to find work in the area and move west after the baby is born. I don't mind telling you, I'm frightened. I know what we did was wrong, and we're paying for that, but I feel it would have been just as wrong to marry Rylan. He's a good man, but. . ."

Judith grinned. "What you feel for Jackson isn't the same as what you felt for Rylan."

"Exactly. It didn't start out that way. The first year Jackson would just check in on me, see how I was faring, that kind of thing. But then we started to talk and talk, and things just escalated from there. For a year I've been trying to write Rylan and tell him what happened. For a year, Jackson refused to marry me until I told Rylan about us. Then it happened. We announced our engagement and married before my parents could notice my condition. When they found out. . ." She shook her head and buried her face in her hands.

"Judith," Rylan called.

She handed Margaret a cool, damp cloth. "In the kitchen."

"Judith, Jackson and Margaret will be staying with us for a little while." Us. Her heart raced.

"All right. Dinner is just about ready. I'll see you later." Judith stepped toward the door to leave.

"Hang on, Judith, we need to talk. Excuse us, Jackson, Margaret." Rylan gently grabbed Judith's elbow, led her up the stairs to one of the spare rooms, and closed the door. "I'm sorry, this isn't the way a newly married couple should live, but they're in trouble."

"Real trouble." She sighed.

"What did she tell you?" he asked, sitting on a chair.

"That she's with child."

"Yeah, Jackson told me about their relationship before and after they married. I'd like to wring the man's neck, but he's done enough of that to himself. He's skin and bones from worry."

"I imagine so. Is her father that cruel of a man?"

"I've heard rumors to that effect. I know some fathers do it, but I can't imagine throwing out your own child like that."

"Me, either."

"Judith?" He captured her hand and pulled her toward himself. "We can do a couple of different things here. We could get the parson to come over after the service tomorrow. Or we could go and see him tonight. In either case, I want to take you away from here. For a day or two, I want it to be just you and me.

Helping Jackson and Margaret is going to take a lot of patience and a whole lot of God's grace, but I want us to start our marriage on our own. Just you and me. What do you say?"

"I say you're the most wonderful man in the world, and I'll follow you anywhere."

He pulled her into his embrace. "Marry me, Judith, and make me the happiest man alive."

"You silly oaf, of course I'll marry you. How about tonight?"

Rylan groaned and captured her lips. "Tonight's just fine, my love. Let's get word to your parents, the parson, the entire town!"

Judith chuckled. "In a minute. I'd like another moment with you all to myself."

Rylan picked her up and carried her down the stairs.

"Don't you have this wrong?"

"No, Ma'am, we're doing it right. First the marriage, then the threshold. I'm just practicing the carrying part." He kissed the top of her head.

Epilogue

September 1856

"Come on, Honey, the fair is going to start without us," Rylan called up to his wife.

"Hold your horses."

He roared. "That's the problem, they want to win again."

"Tell them to behave themselves or I won't be giving them sugar tomorrow."

Rylan smiled as he watched his wife descend their stairway. "I hope you and your mom made the black raspberry tea again. I know I'll have a powerful thirst today."

"More than you know. Sit down, Rylan. I need to make a cup of tea."

"Are you feeling all right?"

"I'm fine, nothing a few months won't take care of."

Rylan gazed down toward his wife's stomach. "You mean?"

"Yes."

"Ye-ha!" He grabbed her into his arms and twirled her around. She paled. "Oh, sorry. Can I get you anything? Sit down. Honey, are you all right?"

"I'm fine." Judith smiled. "Crackers, dry crackers would be nice. At least that's what Mother said would help."

"Honey, we can stay home if you're not up to it," Rylan offered.

"No, you've been working that team too hard not to let them compete. Besides, I like watching the way your muscles play on your back. It was the first thing that attracted me to you."

"It wasn't my winning personality, huh?"

"Nope, pure physical attraction."

Rylan roared again. "Don't ever change, my love. I love you just the way you are. Pure, honest, and straight to the point. God's blessed us."

"Yes, and I'm so glad Jackson and Margaret are in their own place now."

"Me too. Your father is amazing with numbers. The town will benefit from the new bank he's organizing."

"I pray it remains stable."

"It will; he won't make the same mistakes."

Rylan pulled her into his arms.

"I love you, Judith. Thank you for becoming my wife and the mother of our children."

"I love you too, Rylan. You're right, I fit into life here much better than I ever did back East."

He kissed her, a kiss that spoke volumes in commitment and love. Life was definitely better. . .after the harvest.

LYNN A. COLEMAN

Lynn makes her home in Miami, Florida, with her husband of twenty-eight years, serving the Lord as pastors of Christ Community Church. Together they are blessed with three married children and seven grandchildren. Lynn loves writing and speaking for the Lord's glory. She also hosts an inspirational romance writing workshop on the Internet and serves as advisor of the American Christian Romance Writers, an organization she co-founded. She enjoys hearing from her readers. Visit her Web page at www.lynncoleman.com.

A Test of Faith

by Freda Chrisman

Dedication

To my grandchildren:
Dave, Jon, Melly, Josh, Beth, and Joey.
Never forget how much you're loved.

*"Because thou hast been my help,
therefore in the shadow of thy wings will I rejoice."*
PSALM 63:7

Chapter 1

"But it can't be, Aunt Sarah!" The telegram dropped from her hand as Anita Gaines yanked at the bonnet ribbons choking her. "When Father left us, he said he'd be back in Prairie Center in a week! Now it's a month and three days, and he's returning from Topeka with a wife and a sixteen-year-old stepdaughter!"

Sarah Gaines scooped up the shocking telegram and led Anita outside of the telegraph office. Encircling an ancient maple tree, a wooden bench offered the weak-kneed girl a quiet place to regain her poise. Aunt Sarah untangled Anita's ribbons and removed the ruffled bonnet that matched the girl's blue gingham dress.

"Let's keep our voices down, Dear," Aunt Sarah whispered, handing the bonnet to Anita. "Brodrick wouldn't like us discussing this until he has time to explain."

Anita's hands would not obey her. The bonnet slid off her lap. "It must be a mistake! How could Father become so attached to a woman that he'd marry her in such a short time?"

Aunt Sarah picked up the bonnet again and placed it on

the bench beside her. She took Anita's hand. "I suggest we make our way home as calmly as possible and let our minds absorb this as we walk. Can you do that?"

"Yes, Ma'am." Her aunt's firm voice gave Anita strength to obey. She got up slowly, donned her bonnet, and marched forward with her back straight and her head held high.

Unhurried shoppers strolled around the town square. Anita and her aunt had intended to shop for lace to trim a dress, but neither cared to shop after reading the telegram from Anita's father. In the western sky beyond the corner buildings, dark clouds gathered, underscoring Anita's somber mood. Fluttering in the Kansas breeze above them, banners lettered in red and yellow announced the upcoming Prairie County Fair of 1905.

Determined not to cry, Anita set a fast pace her aunt's short legs couldn't match. Aunt Sarah was spry, however, and her pretty face was unwrinkled at age fifty. Anita waited for her while wondering if she was being unfair to her father. Maybe. Yet, wouldn't any girl feel slighted upon hearing of a new stepmother? A stranger? With a daughter just two years younger than herself? Her hand moved to her trembling lips. Why hadn't her father warned her of the possibility of his marrying? It's cruel, and so unlike him.

They swept onto Walnut Street, colliding with a burly youth with reddish hair who staggered awkwardly to regain his balance. Like a hungry puppy, Gilbert Boone's brown eyes seemed to devour Anita. She tensed, intending to move away until she felt Aunt Sarah's deterring hand on her arm.

"Hello, ladies!" Gilbert greeted them enthusiastically. "Imagine meeting you here when I'm on my way to your house."

His words came wrapped in sweaty smiles, induced by the Yale sweater he wore under his jacket. He'd be a sophomore at the Ivy League school that fall and never left the house without advertising the fact.

"I'm sorry, Gilbert," declared Aunt Sarah. "You'll have to excuse us. I've asked Anita to help me shop for a particular lace for my new walking dress. I intend to look my best at the county fair, you see." She pulled off a white cotton glove and fanned herself with it.

"Maybe another day," Anita called as they stepped along. "Good-bye, Gilbert!"

Trailing them, the man persisted. "Wouldn't you like to stop at the pharmacy for a cool cherry phosphate? I know I'd like one," he said, running his finger around his shirt collar. "Has your father come home yet, Anita? What do you suppose is keeping him so long?"

Aunt Sarah turned calmly. "Gilbert, we really have to shop for my lace. You have a phosphate without us. You do look rather warm. Maybe it's fever. Now wouldn't that be a shame? And it's so close to fair time too. I hope you don't miss it." The older woman pulled Anita toward the entrance of a nearby dry goods store.

"All right," Gilbert lamented. "I'll see you soon, Anita."

Seconds later the sound of his footsteps diminished behind them. Making their purchase, they took an indirect route home so as not to run into Gilbert again. Anita felt guilty, but his tedious company would be intolerable just now.

Minutes later they climbed the steps of the porch to Sarah Gaines's yellow frame house. As she opened the frosted half-glass front door, Aunt Sarah and Anita were enveloped in cool air from the darkened house. In the parlor, Aunt Sarah opened the green velvet drapes a few inches, and rosy cherry wood furniture gleamed softly in the half-light, emanating a sense of serenity.

"Just put your things away and come in the kitchen. We'll talk while we have tea." The little gray-haired woman took off her hat as she left by the hall door to go to her bedroom.

Later, in the kitchen, Anita took glasses and sugar from the cupboard, carried them to the table, and opened the icebox for tea and a dish of lemon slices. She smoothed her pompadour with her palms and sank into a kitchen chair.

Sarah's spool heels clicked across the linoleum floor. She stopped behind Anita and placed her hands on the young woman's shoulders to rub the back of her neck. "You have such beautiful black hair, Anita. It has just enough body and curl to make it easy to care for. Mine is like mouse hair. And you have pretty eyes too. Deep sky blue. The only thing missing is a big smile to show those perfect teeth of yours."

"Oh, Aunt Sarah, who do you think you're fooling? I like your compliments, but unfortunately they don't take away the sting of what's happening."

"I know, Dear. But I hoped I could get you to relax and look at this thing rationally. Nothing can be done about your father's marriage. We must accept it, so let's give your confidence a boost. You do have the assets I mentioned, and with God on your side and your good nature, those ladies will bless the day they met you. You'll be a happy family again."

Anita's aunt opened the icebox, and with an ice pick she hacked a chunk of ice from a fifty-pound block. She chopped it in small pieces in a bowl and filled their glasses. The ice crackled and split as the tea splashed over it.

Anita added a spoonful of sugar to her glass. "My mind's still spinning, Aunt Sarah, but I'm trying my best to form a better attitude." She stirred her tea slowly. "They'll be here tomorrow night. I'll have to go over early in the morning and get the house aired out and dusted before they arrive. May I take some of your roses for the entryway and the dining table?"

Aunt Sarah set her tea down and patted Anita's arm. "You would think of that. Of course, you may. I'll help you get the house ready tomorrow. Not that it's dirty, but together we'll have your home so pretty, they'll think they're in heaven."

Anita jumped up and hugged her aunt's shoulders, resting her cheek on her hair. "You remind me so much of Mother. Promise you'll always stay close even after they get here."

"I will, Dear. Don't worry about that. Now, let's decide what we'll prepare for a nice welcome-home supper for your family."

❇

They were home! Anita peered out from behind the curtains covering the front window as her father led his new wife and daughter up to the front door. As they came through the entrance, Anita and Aunt Sarah stepped forward to greet them, and Anita's father offered simple introductions. Anita's new stepmother asked that Anita call her by her first name, Marilla.

"My, it's so dull and shadowy," exclaimed Marilla, examining her new home with a scrutinizing eye. "It's not at all what I expected a banker's house should be. But I guess we'll make the best of it, won't we, Laura? At least until we have a chance to pour our own personalities into it. Before long you won't know it's the same house!" Marilla's laugh changed to a giggle at the expressions of Anita and Sarah.

Laura's eyes studied Anita. "I suppose so, Mama, but I thought you said we'd have a housekeeper."

Dressed in a white middy blouse and blue skirt, Laura took off her wide-brimmed straw hat. With a shake of her head, her blond curls tumbled about, framing a round face with a button nose. Colorless eyebrows and lashes failed to rescue her dull features. Her downturned mouth hinted at a bad disposition.

Anita's father slipped an arm around her shoulders. "To tell you the truth, Anita keeps the house so clean, I never thought of a housekeeper until this very minute."

His brown hair glinted with silver streaks, yet in his dark blue pinstriped suit, he was a handsome figure. Solidly built, he had warm brown eyes and a smile that invited friendship. Anita thought it no curiosity that women were attracted to him.

"Oh, don't do that on my account, Brodrick dear," Marilla said, presumably delighted. "If keeping your house satisfies Anita, I'm sure I wouldn't want to spoil her pleasure. Now if Sarah or Anita will show us to our rooms, we'll get settled." She stepped to the door and called to the man they had hired at the railway station. "Bring the luggage into the house, if you please. Be quick now!"

Anita cast an embarrassed glance at Aunt Sarah. The man was an acquaintance whom she believed had done her father a favor at the railway station by offering his cart to haul the mountain of luggage home. However, as her scrupulous father left the house to take charge of the luggage, she courteously stepped ahead of Marilla and Laura to lead them up the stairs.

"I wondered if you'd like the bedroom on the north side, Laura. That room's usually cool in summer because of the big maples that shade the house. You have several choices for your sitting room, Marilla."

Anita had prayed for a diplomatic approach to the sleeping arrangements for her father and Marilla. Despite her prayers to forget, thoughts of her mother's presence persisted, though it had been five years since her death.

Marilla turned a dainty foot toward a large room at the left of the stairs. Atop her black hat, a tiny bird in a nest of violet lace bobbed with the movement of her head. Though she'd been traveling, her sandy-colored hair was neatly up-swept and her black traveling suit hardly creased. Her hazel gaze scanned the hall.

"This is a pretty room," she said, pointing straight ahead. "I think I'll take it. What about you, Laura?" she asked. "Have you picked out yours?"

Having looked in every room upstairs, the girl sashayed into and around the room, stopping at the center. "I want this room! You took the best room, Mama. Why can't I have it?"

Aunt Sarah, carrying a small canvas bag and a hatbox, preceded Anita's father up the stairs. "I beg your pardon, but that's Anita's room. It's been hers since she was born."

Clasping her hands tight to keep from crying, Anita feigned a cheerful attitude. "It's all right, Aunt Sarah. I'll take the room I'd planned for Laura. Unless you'd like it, Ma'am."

Noticing her husband's presence, Marilla smiled brightly. "Now don't you worry about me. I can use any old room for my sitting room. We just want our sweet daughters satisfied, don't we, Brodrick?"

He smiled broadly. "That's right, my dear, though I'm sure Anita doesn't mind moving, do you, Anita?"

"No, Father. Excuse me, please." Anita averted her gaze as she slipped almost unnoticed down the stairs.

She spoke to the man carrying two suitcases inside and turned toward the kitchen. A moment later, as she took a chilled pitcher of tea from the icebox, Aunt Sarah came to stand beside her.

"We knew there was a chance it might not be easy, didn't we?" she asked softly.

Anita set the pitcher down and turned to her aunt in tears. "I didn't think it would be this hard. I'm going to need your prayers every day."

Chapter 2

That night the family seated themselves for the dinner Anita and Aunt Sarah had painstakingly prepared in honor of the newlyweds and Laura.

Gingerly pinching a slice of Aunt Sarah's excellent bread, Marilla declared, "When we get settled, Anita, I'll teach you the secret of making the lightest bread you ever tasted."

"Marilla's a marvelous cook," exclaimed her father. "While I was away I seldom ate at my hotel. She insisted I have almost every meal with Laura and her in their home."

So that's how the friendship developed so suddenly. Home-cooked food to a widower on a business trip might seem like heaven.

"We-ell, I admit I have my share of culinary talent. So has Laura," Marilla said, smiling at Laura's petulant face.

Anita smiled. "Then you've arrived just in time. The Prairie County Fair will take place next month. There will be a week of competition in food preparation, crafts, and all kinds of needle-work. A display of quilts is also a matter of pride to the women of Prairie Center, and the men exhibit farm products and livestock for the judging."

"Aren't we lucky to have arrived at this time, Laura? The fair will give us a chance to show these country folk how we do things in Topeka. I doubt we'll have any difficulty winning prizes in the ladies' competitions. May I ask what events you two are entering?" Marilla added, looking at Anita and Aunt Sarah.

Anita carried plates to the kitchen as her aunt answered. "I plan to enter several categories. I make a passable angel food cake, and my jams and pickle relish will be entered." She held up a forefinger. "Oh, yes. I also have a quilt for the judging."

"My, you are ambitious, aren't you? We must get busy right away, Laura." Marilla slanted a wink at her daughter.

Anita brought their dessert to the sideboard. She cut her father's favorite, a raisin pie, into equal portions and set them on crystal plates. Bulging with creamed raisin filling, the crisp golden crust broke at the touch of a dessert fork.

She served coffee, and her father smiled his pleasure. "You've outdone yourself on this pie, Anita. It's your best. Um-um-umm!"

Marilla's busy stirring of sugar into her coffee presaged her irritation. "Brodrick, you sound like a little piggy!" She laughed aloud at her fine joke. "Should we enter you in the Prairie County Fair?"

Lowering her head, Anita glanced at her aunt and saw her own emotions reflected. Silently, she prayed. *He's embarrassed, Lord. Let Marilla see that, and help them get along with each other. It's important to all of us, so help me bring harmony and not strife to their lives. Please let this marriage turn out well. In Jesus' name. Amen.*

❋

Anita emptied the coffeepot and washed it for the next morning. She was filling it with water when her father slipped quietly into the kitchen.

"Sorry the girls were too tired to help with the dishes tonight. Next time, I'm sure they'll pitch right in."

Anita turned and hugged her father. "Aunt Sarah and I didn't mind. We always have good talks in the kitchen. She left for home a few minutes ago. The moon's shining bright as day."

"I should have mentioned taking her in the buggy, but so many things happened today, I guess I just didn't think. Marilla wanted some things moved, and I was occupied with that."

Sensing her father wanted to talk as they always did, Anita made quick work of adding coffee to the pot.

"Daughter, come sit beside me."

Anita rinsed and dried her hands and took one of the chairs with him at the round oak table. Her father rested clasped hands on the blue checked tablecloth and sighed. "I expect you're puzzled by my actions this month."

Anita glanced at the wall clock and faced him honestly. "It was a shock. But I've prayed about it, and if you feel this is God's plan for you, I'm willing to do all I can to help."

Her father massaged his temples with his fingertips. "I may have been impulsive, but so far, Marilla's been a comfort to me. I hadn't realized how much I missed the companionship of a woman. When we went out together, I felt like I used to when your mother was alive. After we got married, the feeling grew. I wasn't just a father and president of a bank anymore, I was a husband again, and I seemed to have new respect for myself.

That's the best way I can explain it."

Anita stood, wrapped her arms around her father's shoulders, and laid her cheek against his. Regret filled her voice. "Father, I owe you an apology. I've been thinking only of myself and of the surprise I felt. I understand now. I hadn't realized how lonely you were." Quietly, she took her seat.

"I guess you're too young to grasp the enormity of it. You'd have to live more of life and fall in love yourself before you'd know how I feel." He took Anita's hand. "Will you try to go more than halfway with Marilla and Laura? Marilla has had a hard life. She went into a long depression after Laura was born. Then her husband died, and although she had their house, she had to take in a roomer and do ladies' sewing to maintain their livelihood." He looked deep in her eyes. "I know you try to live your life by what Jesus taught, so I'm hoping you'll put them at ease and make them feel welcome in our home."

Anita recalled Jesus' words in the Gospels: "Judge not, that ye be not judged." She looked away, ashamed. "Yes, Father, I'll try my best. I promise."

Looking up at him again, she added, "Father, Aunt Sarah and I had planned to work on our entries for the fair at our house because we have more kitchen space. But now I believe I'll work at her house. Marilla and Laura need room for their projects, and that way they won't feel as if I'm looking over their shoulders all the time. Don't you think that's a good idea?"

"Why yes, I do. Just be sure to tell me when you need additional supplies, and I'll give you the money. But don't be too standoffish, Anita. They might think you're trying to avoid them."

"I give you my word, I'll try to be a daughter to Marilla and a sister to Laura." Rising again to go to her room, she kissed him on the forehead. "I love you, Papa. Good night."

Tired, Anita went to bed, sure in her heart that she could fulfill her promise. She wanted to be like Jesus. Every day she would make a conscious effort to treat Marilla and Laura as He would.

❄

A week later, Marilla approached both girls at breakfast. "Here's our plan for the day. Brodrick has ordered the produce we need for our canned vegetables and fruit for the fair, and we'll all work on preparing them. But first, Anita, you should go to the store and buy lids for the jars and the paraffin to seal the tops of the jelly glasses. Here. I have everything written down for you." She handed Anita the list. "Now don't dawdle. I need you back here. There's a lot of work to be done."

Anita stepped away from the cabinet where she had been putting away dishes she had done. She took off her apron. "I'll go right away. Let me change my dress, and I'll—"

"The dress you have on is fine. Here's the money. Go on now."

"But I can't go to town looking like this," Anita cried, gesturing to her old blue skirt and waist. "These are my work clothes. Please, Marilla."

"Kindly do me the honor of obeying, Anita," Marilla snapped as she carried a big pan of water to heat on the stove. "Don't hold us up with your complaining."

Remembering her promise to her father the night he got home, Anita clamped her lips shut to avoid being "sassy" as

Marilla had described her to her father a few days before. She stuck the note and the money in her pocket and left by the back door, hoping desperately she would meet no one she knew between home and the store.

Out of Marilla's sight, Anita prayed she'd hold true to her promise, but even as she prayed, she recognized the grudge she still clasped to her heart. *Lord, why can't she talk to me in a normal voice? Why is there always a bite in what she says to me? We're going to be close to each other the rest of our lives. Can't You make her behave?* Anita caught her breath. She'd snatched another fault from the past. Laying out plans for the Lord to put into effect was a bad habit she must break. The Lord was in control, not her. *Please, forgive me again, Lord Jesus. Help me trust You to—*

Anita's feet left the ground, propelled by the force of a huge black dog dragging a leash. She hit the macadam road as the leather untangled from her foot, and the dog raced on. Her left arm took the worst punishment. Blood appeared on a deep scrape below the elbow. A few feet from her, a horse and buggy pulled to a stop, and she reached to pull down her skirt, which had fallen indelicately across her knees.

"Lie still, Miss. Wait until I see if you're all right!"

The command came from a dark-haired, physically perfect man, who jumped agilely from the buggy and ran to her. His mahogany brown eyes assessed the scraped arm, then gave her a quick once-over for other injuries. Finding none, he helped her to her feet. Anita recognized the young veterinarian, Clifford West. She and her father were patients of his father, Dr. West, and half the girls in town were infatuated with the young man. She had no more than a nodding acquaintance with him.

Anita found her face burning as the much-admired animal specialist caught her gaze and smiled, revealing laugh lines around his eyes and mouth. Firm-jawed, his nose was narrow and straight, and his forehead wide, balancing his face in a fascinating mix. If memory served, he was twenty-six.

She found confidence woefully missing. "I–I'm all right. Thank you for helping me. It's only a scrape," she said as he held her arm to examine it again.

"This needs to be cleaned and treated. I'll help you into my buggy, and we'll run you to Dad's office."

Anita remembered her assignment. "Oh, no! I have an errand to do for my stepmother. She's in a hurry for some canning supplies. I'll bandage my arm when I get home."

The look in his brown eyes grew more fervent. "Not until your arm is treated." He fished around in his pocket. "Here," he said, drawing out a fresh white handkerchief. "Wrap this around it until we get there. You're bleeding on your clothing."

Anita did as she was told, at the same time wondering how Marilla would treat the incident. Would she even believe her? She had looked like a beggar before the accident; now, she looked worse. Streaks of blood stained her skirt, and her arm was bloody and painful. There was no choice. Raising her eyes, Anita smiled. Clifford smiled in return and led her toward his buggy.

Conscious of his gentleness as he helped her into the conveyance, she felt her face warm again. She tried to distract him. "My father will pay Dr. West as soon as he learns of my accident. But we must hurry. I'm expected at home as soon as possible, and I have yet to purchase the lids and paraffin my stepmother sent me for."

"Set your mind at ease. After Dad treats the arm, I'll run you home. I'll explain to your stepmother that as I took him home, the dog in my care jumped out of my buggy and tripped you." He chuckled. "I suppose he thought the ride was taking too long, and he knew a shortcut."

With a glance at his smiling face, Anita laughed too. He climbed into the other side of the buggy, and they started off.

Dr. West's hands were as gentle as his son's, and Anita's arm was treated in a jiffy. Telling her how to change the dressing and apply the salve the next day, the doctor released Anita, and his son took over her care once more. He drove her to the store, waited while she made her purchases, and carried them back to the buggy for her. He also stopped by the house of the dog's master to make sure the animal had arrived home safely, and the owner thanked him for coming to explain.

When they were on their way again, Anita decided to satisfy her curiosity. "May I ask a question?"

"Certainly. What would you like to know?"

"Why did you decide on veterinary medicine instead of general practice like your father?"

He smiled. "Two reasons. First, animals don't talk back. Second, they can't speak for themselves, yet they need medical help the same as humans. And I like animals."

He spoke with such satisfaction, Anita thought he must be a fine veterinarian. However, there was no more time to assess his character. They were approaching her home, and she was surprised. She'd given no directions.

"How did you know where I live?"

"You're a Gaines. Where else would you live? Gaineses have always lived in this big white house that just keeps growing."

"Grandfather Rylan Gaines started the house. He willed it to my father. Aunt Sarah insisted on caring for my grandfather and grandmother until they died. Because of her kindness, the family deeded her the little house she lives in. They wanted her to always have a home of her own."

"Why didn't she ever marry? A lady like her?"

"She had a beau. He was killed by his own artillery during the worst days of the war between the North and South. She never wanted another. Instead, she's devoted her life to Christ."

"She certainly has. All this was a little before my time, but I'll bet Dad remembers it. Seems I'm fortunate you came along in my time." Sending her a devastating smile, he made a move to get out of the buggy.

Juggling the package she held and protecting her arm as best she could, Anita made an unladylike exit from the buggy and sped up the path to the house. Her face burning, she dared not turn back to say thank you or even wave. Had he actually flirted with her? No, not Cliff West. She was too young to interest him, and he was the handsomest bachelor in town.

Chapter 3

Marilla was livid. "Where have you been, Girl? I told you I needed those lids as soon as possible!"

"Yes, but I had to go to the doctor's office." Anita held up her injured arm.

"Another excuse. It couldn't have been bad enough to bother a doctor. Now your father will have another bill to pay!" Her stepmother jerked the package from Anita's hand and ripped it open at the cabinet. "Let's have no more talk. Help Laura with the cucumbers, then get busy looking over and washing the berries. Brodrick found good quality produce at a farm the bank took over, and we have to process it quickly so it will keep its color. Nothing impresses a judge like color."

Canning and jelly making were not new to Anita. Year by year, her father bought vegetables and fruit from the farmer who offered the best deal, and she and Aunt Sarah canned all of it. Even meat was successfully canned. The cellar provided savory meals for the Gaineses, Aunt Sarah, and their friends throughout the winter. Produce for their fair entries would have been delivered at both homes today. If she finished helping at home in time, Anita would do double duty tonight at her aunt's.

A single cucumber had Laura's concentrated attention during the interval, and casting a glance at her mother, she declared, "Mama, since Anita took time out, don't you think I should be allowed time to rest too?"

"It will be hard to do without you, Darling, but we'll try. Anita, that means you'll have to finish the cucumbers also. You shouldn't have wasted so much time in town."

Laura snickered at her mother's words and broke for the back stairs to her room.

After a bowl of stew at noon, which Anita prepared and Laura wandered back to share, the three women spent the afternoon in earnest labor. Packing ten-gallon crocks with cucumbers, then filling them with brine, Anita inverted a plate over each crock with a brick to hold the cucumbers down, and the pickling process began. Tomatoes dipped in scalding water peeled easily, then they were canned whole or as juice.

Anita had peeled apples for apple butter since she was eight, but she always found the job a pleasure. She liked the preparation process: spices cooking with crushed apples and sugar, then adding red hots to give them color and flavor. The scent was intoxicating.

Fastidious, Marilla separated the best of the fall blackberries for her jelly. After cooking and crushing them in a colander, she cooked the juice with pectin, sugar, and a splash of lemon. She tested the product's consistency by rolling a sample around the inside of a jelly glass periodically. The mark of a superior jelly maker meant seeing not one bubble in her final product.

Anita finished washing pots, pans, and dishes they'd used and was ready to leave for Aunt Sarah's house earlier than she'd expected.

"I hope you'll prepare supper tonight, Anita," Marilla moaned. "I'm simply too tired to attempt it. When I get the paraffin seal on these glasses of jelly, I'm going to take a bath and freshen up." She poked at the melting paraffin shavings in a pan on the stove.

A bath! How Anita would have enjoyed the same luxury. She pumped another pan of water at the sink and put it on the stove for potatoes. Thankful that plenty of beef roast and broth remained from the night before, she transferred the leftovers to a metal pan, covered it, and slipped the meat into the oven to warm. A plump green cabbage was prepared in minutes; then opening a can of beets from her last summer's store, Anita soon had supper on its way.

Fresh and clean, Laura sauntered through the door, drawn by the enticing aromas.

"Oh, Laura, I promised Aunt Sarah I'd help her with some chores tonight," Anita exclaimed. "Would you be a dear and set the table for me? Then when Father comes in, would you please take up the meat and vegetables? They're almost ready, and there's half a cherry pie in the cupboard. Also a dish of green tomato relish."

"Can't you do it? I'm tired." Laura screwed up a forlorn face.

Anita grabbed a fresh apron from a cabinet drawer. "I just have to go, Laura. Please, do this for me."

"Oh, all right. But you'll have to pay me back."

Remembering Laura's final remark, Anita left by the back

door and hurried toward Aunt Sarah's house. What would Laura's "pay me back" incur? She'd promised her father to help her new family feel at ease and welcome. Today, it had taken all her patience to keep quiet. Marilla and Laura seemed determined to arouse her temper. She hadn't let them. She'd prayed to keep a civil tongue, and God had helped her do it.

"Anita! Where are you going? Wait, and I'll take you."

She looked back to see Cliff West in his buggy coming up the road. Why did it have to be now? Once again she was looking her worst. She had cut through a pasture in her haste, and her cotton stockings were covered with stick-tights. She hadn't taken time to comb her hair, either, and her skirt and blouse were limp and dirty. What a mess! But she stopped and waited for him.

"I'm on my way to my aunt's," she explained.

Cliff's eyes were mesmerizing; Anita found it hard to concentrate on her original objective.

"That's too bad. I was in hopes you'd accompany me on a call to the Lewis place. They have a calf in trouble that they plan to enter in the livestock show." He scooted over. "Get in. I can at least save you the walk."

He held out his hand to assist her into the buggy. To cover her nervousness and satisfy her curiosity, she stammered, "Uh, what's wrong with the calf?"

Still holding her hand, Cliff whispered, "I can't tell from here." He grinned. "It's probably nothing serious. The Roland Lewises are anxious because they're positive the calf will win a blue ribbon at the fair." He flicked the chestnut's reins to move on.

"Oh." Anita smoothed her wispy hair as they turned at the corner and passed beneath a row of maple trees, trying to think of something else to say. Some of the leaves had turned upside down, which old-timers vowed was a sure sign of rain. She decided that would work. "Do you think the tree leaves turn over like that when it's going to rain?"

"I'm not sure," he said with a chuckle. "The weather's a good subject to fall back on, but don't you think we could find a more interesting topic of conversation? For instance, what errand are you hurrying to accomplish this time?"

"Not an errand. As I said, I'm headed for my aunt's. We're going to work on our entries for the fair. Father and I agreed we should let his new wife and stepdaughter have the house for their projects." Suddenly realizing how unfair that sounded, Anita tried to rectify the mistake. "I'm afraid that sounded self-sacrificing, but it wasn't meant to. They have only a short time to get their entries done, and our kitchen is larger, and the cellar is right there, and—"

"I think it sounds like a very considerate girl trying to make her new stepmother and stepsister feel at home. Uh, did you help them get started today?" he asked in an odd voice.

"Yes, then it was time to make supper. Laura, my stepsister, told me she'd take things up, and I headed for Aunt Sarah's. You stopped, gave me a ride, and that's the end." She smiled up at him. "Thank you, by the way."

"You're very welcome," he said, looking deep into her eyes.

When they pulled up in front of Aunt Sarah's modest home, Cliff bounded out of the buggy and in seconds stood ready to help Anita down. She was ashamed to have him get a closer look at her downtrodden state, but she took his outstretched hand.

"I'm sorry I look so terrible. I hope I didn't embarrass you driving through town."

"Of course not. I just assumed you'd been working hard all day and had more work to do tonight." He looked thoughtful. "I'd like to help you out, though. What if I pick you up when I come back from the Lewis farm and take you home? Wouldn't that help?"

She stepped away. "I don't know what time I'll be through. And, uh, I'm afraid Father wouldn't approve of my being out so late with, uh, an older man without his approval."

Cliff took her arm and walked with her to the gate of the white picket fence surrounding the yard. "I'm going to your house, where I'll catch your father alone and ask him to let me bring you home. You'll need a lift by then."

❋

As she walked up the path, Cliff imagined Anita working beside her aunt with the amazing energy and enthusiasm he'd seen in her as she matured into a young woman. It embarrassed her that she had been dressed less than handsomely, yet it made no difference to Cliff. Anita Gaines would be attractive no matter how she dressed. She had no idea the effect her enchanting blue eyes had on someone already enchanted.

He had watched her grow up, though during her so-called awkward years he'd been away, learning his profession. When he'd come home to start his practice, his bachelor status and availability had produced a frenzied wave of anxious young women vying for his attention. They saw him as a candidate for a "happily ever after" life. Anita had never participated.

Cliff was a Christian, and he saw Anita as the only young woman he knew with real commitment to Christ. She sang in the church choir, and during the pastor's sermons, her rapt gaze left the speaker only when she searched her Bible. Children raced to hold her hand or to sit with her. At prayer she seemed in a world apart. Yes, he had noticed her when she was not in working clothes, and she was charming.

Sarah Gaines's front door closed behind Anita, and feeling the void Anita's absence created, he slapped the reins of the horse to continue on his route to the Lewis farm.

❋

"Anita, that's enough for tonight," declared Aunt Sarah while drying a stewer she'd scalded. "You've ground all the green tomatoes and cucumbers you're going to. I'll finish up, and we'll continue when you can get away again. I have my quilt to work on when you're not here. Now, scat, and get a good night's rest." The older woman gave her young helper a quick hug and kiss.

"I have to admit, bed sounds sooo tempting," Anita said.

"I'm glad we had this chance for a long talk about your home situation. Off with you, now, and I'll be praying for you. Don't let your temper get away from you. You can avoid it. Remember, I Corinthians 10:13 says, 'There hath no temptation taken you but such as is common to man: but God is faithful, who will not suffer you to be tempted above that ye are able; but will with the temptation also make a way to escape, that ye may be able to bear it.' "

Anita clasped her aunt's hand and kissed it. "I'll remember."

She walked wearily to the front door, Aunt Sarah following, carrying one of the kerosene lamps. A rap at the door stopped them both. Aunt Sarah stepped ahead and tugged the door open. Cliff stood outside. Smiling, he hesitated only a moment.

"Hello, Miss Gaines," he said politely. "I just came from talking with your brother, Brodrick. He gave me permission to take Anita home. I saw her earlier, and I knew she would be tired. Mrs. Gaines thought I was exaggerating, but she was wrong. I'm sure Anita can use a ride."

"You're right. Go along, Anita. Now that I know you're with Dr. West, I feel much better," she said, ushering her niece out the door.

Almost in a daze, Anita managed the front steps only because Cliff assisted her. Had her father really consented to let him take her home? Of course, he did. Cliff wouldn't lie. He took her hand to help her into his buggy, and a thrill trembled through Anita's body. He'd come back for her! He set the horse in motion, and the trip became a dream come true. What was even more remarkable was that they were conversing together. . . laughing, chatting, changing subjects as if they'd been friends forever.

Soon, they reached her house. Cliff jumped out and came around to help her down. It was then that she saw Gilbert Boone's horse and surrey pulled up to the side of the house.

"Oh dear, Father has company," she said with a little sigh.

"Aren't you the lucky one? It looks like Yale's pride, Gilbert Boone." He lifted an eyebrow. "I forget. Is he your beau?"

"No!" Then seeing his grin, Anita smiled too. "He's a friend."

"That's good to hear. Let's go inside."

Anita giggled, and they dashed up the steps, entering the house in a burst of laughter.

Marilla's skirts swirled as she spun toward the parlor door with an angry face. "Anita! So you're here at last! I had no idea this man was invited here tonight, and here you are, arriving with another one, abusing my hospitality further. Brodrick had an obligation to see a man about his mortgage, but he'll be back soon. You'd better have a good explanation for this intrusion when he gets here!"

Anita hung her head, too embarrassed to look at Cliff.

Chapter 4

Shocked by the woman's outburst, Cliff reached for Anita's arm to pull her back. Anita still could not look up.

Marilla continued her tirade of Anita's faults. "Well, what have you to say for yourself, Girl?" she said in conclusion.

"About what, my dear? I heard you all the way down the hall." The entry of Anita's father through the doorway at the rear of the parlor had gone unnoticed.

Marilla turned a pale face toward him and touched a quivering hand to her hair. "Why, Brodrick dear, I didn't know you were back."

"My errand didn't take long."

No one spoke.

"What's going on here? What has Anita done?" His gaze swept the room.

Cliff and Anita stood just outside the parlor door, cemented there by Marilla's outburst. Gilbert, hardly a stranger, sat on the far end of the sofa from Laura as if petrified by the proceedings.

Anita's father cleared his throat self-consciously and laughed.

"You'll have to excuse me, folks. In this light I failed to notice we had company. Marilla and Laura, it looks as if you're already acquainted with Gilbert Boone, whose father is Gilbert, Senior, one of the bank's founders." Mother and daughter blinked and tried to smile. "But I don't believe you've met Dr. Clifford West, our finest veterinarian." More blinks and smiles.

Cliff laughed. "And the only one. No, we haven't had a chance to be introduced. Anita and I just got here." He gave Marilla a little bow and nodded to Laura, who momentarily lost interest in Gilbert to stare at Cliff.

Marilla's pale face changed to a mild violet, but she sought to extricate herself from censure by blaming Anita. "You should have explained," she sputtered. "You had Laura and me at a disadvantage." Actively wielding her bamboo fan, she declared, "We're happy to have you in our home, gentlemen. May I invite you to have a glass of tea or lemonade?"

Gilbert leaped up and strode toward Anita. "I'd like a lemonade. Anita, may I help you serve it?"

Before Anita could answer, Marilla pulled Laura's arm. "Now why don't we let you and Laura get the lemonade while Anita entertains Dr. West?" Pushing Laura forward, she planted herself between Anita and the two she'd paired off.

"Good idea," said Cliff. "Anita, let's take seats over here on the sofa and talk. Mr. Gaines, would you join us?"

Anita's father plopped into his big wing chair next to them. "You talk while I rest. This has been a long day."

Forgetting her own embarrassment, Anita suddenly realized her father did look tired, and she hoped the evening would continue peacefully.

After directing Laura and Gilbert to the kitchen, Marilla chose an overstuffed chair close to her husband's and settled into it like a mother hen.

"Dear," she addressed him, "you simply must hire a housekeeper. There are far too many duties here for one fragile woman to manage."

"I agree. It would give Anita more free time. I'll place an advertisement in the newspaper in the morning. I should have done it long ago."

Though she felt airing their personal problems before Cliff inappropriate, Anita breathed a thank-you to God for the gift He had given. A housekeeper would lessen the friction in their home considerably.

"Well, I never!" Marilla sputtered. "Not a word of concern for me. Only for Anita." Her pout became a pitiful tremble.

"Now, I didn't mean to slight you, my dear. My thinking is that if we can find a housekeeper, it will benefit both of you. I don't want to see either of you overworked."

Anita wondered if her dowdy appearance had swayed her father toward the idea.

"I suppose your clothes looking so forlorn make you look more tired than usual, Anita," he said, as if reading her thoughts. "I'm used to seeing you fresh and clean. That is, until lately." Frowning, he scratched his head. "I think I'd better put out a few feelers and get a lady in here as soon as possible."

Although sorry the scene had taken place in front of Cliff, Anita needed the support her father had just given her. The incidents were minimal, but now and then, her father and Marilla crossed verbal swords. After one such episode, Anita had seen her father reading his Bible. Could he call up neglected spiritual values to bring them together in Christ? She must do her part to support him in his marriage.

"Well, Cliff, how do you think Teddy Roosevelt will do as president in his own right?"

Anita relaxed a little, grateful her father was trying to change the subject from such personal issues.

"I hear he has some ambitious ideas," her father continued. "When McKinley was killed in Buffalo, he slipped into the office out of necessity, and so far he's done well. Mine owners and workers are speaking again. I'm ready to see what he'll do next."

"The president and I see eye to eye on conserving our natural resources," replied Cliff. "His view of railroad regulation is beginning to interest me too."

Her father smiled. "Well, he has his 'bully pulpit,' as he once called the White House. And he has the energy and the confidence to do some good things. Let's hope he does them."

Anita enjoyed listening to her father and Cliff. Marilla, however, waited only for a pause in the conversation before interjecting her own questions.

"What do you think of the fair, Dr. West? Finding that Laura and I have never had the experience, Anita and Brodrick seem to think our education has been sadly neglected."

Anita cringed and dared not look at her father.

Cliff answered boldly. "The Prairie County Fair is very popular. Even if they don't compete, folks come from all over the state to attend. It's an annual event that's been going on for fifty years that I know of."

Before Marilla could reply, Laura and Gilbert appeared with a tray of lemonade. Anita noticed Laura had used the everyday glasses and waited for Marilla to apologize or send her back to the kitchen for the best ones.

Carrying the tray with uncommon finesse, Gilbert spied Anita beside Cliff on the sofa and stumbled awkwardly over a small stool. Lemonade and glasses flew through the air and crashed like a thunderstorm to the floor. Laura wasted no time deriding her poor assistant, who no doubt had thought to impress her with his Ivy League manners.

Marilla, on her feet and aghast at the breakage, apparently remembered the wealth Gilbert represented and broke into a wide smile. "Oh dear, such a shame. Laura and I will prepare a fresh tray. You men be seated while we go to the kitchen. Anita," she snapped, "until we get a housekeeper, it's your place to get rid of the glass and mop up the lemonade. Quick now!"

Marilla turned and, tugging at Laura's sleeve, exited the room with her daughter.

Anita's father sat as if flabbergasted, and Cliff sprang to her aid. "Anita, you get the broom and mop, and I'll pick up the larger pieces in a—"

"Get that little wicker basket by the desk, Clifford," said her father. "Marilla uses it for waste paper when she does her letter writing. Anita, we'll all help," he said, rising.

Gilbert, finally revived from stark humiliation, stepped back away from the shattered glass. "Yes. I'll help too."

Cliff's frown and raised eyebrows gave Anita a clear picture of how much help he thought Gilbert would be.

"Don't worry, Father. I'll have it taken care of in no time," she said, not glancing at Gilbert.

"We'll have it taken care of—I insist on assisting, Anita," said Cliff with a grin.

When Anita came back from the broom closet, she and Cliff worked together until the accident scene was cleared. Gilbert pouted and took a seat out of the way. By the time Marilla and Laura brought a second tray of lemonade to their guests, the last of the debris lay in the basket, which Anita carried out to the trash.

"Well, I see you've cleaned up," Marilla observed. "It wasn't as bad as I thought."

"We managed quite well, Mrs. Gaines. But I'm afraid I can't stay for refreshments. I have a busy day tomorrow at the fairgrounds," replied Cliff. "The committee in charge of the fair has decided I need to completely inspect the pavilion and stock enclosures."

"Oh, surely you can stay just a moment longer. Laura made these delicious cookies yesterday. You and Mr. Boone must try some." Marilla held the plate in front of him with both hands.

"All right, I'll try this one," said Cliff, and he took a small bite of the morsel, while Marilla offered the plate to Gilbert. Cliff turned to his host. "Mr. Gaines, I'd like to call for Anita to drive her to church Sunday morning. May I?"

So fatigued she had almost lost track of the dialogue, Anita realized a miracle had taken place. She returned Cliff's look with a self-conscious smile.

Marilla shoved the plate of cookies into Laura's hands. "No! Dear, I think we should all go as a family. That is, if we're going," Marilla recanted with a look of irritation.

"We'll decide the issue later," replied the tired banker. "Meantime, I see no reason why Anita and Dr. West shouldn't go together."

"Thank you, Father." Anita aimed a full-blown smile at Cliff. "Thank you, Cliff."

Cliff's eyes warmed as he answered, "You're welcome."

Laura broke in. "I think we should all go as a family too."

"Ahem. . .Laura?" Gilbert said with a vengeful look at Anita. "I was just on the verge of asking if I could come by to take you for a ride Sunday morning."

"Me? Oh, I'd love to go, Gilbert. I may, may I not, Mama?"

"Well. . .I. . ."

"I think we can trust these young men with our girls, don't you, Marilla?" Anita's father intervened.

Marilla sputtered no longer. "Of course, of course! If Laura would like to ride to church in Mr. Boone's surrey, the honor is hers," she gushed.

Gilbert marshaled a wide smile, obviously glad to put his earlier clumsy exhibition out of their minds.

❋

Sunday morning progressed far differently than Anita had imagined. Gilbert arrived to take Laura for a drive in his father's elaborate buggy and later to church, and Marilla beamed with approval.

When they left, Marilla sprang her surprise. "I simply can't let both of you go when we're expecting guests. You're the oldest after all, and with no housekeeper, it falls to you to stay and help. Gilbert Boone is Laura's only friend in Prairie Center, and it's good that they have this chance to get better acquainted."

It was not the time to tell Marilla, Anita realized, but she knew Laura would have more friends if she'd only make the effort. The young people at church had asked Anita about the new girl and hoped to welcome her soon. Gilbert hardly qualified at a religious leader. Seen rarely at church, his attempts at piety failed to convince.

Her attention shifted back to Marilla. "I don't understand. We're having guests? I didn't know anyone was coming."

"I don't believe I need your approval to invite company. Your father has not entertained his staff and their wives since your mother's death. I've decided to have them over for luncheon today. I need your help, so I'm calling Clifford West's home to cancel your church outing."

Astounded, Anita listened to the brief staccato conversation on the wall telephone. Before she could react, Marilla hung up.

"Now. That's taken care of." Marilla reached into a shelf under the cabinet and brought out a big bowl to mix bread. "I bought green beans from a peddler at the back door this morning. They're in the pantry. Get them washed and snapped. Then set the dining-room table for ten with the best china. I'm going to the cellar for my spices. Get busy."

As Anita washed the beans, she relived the moment when Cliff had asked her father to take her to church. Even if she didn't get to go, she'd always have that. He had asked her. Cliff West! He was handsome, kind, a Christian, and happy with his occupation. He was a man she could fall in love with.

Thirty minutes later, she finished the beans and set them on the cabinet, ready for cooking. Taking a tea towel, she set the table, polishing every dish and glass, then placed a bowl of flowers Marilla had ordered for the centerpiece. Next she peeled fruit to cut up for a salad.

"Be sure to add lemon juice to the fruit to keep the taste and color, Anita." Marilla dusted flour on the breadboard once more to knead her roll batter.

"Yes, Ma'am." Anita's mother had taught her how to cook from the time she could understand instructions, but Anita kept quiet and did not tell Marilla so. Setting the bowl of fruit in the icebox, Anita got out a roaster for the meat.

The front door knocker sounded.

Anita started to answer, but Marilla, drying her hands, stopped her. "Never mind. I'll go. You get the roast in the oven."

Her voice allowed no argument, and Anita seasoned and floured the roast to brown it.

"We have a visitor," Marilla said without smiling. "Is the coffee still warm? I'm sure Dr. West would like a cup."

Anita thought Marilla's tone unfriendly, and she wondered how Cliff had charmed his way inside.

"Good morning, Anita," he said with a smile. "Can you use some help? When Mrs. Gaines told me about all the work you had to do, I thought if I volunteered to help, you might still have a chance to go to church. You'd allow that, wouldn't you, Ma'am?"

In utter joy, Anita wondered if Cliff was God's special gift to her this day.

Chapter 5

What's going on here?" asked Anita's father, taking off his hat as he entered the kitchen. "Hello, Cliff! What are you and Anita doing in the kitchen? Anita, you should be getting ready for church."

Cliff, washing a head of lettuce, nodded. "I came to help with lunch preparations," he explained. "It's a cooking party. All hands welcome."

Marilla simpered an excuse. "We invited your staff and their wives for luncheon, Brodrick dear, don't you remember?"

"You said sometime, Marilla. I didn't mean this Sunday."

He took off his coat and started rolling up his sleeves. "I'll take you up on the offer to help, Cliff, on one condition. Anita, go dress in your Sunday-go-to-meetin' clothes, and I'll help Marilla wind this up for you. You and Anita keep your date, Cliff. Take as long as you like."

Smiling, Anita kissed her father's cheek. "Thank you, Papa." Her childhood name for him conveyed thanks for his trust, and she felt her first sense of freedom since Marilla had arrived.

Running up the stairs, Anita contemplated what she would

wear. Should it be the blue or the yellow print? Her white lacy brimmed hat would go with either. Smaller than the top-heavy monstrosities fashionable women chose, the hats Anita wore featured what to her seemed a simpler, tasteful size. She suddenly became aware of the need to update her wardrobe. Most of her clothes were at least two years old. With the house to run, she hadn't bothered to stay in style.

Anita dressed quickly in the yellow, and adding the little hat and grabbing her Bible, she hurried downstairs. Cliff had regained the Sunday-go-to-meetin' look her father had joked about. His dark gray suit looked particularly smart, and Anita's heart filled with pride when he offered her his arm to leave.

❋

The two were the center of attention when they walked into church together. Smiling brightly, Anita's friends rushed to say hello before taking their seats. She was sure her popularity could be chalked up to her escort for the day.

Pastor Brownlow's wife approached them. "Oh, I'm so glad you're here, Anita. You too, Cliff. The choir director was called out of town, and I'm substituting. I'm missing two or three strong voices, and I need you both. Cliff, I know you can sing. Persuade him, Anita. Will you?"

Cliff grinned at Anita. "Want to?"

Anita didn't really. This Sunday she'd wanted to sit beside him in the congregation. But she said, "If you do."

"Looks like you have two more volunteers, Mrs. Brownlow."

All three made their way to a side room where fewer than a dozen other singers had congregated. They were told the hymn they would sing as special music, and they marched single file into the choir loft. Cliff sat directly behind Anita, so she could hear his resonant bass voice through every hymn.

Pastor Brownlow's message drew Anita's mind away from Cliff and all else except worship of the Lord. A small, calm man, the pastor's presence commanded exactly that worshipful attitude.

The text of his sermon went straight to Anita's heart. It came from Matthew 24: " 'Watch therefore: for ye know not what hour your Lord doth come.' " Looking back on her life since Marilla and Laura had arrived, Anita had to admit that many times, if the Lord had come, she'd have been ashamed of her thoughts and attitude.

"Let me ask a question," said the pastor. "Are we as eager for Jesus to come again as we are for the Prairie County Fair to arrive? Everywhere I go, people talk about the fair as if it's the most important thing in the world. We're preparing to the best of our ability: our family's clothes, our schedules, and our entries in the different competitions. When the day comes, we will know it, right down to the minute the gates open. We look forward to great happiness during the week; but at the end, the fair will close, and it will be over until it comes again. Which, of course, the fair will do.

"More surely," the pastor continued, "Jesus is coming. How eagerly do we anticipate His appearance? Is it the most important thing in the world to us? Are we talking about His coming to each other and talking to others who don't know our Savior personally? I wonder if we're preparing to the best of our ability: studying God's Word, praying for our unsaved friends, making sure we've done all we can as Christians to welcome Christ to our contemporary world. Unlike the county fair, we don't know the hour. But Jesus will come. If we are not prepared, there will be no second chance. If Christ's call to our hearts is rejected, it may not come again."

Anita listened with a full heart to all Pastor Brownlow said. When they finally bowed for prayer, she regretted the sermon had ended.

The same emotions seemed to surround Cliff's thinking as they left the church and approached his buggy. "I'm reluctant to take you home, Anita. I want to capture the mood. You and I believe the same, and we think alike. We always seem to be of one mind. I'd like the chance to talk with you for awhile." He handed her into the buggy. "My folks are having lunch at my aunt's home today. How would it be if we stopped by my house, made a few sandwiches, picked up some fruit and a jar of tea, and had a picnic? We could drive out by the river."

"Won't your mother mind our taking food she might be planning to use for supper?"

"Naah, she's used to me inviting people to eat with me. Say yes, Anita."

"Yes."

After preparing a basket of chicken salad sandwiches, apples, and coconut cake, Anita and Cliff set off, spinning along toward the river in his buggy.

"It's a beautiful day for a picnic, isn't it?" Anita asked, taking the hatpins from her hat and placing it gently in her lap.

"As beautiful as your pretty hat," said Cliff. "You know, some of the hats women wear these days are frightening, but I've noticed your little bonnets and hats show much better taste."

"Oh, Cliff, you never even looked in my direction until a few days ago."

Cliff propped a polished half-boot on the side of the buggy. "That's where you're wrong, Anita. You've always been a fascinating character to me."

"Being a character's not a compliment. Makes me sound old."

"Let me rephrase that. I have always been fascinated by the high quality of your character."

Anita shifted in her seat to face him more directly. "How could you possibly know that much about me?"

"I've seen your loyalty, your concern for people, and your ability to keep your father's house at such a young age. Best of all, your Christian values have shown the serious kind of person you are." He turned the horse to climb a slight embankment and stopped the buggy under a large sycamore tree.

Instead of moving to get out, Anita sat still, thinking of what he had said. Cliff was one of the most interesting people she had ever met, and he had noticed all those facets of her personality. Her face warmed. Cliff was waiting to hand her down from the buggy, and she felt still more frustrated that she'd been daydreaming and hadn't seen him get out. She smiled, calming herself, and stepped down.

They spread a checked tablecloth on the grass, and Anita took their food out of the basket.

Cliff sat in the grass opposite her. "Shall we thank God for our food?"

"Would you?" said Anita, bowing her head.

Cliff voiced a brief but sincere prayer, and when they opened their eyes, their gazes held for a long moment.

Anita reached for the tea. "This is still nice and cold," she said, handing him the glass she poured.

"Just what we need after a ride in the sun. A sandwich, please."

Anita obliged and helped herself. "This is such fun, Cliff. Thank you for thinking of it. Aunt Sarah and I have been preparing for the fair. I haven't had much time to simply relax."

"So you go to your aunt's every night?"

"Just about. We're close to the end now. I'm always glad when we finish because most of our canning is done for the winter. We take special pains with those items that go to the fair."

"I know. Mother does the same. But aren't you working too much, Anita? Doing so many things at home, then doing another day's work at your aunt's?"

Anita wiped her lips with her napkin. "I admit it hasn't been easy, but being with Aunt Sarah is a joy. When I talk with her, she brings Jesus so close, you feel Him in the room. She's meant a lot to me spiritually since my mother died. After her death, Father lost interest in the church, I'm sorry to say," she added, her eyes downcast. "Uncle George reminds him when he's around, so we haven't seen him much in the last five years—nor my cousin Ben, whom I miss terribly. I have to be careful what I say too."

"But you haven't lost interest. Among the Christians I know, I see you as the clearest picture of what a true believer is. You're a more adult Christian than many who occupy church pews every single Sunday morning. I admire you, Anita."

She smiled. "I'm not a very productive Christian. Remember what the pastor said about being a positive influence? I'm not a positive influence on my father, or Marilla, or Laura. It makes me sad that I can't seem to live in harmony with them. I'm always asking God's forgiveness for things I shouldn't have done or said or thought." Anita looked away, across the gently moving water. Opposite them, another family had set out a picnic lunch under a tree by the river.

Cliff took a drink of tea and swallowed. "Maybe not everything is your fault, Anita. I've seen Mrs. Gaines's actions toward you when I've been around, and they weren't exactly friendly."

Anita faced him abruptly. "Please don't encourage me, Cliff. I have enough trouble being a true Christian when those things occur. I want to get along with Father's new wife and her daughter, and I know that with Christ in control, I can do it. Pray for me, but don't urge me to fight back. I must cooperate for my father's sake."

Cliff reached for her hand. "Sweet, fair Anita. I will try to do as you ask, but I have a notion things will come to a head with or without the two of us. God can't honor disobedience."

Three weeks later, Marilla's quilt wasn't finished, and she had only two days left. Nearly frantic, she pressed both Laura and Anita to help. Anita had expressed doubt that Marilla could finish when she started, but Marilla would not be talked out of the project. Anita agreed to help, at the same time filled with pity that her stepmother had taken on such an impossible task. Laura used any excuse to get out of the job. This included time with Gilbert, to whom Anita had explained the entire situation earlier.

"It's only a quilt at a hick fair," he had retorted.

"But it means so much to Marilla, Gilbert," Anita pleaded. "I know she can't finish soon enough to win a blue ribbon, but she needs to try for her own satisfaction."

"Tell you what. I'll stop asking Laura out if you'll go instead," he said with an insidious smile.

"No, we both need to help Marilla."

"Sorry. That's my best offer."

That very evening Laura had gone with Gilbert for a ride in his surrey. Anita found Marilla in tears, and she attacked the quilt with renewed energy. For the first time, a chink in Marilla's armor appeared.

"I must say you've been good to support me in this endeavor, Anita. I just didn't have enough time."

It was the closest thing to a compliment Anita had received from Marilla. She was so happy, she slipped around the quilting frame and gave her stepmother a hug. "We'll just keep working. Maybe we'll finish yet."

Marilla's face reflected total surprise.

Chapter 6

Aunt Sarah's angel food cake, expected to win first prize again, would compete with Marilla's. The fair's fresh-baked-goods competition took place on the first day.

After church the day before the fair opening, Marilla demanded all of Anita's time. That night Anita walked, exhausted, to Aunt Sarah's, bathed, and dropped into bed. Still unmade was her raisin cream pie, and her pickle relish and apricot preserves had to be packed for transporting to the fair.

At four o'clock in the morning, she got up, made the pie, and started her last-minute tasks. By the time Aunt Sarah's would-be suitor, Oliver Palmer, came to pick up their entries to deliver to the fairgrounds, she was nearly ready.

"The cart's at the front gate, Anita," Aunt Sarah called, and Anita rushed to help. "First, take your canned goods out and come back for your pie. Oliver, you carry the heavy box by the door. I'll carry my quilt and my cake."

A ruddy-faced man of medium height, Oliver's bald pate reflected the morning sun's rays streaming through Aunt Sarah's kitchen windows. "I'll take everything, Sarah," he insisted. "No need for either you or Anita to lift a finger."

Outside the kitchen door, Cliff raised his voice. "That's right, Oliver, with two of us to help, there's no need at all!" Grinning at Anita, he added, "I thought I'd drop by and see if you could use an assistant."

Exchanging greetings all around, the four shuffled boxes into the two conveyances traveling to the fair. Aunt Sarah waited until Anita had changed her dress, then she and Oliver started off. Hitched to Oliver's neat blue cart, the pinto pony sped away, trotting smartly at his chore.

Cliff waved good-bye, then held out his hand to help Anita step up into his buggy. "As usual, Miss Gaines, you look as pretty as a girl has any right to. How do you manage that?"

Anita laughed. "I'm not sure you mean it, Cliff. Maybe it's just the glow of a morning's hasty work. We had lots to do."

"You can't talk me out of it, Milady. Any time you make an appearance, you're beautiful."

Anita's face burned again. To hear such longed-for words from one whose friendship she had begun to treasure lifted her expectations of the Prairie County Fair to a new level.

A pleasant breeze cooled Anita's face and rustled her hair as the horse jogged along the rock road toward Main Street. Done with her feverish activity, Anita sat back, relaxed, and scanned the houses, trees, and reddening sumac lining their route to the Prairie County Fair.

Following a bend in the road, the buggy brought them to an abrupt change of scene. "Cliff, look!" cried Anita. "It's Oliver's cart! Oh, no!"

"It sure is. What a mess! The horse must have sidestepped into the culvert and fallen. Let's get out, quick!" He jumped out and ran to the couple sitting on the ground beside the overturned cart. "Are either of you hurt?"

"No, nothing but our pride," muttered Sarah.

"Are you sure, Sarah dear?" said Oliver, gingerly standing.

"Oh, go see to the horse, Oliver! And don't call me dear, or you'll have everybody in town gossiping," chided Sarah.

"Aunt Sarah, try to stand by yourself so we'll know you're all right," said Anita, finally reaching her.

Sarah pointed to a white box perched perilously on the edge of the overturned cart. "I hate to look. Would you do it?"

Anita whisked the box away before it could fall and opened the lid covering the angel food cake. The cake lay smashed against one side. Anita reluctantly raised her eyes to meet her aunt's gaze.

"It's ruined, isn't it?"

"No, I'm sure it still tastes delicious. It just doesn't look quite as good as when we left the house."

Sarah got to her feet to inspect the cake. She threw up her hands. "Ooh! I'll never win with that. I'd be ashamed to show it. I'll just withdraw."

"No, you won't, Aunt Sarah. You'll get in the buggy with Cliff and me, and you'll fix it the best you can when you get to the fairgrounds. It's still the best cake in the county. Now, come on," said Anita, and she carried the cake in its box to Cliff's buggy.

Cliff and Oliver had made sure the pony was not hurt and set the cart up straight. As they reloaded boxes, they inspected the contents and found the glass jars intact.

"We'll see you at the fair, Oliver," said Cliff. "You can handle the rest while I take care of the ladies, can't you?"

"Sure can. Go on so Sarah can fix her cake." To Sarah he added, "Don't you worry. I'll get the other boxes there safe as can be."

By the time Sarah was persuaded to enter her somewhat lopsided cake in the contest, the rest of Anita's family had arrived. Marilla carried a box containing her angel food, meticulously decorated on a crystal pedestal cake plate.

"My dear! Whatever happened to your poor little cake?" queried Marilla with a delighted, yet withering smile.

"I'll bet it still tastes as good as ever, Sarah," Anita's father inserted, trying to offer brotherly encouragement.

"Not as good as mine, Dear," Marilla reminded grimly.

The man did not reply. Instead, he eyed Anita's old dress and cast a glance at the two beside him who had shopped for new clothes during their first week in Prairie Center.

"Anita, you should have had some new dresses for the fair. I'm sorry I didn't see it before."

"She looks lovely to me, Mr. Gaines," Cliff said, drawing a smile from both Anita and her father. "I've tried to convince her since we arrived that it's the general opinion on the fairgrounds too. Say, Laura, I don't see Gilbert. Aren't you seeing the fair with him?"

Obviously disturbed by the question, Laura answered simply, "He couldn't be here this morning."

Anita knew the real reason. Gilbert's pursuit of Laura had cooled over time. Anita had seen two other girls enjoying the comfort of Gilbert Boone's stylish surrey. After taking Laura for a ride the night Anita helped Marilla with her quilt, Gilbert had not asked her to the opening of the fair. Laura was embarrassed to be with only her mother and stepfather. Anita felt Cliff's sensitivity. He did not mention Gilbert again.

"All right, now. Anita, since we have the cakes and quilts in their assigned stalls and yours and Miss Sarah's canned goods on display, why don't we take a walk down the midway to see the fun part of the fair? Then, if you like, we can walk to the livestock pavilion so I can show off my charges who are vying for prizes."

Marilla, incensed, spoke her mind. "Brodrick, do you think your daughter should be wandering around the stock pavilion like a man? How do you know she won't be injured or embarrassed?"

"I assure you I won't let that happen, Mrs. Gaines. Anita will have my closest attention," Cliff replied heartily.

Anita's father quickly agreed. "Marilla dear, Dr. West is a fine Christian man. I trust him as I would trust Reverend Brownlow at the church. Anita is in good hands."

Marilla turned a tight-lipped countenance away from the group, supposedly inspecting the crowd.

"Be on your way," Anita's father said to the young couple, "but be sure to come back for the cake judging."

Aunt Sarah chuckled. "After all our trouble, you can't miss that! Poor Oliver will never forgive himself."

"We'll be back. You can count on it. Have a good time," Anita called to the group, and she and Cliff hurried away.

Out of sight, Cliff bent to whisper in Anita's ear. "I've seen lots of sixteen-year-old girls cry, but that's the first time I've seen a grown woman pout like one."

"Cliff, stop it! I told you not to encourage me," scolded Anita, determined not to smile at his observation.

"All right. Let's see what we'd like to ride tonight. Maybe we'll start with the merry-go-round."

"Yes. There it is!" A blast from the calliope split the air and immediately went quiet. Anita covered her ears, awaiting the next blast.

"I guess they're still working on the equipment, making sure it works right," said Cliff.

Unstopping her ears, Anita remained skeptical. "Let's hope we have music with our ride tonight."

"We will. It'll be grand." He took her arm to lead her around a tree stump in the middle of the midway. "Maybe someday we'll raise enough money to improve the fairgrounds. It's just a field with an odd stump or two now, but we'll get them dug out as time goes on. It's still a good place to have the county fair because of the macadam road along one side."

"And we still have the trees on that side. I hope they leave those in the back too. We need the shade on hot days."

"I agree," said Cliff. "Would you think I'm bragging if I told you I've been asked to be in on a little civic group to plan for things like that? It's not quite a city council as they have in big cities, but it's a bunch of us that want Prairie Center to grow while maintaining its best assets. If we do, it will bring more people to the Prairie County Fair. Your dad and his brother, George, will join us soon. They should have some good ideas."

Anita fought the temptation to say, "If Marilla lets Dad," but she immediately chided herself. You tell him not to encourage you, then you downgrade Marilla in your mind, all by yourself. *Oh, Father God, help me stop doing that. Every time I have a bad thought against her, it undermines my determination to love Laura and her. I'm really trying, but I need Your help.*

Anita smiled. "I imagined you would be interested in the town's progress. Also the fair. My father seems to have great respect for you, Cliff. So do I. I know you're wonderful with people. What kind of a vet are you?"

"A dependable one, and I'm grateful for your respect," he said with a smile. "Speaking of my job, why don't we make a jog by the livestock pavilion? I have to pick up the examination forms required for the heavy stock. The animals should be ready for me to begin checking them for infections later today. They have to be healthy, you know. If they aren't, we could have a pavilion full of sick animals."

Anita hadn't considered that. "But you'd think they'd all be healthy. That's why they're entered, isn't it, to prove how perfect they are?"

"Yes, but let's say a man had been working hard for months, grooming a calf for the fair. Can you see how he might be tempted to fudge a little? We can't have that." He reached for her hand. "Come on, we'll see if the Lewis's calf is here yet. Would you like to meet her?"

"Of course! I haven't met a single little fat calf today," she said impishly, and when she looked up, she had the strangest feeling that Dr. Clifford West wanted to kiss her.

Chapter 7

Picking up their pace, Anita and Cliff were nearing the enclosure to the pavilion when Laura and Gilbert ran toward them from the direction of the road.

"Wait till you hear, Anita! I'm going to enter the beauty contest for young ladies!" called Laura.

"Beauty contest?" Cliff repeated skeptically. "I didn't know we were having one."

"Gilbert persuaded his father to sponsor one. Isn't it exciting?" Laura jiggled from one foot to the other.

"Looks like it's going to happen," said Gilbert, challenging Cliff with a look. "Why don't you enter, Anita?"

Before Anita could refuse, Cliff asked another question. "Where's this contest supposed to take place, Gilbert?"

"I've arranged for a tent. Other than that, all we need are a few planks to make a stage for the girls to walk across. To make a decision, the crowd must be able to see them well," he said, waving his arms as if directing.

Cliff persisted. "Who are the other contestants? When do

you plan to hold this beauty contest? The fair ends a week from Wednesday."

Still optimistic, Gilbert smiled. "After we work out the location, we'll put up signs and run an ad in the newspaper. Once people hear about it, contestants will come from all directions."

Smiling, Cliff scratched his cheek. "Provided they subscribe to the Prairie Center Reporter."

Anita didn't think her father would approve of his stepdaughter participating in anything as undignified as a beauty contest. But Marilla might permit it. Would it cause trouble between the two? How could it be avoided? Maybe for the sake of her father, she should try to reason with Laura.

She glanced at Gilbert, then turned to the girl. "Laura, I wonder if your mother would approve of your entering a beauty contest," she murmured. "Shouldn't you get her opinion?"

Laura stepped back, her smirking face taut. "My mama believes in me. She'd be the first one to say I have a chance of winning. I intend to enter!"

"Anita, I'm expected at the pavilion. I think we should leave now." Cliff obviously meant to extricate her before she said more, and grateful, she knew he was right.

"Yes, we'd better go." She took the arm he offered, and they walked away. "Thanks, Cliff. I shouldn't have tried that," she said under her breath.

"Are you sure you don't want to enter the contest too, Anita?" Gilbert yelled after them. "We're going to give a trip to Kansas City as a prize."

"I don't think she's interested, Gilbert," called Cliff.

"Probably thinks she couldn't win," Laura shouted, giggling

as if she'd played a huge joke on Anita.

"Just keep walking," muttered Cliff. "Don't fret yourself. That beauty contest will never happen."

Anita didn't look back, but she couldn't keep her fears from Cliff. "I can't imagine what my father will say when he hears about this. I'm sure it will cause trouble."

"Try to forget it for now. I want you to enjoy your trip to the pavilion." He swung open the wooden gate of the enclosure to let her enter. "It's a good idea to follow the planks they've laid for walkways, Anita."

"Yes, Dr. West. I understand," she said with a grin, modestly raising her skirt hem to avoid the danger area.

"Hello, Cliff." A tall man leading a proud chestnut horse passed near them.

"Morning, Frank. He looks like he wants to win." Cliff stroked the animal's shoulder.

"You bet! That's what we're here for."

Similar remarks were aimed at him as they walked slowly through the pavilion, Cliff showing Anita particular animals he thought might win ribbons or first prize in the judging. Anita was fascinated with them all, but the lambs and the white-faced calf belonging to the Lewises were her favorites.

Cliff's charisma drew farmers and townspeople alike, and Anita's admiration for him flourished. Or was it more? A warm glow of reality filled her as she admitted her feelings to herself. She was falling in love.

Anita had watched Cliff charm every girl in town, from her age to his, never dreaming she would ever be close to him, much less have him interested in her. Was he interested? Or was this just summer fun for him? Had he determined to pull the little Gaines girl out of the big white house and show the town he could charm her as well? If so, he had succeeded.

"What is that little frown about, Anita? Are you getting tired of this?" Cliff sounded disappointed.

"No! I'm having a good time. I was thinking about something else."

"Why did it make you so sad?" he persisted, moving toward her.

Cliff's broad shoulders in his blue denim shirt defined a man of athletic ability. His was a vocation not every man could achieve or fulfill even after training. He was muscular yet gentle. Laura's and Gilbert's remarks to her had provoked him, and he had done his diplomatic best to protect her. That was part of his character too.

She smiled to dispel his belief that she was sad. "I'm fine, Cliff. Really." Her eyes followed a couple leaving the building. "I wonder if it's time for the baked-goods competition?" she asked.

"Not going to tell me, eh?" Cliff snapped his fingers. "All right. Time for the baked-goods contest. I'd almost forgotten. By the way, while I think of it, I intend to ask your father if I can escort you to the fair for the rest of the time." He leaned forward, grinning. "Day and night."

❋

White tablecloths covered two long tables displaying pies, cakes, cookies, tarts, and breads of every variety. Excited women stood close, watching every move of the judges as they walked up and down the tables, ready to begin their evaluations.

"Did you have a good tour around the fairgrounds?" asked Anita's father, crisp and neat in his business suit. "I think it's the best fair we've ever had. Business has picked up, the bank's full of people, and wherever you go you see smiles. This is always the best time of year for Prairie Center."

Cliff grabbed the man's hand and gave it a shake. "Good for you, Sir! I feel the same way."

Anita located her raisin pie and Aunt Sarah's repaired angel food cake. Marilla's cake sat elegantly on its crystal pedestal; and dressed in a stylish green crepe and black hat, Marilla waited as if confident she would be called forward as a winner.

One by one the categories were judged for appearance and taste until they came to the cake category. Anita's father, who had taken time off to see this particular contest, seemed undecided as to whom he should root for. Anita could empathize. Though it hardly seemed likely, he would be in trouble if Sarah's cake won over Marilla's. The judges finally huddled, then one came away.

The main judge, a baker from Topeka, made the announcement.

"Ladies and gentlemen! We are in agreement that the first prize blue ribbon be awarded to Mrs. Brodrick Gaines for her beautiful angel food cake!"

A chorus of "ohs" and "ahs" surrounded Marilla, preening like a proud bird of paradise as she accepted their compliments.

"Just one moment, ladies and gentlemen! We have another announcement. Please! Everyone quiet." The crowd silenced. "As your judges, we have decided to give a special blue ribbon award this year." The judge cleared his throat. "Due to circumstances beyond her control, one participant's entry met with an unfortunate accident. The cake's appearance is not the best, but one asset overrides that misfortune. Miss Sarah Gaines, whom we understand has been the winner in this category many times, is awarded a blue ribbon for the best-tasting cake judged!"

Rushing to Sarah, women squealed, clapped for, and hugged the breathless winner. "I knew you'd win something, Sarah! No one could eat your angel food cake and not give you a prize!" said one friend.

All the ladies expressed words to the same effect, and Anita was prouder of Sarah's ribbon than of the one she had been awarded for her raisin pie. Reluctantly she glanced at Marilla. Standing apart, her mouth wore a pout, and cheerless lines creased her face. The woman was jealous! Why? She had won the main competition. How could she resent Aunt Sarah winning a much-deserved honor? She made her way toward her aunt.

At her shoulder, Marilla spat, "Anita, I have a headache, and I'm leaving with Brodrick. You pack both our boxes and get them home. There's a lot of work to be done, so don't stay long. Laura is with Gilbert, and they've gone for a picnic out at the Boone farm." With that she moved to her husband, and they headed for their buggy, Anita's father trying to cheer her with the news that he'd found a housekeeper who could start the next week.

"That's good news for you," said Cliff softly. "But I take it Laura hasn't told her yet about the beauty contest." Anita barely heard him over the noise of the crowd. "I'm sure Father doesn't know. He's far too serene," she murmured, stuffing newspapers around Marilla's cake plate in a box.

"Enjoy the peace. I don't think it will last." Cliff hoisted a box of canned goods and preserves to his shoulder. "I heard your stepmother. To keep her happy, I'll take you home, but I'll be by at seven o'clock tonight. Your father likes me, Anita. I'm confident he trusts you with me."

Each carrying a box, they made their way to his buggy. "I think he does trust you, Cliff, and I have a favor to ask. Will you please pray for my family and me? I'm discouraged about our home situation. We have friction where there should be none. My father should lead the way for Marilla and Laura. Not me. I only add to the friction. We all need the Lord."

It took two trips to get their boxes to the buggy and pack them in safely. At last, Cliff assisted Anita up into her seat. He stood beside her, not letting go of her hand. "If you ask Him, Jesus will love them through you, Anita. They're His children, and He loves them. Trust Him. He'll never fail you. I'll take you home now, and tonight we'll spend time praying about this. They'll come around. You wait and see."

"Where's Laura's mother, Anita?" yelled Gilbert, who sprinted, scarlet-faced, up the middle of the grounds. "I have to find her!"

"Why? What's wrong?" asked Anita, apprehension growing.

"It's Laura. Bees stung her!" he said, the words tumbling over themselves. "Her face is all swollen, and her eyes are nearly shut."

Cliff interrupted. "Where is she?"

"In my buggy by the main entry."

"Let's go! We'll take her to my father's office!"

In seconds, they were streaking down the road in Cliff's

buggy, weaving their way between oncoming conveyances headed for the fair. Inside the buggy, Laura cried with pain in Anita's arms. For the first time, Anita felt the girl reaching for friendship.

❊

While Anita and Cliff explored the Prairie County Fair that week, Laura, her right eye swollen shut and suffering pain from other bites, stayed in her room at the Gaines house. The bad reaction was not unusual with some bee stings. Her distress made Anita and Cliff feel guilty that on that first day, they had hoped the bee stings would keep Laura out of the potential beauty contest and solve their problem. Fortunately, the contest never came to pass.

Anita heard that Mr. Boone, Sr., changed his mind after a group of Prairie Center citizens met with him in his office. Since he was so easily persuaded, Anita wondered if Boone had only agreed to the contest because Gilbert, his only child, was denied nothing. She suspected who had sparked the dissenting group to action. Meanwhile, the incident had resulted in Gilbert's absence from Laura's company.

Anita took time every day to make herself available to Laura. Little by little, Laura's cold facade revealed tiny fractures. Once, when Anita brought Laura her supper on a tray, she experienced an actual breakthrough.

"Why are you being so good to me?" Laura asked. "You know how mean I've been to you," she murmured.

"I'm a Christian, Laura. I'm not being 'good' to you. I want to help. Jesus asks us to love one another, and I try to do His will."

"I see you reading your Bible every day. What's so interesting to you?"

"God's Word is the most important thing in my life. You'd have to read it to understand why that would be so."

"I thought your father was the most important thing in your life," said Laura.

"Jesus is more important to me than my father. Let me tell you why. In the book of Matthew in the Bible, the tenth chapter, verse thirty-seven reads: 'He that loveth father or mother more than me is not worthy of me: and he that loveth son or daughter more than me is not worthy of me.' These words are from Jesus, speaking directly to us."

Laura's swollen eye opened wider. "Do you mean Jesus says Mama should love Him more than she loves me?"

"Yes, but when you become a Christian, you just naturally love Him more than anyone. Jesus means more to me than my life."

The girl turned on her side away from Anita. "I don't want to talk about this anymore," she said softly.

"I'll take the tray downstairs. If I can do anything for you later, let me know. I hope you feel better soon."

She received no answer, but the Lord had given her a divine opportunity. She trusted Him with what happened next. Laura was coming around. Remembering Laura's earlier "pay me back" threat, Anita wondered if Laura was pursuing more adult ways to deal with life.

Chapter 8

Before Cliff arrived that evening, Anita's father and stepmother almost quarreled because Marilla thought Anita hadn't earned an evening out with Cliff. "There's cleaning to be done, and we should be cooking for the weekend! Anita hardly does anything, and Laura is too ill to help. Her reaction to the bee stings has caused her to miss most of the fair, poor thing."

"Now, Marilla, you're being unreasonable!" Anita's father countered. "Do you think I'm blind? I can see how much work Anita does. She deserves a week of fun."

"No more than Laura!"

"But Laura is unable to get out—rather she could, but she doesn't want to be seen. There's no reason to penalize Anita for Laura's decision."

Marilla sank into a kitchen chair, hands dropping into her apron-covered lap. "Well, I never!" she gasped, surprised.

"As long as we're talking, there's something else I have to say." Anita's father paced the kitchen linoleum in front of Marilla. "Next Sunday, we are going to church as a family. I was taught in my youth that the father is the spiritual leader of the family. So far, I've been sorely lacking in that area. But no more. We'll be going to church regularly from now on."

Anita, wiping off the cabinet, felt her heart so full of joy she thought it would explode. Her prayers were being answered. *Thank You, God. Oh, thank You!*

A short while later, Cliff called for Anita. He carried a bouquet of flowers from his mother's garden.

Anita's father invited him in, hands raised, expressing surprise. "My boy, this wasn't necessary!"

Cliff laughed out loud. "They're not for you. And they're not for the pretty girl behind you, either. They're for Laura," he said, smiling at Anita. "She's missed a lot this week. I thought maybe these might help make up for it in part."

Anita took the bouquet and left to find a vase for them. She was happy that her father liked Cliff. But Marilla didn't. Though Laura had spoken to Anita without anger, Marilla's attitude remained stubborn.

Cliff also brought an invitation for the family to join the Wests for a celebration on the last night of the county fair. Anita held her breath. Was it possible this invitation was a measure of Cliff's feelings for her? Cliff was a beautiful man. His body, mind, and spirit were in the possession of his Savior for all the world to see. She would think herself blessed if he had started to love her.

Cliff and Anita enjoyed strolling the fairgrounds during the early part of the evening, but when it was time for the final judging at the quilting booth, Cliff had duty at the livestock pavilion. Anita went to the contest with the rest of the family.

Even Laura was commanded to go, and after days of hibernation, she was willing. Aunt Sarah met them at the display.

"Isn't this exciting, Marilla?" she asked. "How beautiful they all are!" She ran her hands over the quilts displayed on racks and lines around them. The colors resembled a flower garden in bloom.

"They certainly are, Sarah," Anita's father said.

"Look at this one, Father," said Anita, pointing at a wedding ring quilt. "It belongs to Cliff's mother. I think it's one of the best."

Her father and aunt laughed. "I wonder why she thinks it's so beautiful?" Aunt Sarah said.

Marilla, in her usual state of irritation, chided them. "Has anyone looked at my quilt? I'd think you at least would pull for a blue ribbon for me, Anita."

Anita smiled at her stepmother, but she was at a loss for words. She'd sympathized with Marilla's despair as she'd struggled to complete her project and had felt compelled to help her. But Marilla's was not even a pretty quilt. She had hurried a process that should never be hurried, and her workmanship showed it.

"I'm proud of yours for you, Marilla," said Anita's father.

"And don't forget," added Aunt Sarah. "Many of us framed our quilts right after the fair last year. We've been working on ours a lot longer than you did yours."

Marilla took out a handkerchief and dabbed at her nose. "I'm so glad you're proud of mine, Brodrick," she said, obviously pulling at the man's heartstrings with the pitiful expression on her face. Then she added brightly, "Of course, you realize I may win first prize after all!"

How desperately Marilla needed the Lord, Anita thought. She was full of fears and could not stand to be looked down upon. If she'd only let Him, Jesus could give her life a value she hadn't known before.

The judges were pinning blue, red, and white ribbons on the quilts according to different levels of quality and expertise. The first prize blue ribbon was attached to Aunt Sarah's multicolored quilt, its dozens of pieces sewn with stitches almost too small to be seen.

No ribbon was pinned on Marilla's quilt, and Anita saw genuine tears shimmering on her stepmother's cheeks. But her father's arm crept around the woman's shoulders, and that seemed comfort enough.

"I'll start sooner next year, Brodrick."

Slipping away to give the couple privacy, Anita rushed out of their sight to gather her aunt in her arms. "You won, Aunt Sarah, you won!" The two hugged as Anita bounced them up and down. Laughing, she pulled away. "You know we're being absurd, don't you?" A second later they hugged again, giggling.

"Did I miss the big moment?" It was Cliff.

"You sure did. See my blue ribbon?" said Aunt Sarah.

He gave her a kiss on the cheek. "Congratulations!" He dragged Anita away, caught her father's eye, and pointed to Anita. "Mind if I borrow this one?" Her father waved and nodded. "Let's take a trip down the midway, Anita."

Sarah came toward them.

"Do you need help or a ride home, Ma'am?" Cliff asked.

"Thank you, no. Oliver will be by in a few minutes, as soon

as he's sure the hen party, as he calls it, is over."

"Sounds like him." Cliff turned to Anita, grinning. "Come on. Let's have some fun."

They turned and made their way through the crowd milling the grounds. Wide-eyed children clung to their parents' hands, astonished by an array of high covered torchlights and blaring music from the merry-go-round. Older boys darted about game and food booths, testing the limits of adults and teasing girls they knew from school. An occasional feminine squeal marked their success. Cliff bought sacks of popcorn, and they sat on a log bench to rest and eat.

"I love this time of day when the tension's over and it's time to relax," said Anita with a sigh.

Cliff's eyes flashed to her face, examining her. "Are you really under that much stress, Anita?"

"No. I'm probably being a baby because I'm with you."

Cliff smiled and pressed his shoulder against hers. "Do you feel that way with me? Explain."

"I can't tell you the reason except that I always feel, um, safe when I'm with you."

Leaning back, still watching her, he murmured, "That's probably the best compliment I've ever had."

"Hmm, and you like people to depend on you."

"How did you know that?"

"From seeing you grow into an adult."

His smile got wider. "I didn't know you were watching. If I had, we might have been together sooner. What else do you know about me?"

"Although you're eight years older, I don't feel there's a gap between us. I'm very comfortable with you." She took another few grains of popcorn and watched him as she chewed.

"Don't stop now. Please!" Cliff took her popcorn away.

"My, what an ego." Anita grabbed the sack again. "Very well. Here's my list of your assets: I think you love your family very much; you love animals; people like you and trust you; you're practical and thoughtful, always have been; you're a brilliant man because you got your scholastic degree in a short time." She paused, tapping her forehead in thought, and fixed him with mock scorn. "And I shall not give you one more compliment. Your ego has been boosted quite enough."

Conscious of the crowd, the look on Cliff's face made Anita fear he intended to kiss her, and she jumped up. "I thought we were going to ride the Ferris wheel. People have come from miles around just to get a look at it. Most have heard of it, but they've never seen one. We have a curiosity here." Her gaze, captured by his, was not released.

"All right, Anita. We'll ride the Ferris wheel. But our mutual admiration will soon come to an agreement."

"Should we keep that in mind as we ride the Ferris wheel?"

"Indeed we should. Sailing away under the glittering stars is bound to help us agree upon the emotions we feel."

Anita took the hand he offered, and they turned toward the ride. Locked into the seat, they were swooped upward on the wheel until new riders occupied the remaining empty seats. Abruptly, it gained speed, and Anita gasped. Cliff's arm came around her to clasp her shoulders. The descent was swift, and being held by Cliff was comforting.

Their seat zoomed past the platform below, and before

Anita's eyes stood her father and stepmother.

The wheel zipped them up again, Anita wondering what Marilla thought. Would she assign the worst possible implication to what she saw? She hoped not. But she recalled something else, a wonderful thing: It was her father's approving look as he exchanged smiles with Cliff.

Chapter 9

An amateur contest was scheduled for the fair's last night. That morning Mrs. Brownlow, the minister's wife, approached Anita at the fairgrounds.

"Anita, why don't you enter the contest tonight? You have such a beautiful voice. The fair crowd would enjoy a hymn."

A horse-drawn water tank came by, spraying down the dusty grounds, and the ladies stepped aside to avoid it. Anita flipped her long hair over her shoulders. Since Cliff liked her "beautiful black hair" down, she wore it that way more often.

"Mrs. Brownlow, I do fine in a choir or with other singers, but not as a soloist. My goodness!"

"I think you should enter. We—"

"There you are. I've been looking for you." Cliff smiled at Mrs. Brownlow. "What are you trying to talk her into?"

Anita swatted him on the arm. "Stay out of this, will you? I can't sing well enough to enter a contest! Besides, I have no one to play for me."

With his forefinger, Cliff flicked the end of his nose. "Would you be insulted if I offered to accompany you?"

"What? You mean you—"

"I tinker around a bit—privately," he admitted, grinning. "I think I can make you sound good." His eyes suggested he was thinking of situations unrelated to the fair. "We'll be a good team, Anita."

Anita's heart was keeping a musical beat already. She'd begun to believe Cliff cared for her. Before, she'd thought it wishful thinking, imagining he had fallen in love with her. Now, her heart was telling her it was possible.

❋

Later, at home, Marilla objected vocally to Anita's entering the amateur contest, but Anita was too happy to mind.

"She might embarrass us, Brodrick," Marilla declared.

Laura moaned, Anita judged more from envy than dissent.

"Now, stop it, you two," thundered her father. "How do you think this makes Anita feel? She tries her best to help us, and we do very little in return. Maybe we should pray about our attitudes. It might do us all a lot of good."

Surprised by her father's diatribe, Anita was stunned by the flushed, downcast faces of the other two women. Both were polite while the three of them prepared the evening meal.

"I wish you had a new dress for tonight," Anita's father had declared at the supper table.

"She could wear one of mine," Marilla offered softly.

Shock slowed Anita's speech. "I-I appreciate it, Ma'am, but Aunt Sarah altered my pink, and it's my best color."

"I was a seamstress before. I guess Brodrick told you."

"Yes, Ma'am."

Marilla released a great sigh. "Anita, I started out wrong

when I got here. I'm used to standing up for myself, fighting the bad things that always seem to happen. I got in the habit of striking out before anyone could get at me. It was a bitter way to live, and it made me unhappy."

She reached for her husband's hand. "Then I met Brodrick, and he took charge. I'd never had a stable life, and I didn't realize how good it could be. I'm just now learning how to act. I can't say I'll change overnight, and I'm not a religious woman, but I'm going to try hard. I want us to be a family."

Anita's father spoke in a coarse voice. "Then I suggest I lead us in prayer." He cleared his throat. "Father, it's been a long time since I was the spiritual leader in this house, but if You'll forgive me, I'm going to make up for that. Please, lead us all to follow Your will and become a close family. Help Marilla and Laura to believe that I love them and want only their best.

"Now Father, help Anita to do her best tonight and sing for Your glory." His voice broke. At last he croaked, "Lord, it's good to talk to You again. Thanks for waiting. Amen."

Later as Anita got ready to go, Laura came to her room.

"Could I talk to you for a minute?" At Anita's open look, she continued. "Anita, I have to admit you've been nicer to me than I have to you. I'm sorry. If you want your room back, you can have it. I'll exchange with you." She turned, then looked back. "Would you mind if I borrowed your Bible for awhile?"

"Of course you may, Laura." Tears in her eyes, Anita took her Bible from the bed table and handed it to her. "If you'd like one of your own, we'll make sure you get one."

When Laura left, Anita knelt and thanked God. If Laura

came to Christ, there was a chance Marilla would too. She would continue to pray for both of them.

❇

That night at the fair, Anita and Cliff sat with the other entrants, waiting for their turn in the amateur contest. Anita's joyful mind reviewed the last few hours at home. Remembering her father's sweet prayer, an overwhelming desire to edify Christ's name overshadowed her fear. Her name was called, and she and Cliff rose to step up onto the rough wooden stage. An old upright piano sat to one side, and Cliff took a seat in the straight-backed chair in front of it. At her signal, he played a lyrical introduction, and she began to sing.

On a hill far away
Stood an old rugged cross
The emblem of suffering and shame:
And I love that old cross
Where the dearest and best
For a world of lost sinners was slain.

As her voice rose in the night, the emotion in Anita's heart was liberated. She sang as she had never sung before. She had prayed earnestly that her performance would be a true witness for Christ, and He had answered her prayer most abundantly.

Crowding around the makeshift stage, dozens of people were attracted by Anita's song. As more listeners congregated, silence gripped the area. On the final chorus, the crowd joined in. A few at first, then a robust chorus lifted the name of Jesus to the skies. In true accord, the singers smiled warmly as the last note sounded. Total quiet prevailed. An "Amen" here and there became a wave throughout the expanse, glorifying God.

Thunderous applause followed, and Anita stood with Cliff, smiling at the crowd in which both their proud families watched. Since they were the last act on the program, it took only seconds for the decision of the three judges. Anita and Cliff won first prize.

❇

The golden glow of a full harvest moon shone down from a sky full of stars. En route to the Wests' home, Cliff and Anita rode ahead in his buggy, her family following.

Anita used her cape to polish the silver-plated loving cup they had won at the Prairie County Fair. "It's pretty, isn't it?" she said, turning it from side to side.

"Almost as pretty as the girl beside me." He took her hand and kissed it lightly. "You sang beautifully tonight, Anita. I was so proud of you."

"I wouldn't have sung half as well if you hadn't played for me. Together, we're good." The words seemed to take on new meaning, and Anita felt her face flush.

"Exactly."

He spoke the one word and said no more. She needed to talk to relieve her tense nerves.

"Your mother and father have always been nice to me, Cliff, but how do they feel about me now? Now that we've been together practically every day?"

"They like you, Anita. Why? Are you scared?"

"Not scared exactly. Just anxious."

"Don't be. The best is yet to come."

While Anita puzzled over the remark, they reached the West home. To leave the hitching post available for Anita's father, Cliff jumped down and guided the horse to the side of the house, where he handed Anita down from the buggy.

Dr. West appeared at the front door. "Welcome, welcome! Come in, everyone!" he called, turning up the gaslights in front of their red brick two-story house. Anita had never been inside the house, and she was impressed with the delicacy and beauty of the interior decoration. Cliff's tall, gracious mother gave their family a reception of such warmth that Marilla and Laura were visibly affected, and their smiles reflected sincere pleasure.

It was a wonderful evening of good conversation and delicious food in the outstanding company of Dr. West and his wife. Anita and Mrs. West spent private moments together, Anita regretting she hadn't known Cliff's mother well before.

As the evening wound down, Cliff spoke quietly to Anita's father. Then he excused Anita and himself from the room. He led her down the hall to the back door, and Anita caught her breath as they stepped outside.

"Oh, Cliff, what a wonderful rose garden! Smell them! So many different colors. I'm glad the moon is full so we can see them." Walking along a row of white roses, she took several stems in her arms and buried her face in their blossoms.

"Stop giving those kisses to the roses and come with me," said Cliff, capturing her hand. He led her down a slight grade to a willow tree. A stone settee snuggled beneath its branches. Lifting the veil of low-hanging branches to allow her to enter the little cove, he drew her down to sit beside him and gathered her in his arms.

"Do you realize how much more beautiful you are than a rose? In many ways. You've stood up against extreme pressure in your home, and in your sweet Christian way you're beginning to win Marilla and Laura over. I can see that. You're the very best daughter and the best niece in the world. I have that on good authority. You won my heart the first time you looked directly into my eyes, and tonight you sang like an angel. God's given me a miracle, and I'll never let you go until He says so."

"Cliff, I'm not—"

He touched a finger to her lips. Then, tenderly, ever so tenderly, his lips found hers. Anita had dreamed of this moment. Giving herself up to its magic, she slipped her arms around Cliff's broad shoulders, and he pulled her closer, deepening the kiss. Anita felt faint, and she slipped her hands down between them. Cliff pulled his mouth away.

"That was too much for you, wasn't it? I'm sorry, Anita. It's just that I've waited for what seems an eternity to hold you in my arms and kiss you. This is not just a passing thing for me, Darling. Don't you feel what I do? I've found what I want. I want to be with you, go to church with you, come over for Sunday dinners, and play chess with your dad. There's so much I want to learn about you and that I want you to know about me."

He sat back and snuggled her against his shoulder. They were quiet for a few seconds, then Anita laid her palm against his cheek.

"My love, don't misunderstand. I've waited for this too. What I feel is love. We haven't been seeing each other long, but I know I'm right. If you feel the same way, I know you are the man God has for me."

Cliff smothered her face with kisses. "Darling, I do feel the same. Believe me, I do. I want you to marry me. But you're so young, I was afraid if I mentioned it too soon, you might run away from me, and I'd never see you again. I hoped a few more weeks together would convince you we'll have a wonderful Christian future."

"We can still have those weeks, can't we? Let's learn about each other, Cliff. We'll spend time finding out what makes each of us the way we are. We'll build a true love that will last forever."

He covered her mouth with his, and the kiss seemed to last an eternity. When it ended, he murmured against her cheek. "We'll build it as the Lord meant marriage to be. We'll wait as long as you say, Anita, even a year."

With a little smile, Anita slid her arms up around his neck and whispered against his lips, "I don't think we should be ridiculous about it. Do you?"

His ardent kiss was her answer.

FREDA CHRISMAN

Enjoying retirement, Freda and her husband live in the Houston metroplex. Blessed with two children and six grandchildren, they eagerly watch as God develops the Christian character of each. Before publishing her first book with Heartsong Presents, Freda published short stories and articles for Sunday school papers and magazines. Four books later, it is more than ever a sacred trust to write stories nurtured by the Lord. She enjoys speaking, teaching, and encouraging beginning writers. Visit her at www.fredachrisman.com

Goodie Goodie

by Tamela Hancock Murray

Dedication

In memory of my grandfather,
Bryce Anderson Hancock,
who nurtured 150 rose bushes in his backyard.

The wilderness and the solitary place shall be glad for them;
and the desert shall rejoice, and blossom as the rose.
It shall blossom abundantly, and rejoice even with joy
and singing: the glory of Lebanon shall be given unto it,
the excellency of Carmel and Sharon,
they shall see the glory of the Lord,
and the excellency of our God.
ISAIAH 35:1–2

Chapter 1

1946

Number Five. Willa Johnston slid her Apple Avocado Amazement into the empty slot on the wooden table. Her own creation would compete with nine other entries in the best entrée category of the Prairie County Fair bakeoff.

Willa sprinkled her masterpiece with a coating of rat cheese. In spite of its disgusting name, the sharp cheddar would make anything taste good. Not that her hot casserole needed any help. From the corner of her eye she watched Dorothy, one of her old high school classmates, carefully place potatoes around her meatloaf entry. Dorothy raised her penciled eyebrows and sniffed in the direction of Willa's casserole. Her reddened lips twisted as though Willa's dish emitted a foul odor.

What does she know? My Apple Avocado Amazement must be just fine for my brothers to tell me to enter it in the contest. How could meatloaf possibly win? It's just plain as plain can be. No imagination or creativity.

Willa gave her steaming concoction a nod of approval and tried to ignore Dorothy's look, which had changed to one of amusement. Willa knew she'd have to forgive Dorothy's merriment. Today was the first Saturday of the fair, a weeklong extravaganza of fun, food, and games, the likes of which hadn't been seen in Prairie County since the fair's hiatus from 1942 to 1945, thanks to the war. An abbreviated version had been hastily thrown together after the Japanese formally surrendered last year on September 2. But for 1946, the fair had returned in all its glory, finding a receptive audience ready to cut loose.

Earlier, as she walked through the fairgrounds to the site of the bakeoff, Willa had noticed that each seat of the Ferris wheel was filled with squealing adolescents. Adults and small fry alike glided on carousel horses in rhythm to circus tunes. Carnival barkers shouted over the tinny music, wheedling high school boys to try to win cheap trinkets for their sweethearts. Sizzling wieners and burgers emitted appetizing aromas, but apples glazed with a sugar coating the color of garnets, along with pink cotton candy, tempted the sweet tooth.

A man's voice brought Willa back to the present. "What's this?"

Raising her head, Willa saw the owner of the voice was holding hands with a woman whose swelling belly indicated they would be parents come late winter.

"Oh, it's just the bakeoff," the woman said, shrugging. Her eyes meeting Willa's, the woman realized she was a contestant. With her face reddening, the woman wished her luck.

The young man put his arm around his wife's shoulders. "All this food is making me hungry. Would you like a burger, Honey?"

"That sounds just wonderful!" She gazed into his face. He squeezed her shoulder, and they headed toward the nearby concession stand.

Willa's stomach knotted with envy in spite of her best intentions. She clenched her teeth and tossed an extra handful of cheese on the dish. *If God had intended me to be married now, I would be. Besides, I'm only twenty-six. There's plenty of time.*

Interrupting her melancholy, Dorothy grabbed Willa's forearm and pointed to someone in the crowd. "Look. It's our judge. Garrison Gaines."

Willa peered into the throng. "You mean the one who's towering over everybody else?"

"You got it! Tall, dark, and handsome. Isn't he a dreamboat?"

Willa didn't want to concede her agreement to big-mouthed Dorothy. "Who did you say he is?"

Dorothy looked at Willa as though she had taken leave of her senses. "Garrison Gaines. Haven't you heard? He inherited the old Gaines place."

Willa remembered the white two-story house a couple blocks from Prairie Center's business district. The house had been built by one of the county's founding fathers, Rylan Gaines, in the mid-1800s and had since remained occupied by a member of the Gaines family.

"Then how come I've never heard of him?"

"Oh, he's from back East. Maryland."

Willa was struck by the way his hair was the color of semi-sweet chocolate poured into perfect waves. Stylish clothes made him seem as though he hailed from a city. "Where in Maryland?" she asked. "Baltimore? Annapolis?"

"Oh, no. Somewhere around the Chesapeake Bay area." Dorothy gave Willa a scheming look. "I suppose the only way to find out more is to talk to him. I think I'll go on over and say hello."

Willa eyed her fellow contestants ingratiating themselves to the handsome Mr. Gaines. As if he sensed she was staring, he looked her way. For an instant, his face became alight with interest, his eyes burning into her as if beckoning her to take Dorothy's suggestion.

His glance left Willa wanting to swoon like a bobby soxer in the presence of Frankie Sinatra. She wished she had Dorothy's courage to walk right up to him and introduce herself. But the icy grip of shyness kept her feet attached to the dusty spot on the ground.

❋

Garrison was trying not to be rude to the women flocked around him. He might have been flattered by their attention had he not known the attraction stemmed from his position as a bakeoff judge rather than his person. Before this moment, Garrison hadn't realized how seriously the contestants took these friendly little competitions.

Summoning instructions from every lesson his mother had drilled into him about behaving like a gentleman, Garrison answered their questions about the other Gaines relatives, those who hadn't been fortunate enough to inherit the house. Judging from the women's knowledge of its long-deceased builder and of the alterations various owners had made over the years, Garrison deduced that the house had become a famous local landmark. One of which they were obviously proud.

If only he could share their enthusiasm. He shuddered as he recalled the hideous journey from the East. Garrison's buddy at a Ford dealership had managed to snag him a new woodie wagon, procured with savings from Garrison's tours of duty in the navy. Goodie Woodie was an investment in his business, and Garrison begrudged every one of the 1,233 miles the mind-numbing trip through Maryland, West Virginia, Ohio, Indiana, Illinois, and Missouri registered on her odometer. As hills and mountains gave way to vast stretches of level land, he felt the sensation that the car was moving but not making any progress. He could only imagine what the journey had been like for the pioneers traveling nearly a century before in covered wagons. No wonder they'd had to bribe people with 120 acres of land to get them to settle in Kansas.

Garrison was proof that bribes continued to work. He'd abandoned Maryland because his sister, too much in love with her beachcombing war hero, refused to leave the East Coast. Her refusal left Garrison with no excuse not to take the faraway house. The ink was barely dry on his papers granting him an honorable discharge from the navy. He had no job in Maryland to hold him and no wife to protest a move. Of course, had Maude been willing, he would have brought her to Prairie Center as his wife. But true to her selfish ways, she chose her native Maryland over him. He was grateful the Lord had used the house to lead him away from a woman he thought he loved. Her reaction to the move meant she had been wrong for him all along.

As wrong as the little town of Prairie Center. He just couldn't see himself living in an old farmhouse out here, eons from the nearest beach, forever. But for the time being, he could live rent free and take as many catering jobs as he could. As soon as he saved up enough money, he'd sell the old house and move. Somewhere, anywhere, on the East Coast. Preferably right beside the ocean, where he could fall asleep each night listening to the lullaby of lapping waves.

Feeling as though someone were concentrating on him, Garrison looked over to the table where most of the contestants had placed their entries. Gazing back was a gorgeous blond. Caught in the act, she turned to a bespectacled woman with gray hair and began speaking to her. But Garrison had gotten a good look at the blond's face, with its defined cheekbones and big brown eyes. Donned in an apron edged with lace, she was the image of a happy housewife waiting with a home-cooked dinner for her husband upon his return from a hard day at the office. Which is probably what her life was really like.

He restrained himself from letting out a resigned sigh. He didn't have time for women anyway. Not if he wanted to hightail it out of Prairie Center. And soon.

❋

As the judging began, the contestants scrambled to one of the chairs in front of the tables so they could watch. Willa felt the air ignite with tension. Contrary to her feelings only moments before, she realized she cared greatly about winning the contest.

Willa had entered only after her brothers, Don and Ron, prodded for weeks. "Do it for Mother. She'd want you to win prizes for cooking, just like she did. Please? Please?"

She shook her head at the memory of their faces, wondering

what the rest of Prairie Center would think if they observed two of their war heroes acting like juveniles.

At that moment, Willa heard an intake of breath as Garrison and two other judges sampled stuffed pork chops. The judges made their way around the table, biting into each dish, then conversing and taking notes. With the assessment of each entrée, the woman responsible visibly tensed and held her breath. After they tasted Dorothy's meatloaf, Willa cut her gaze to her rival. Dorothy couldn't contain a self-satisfied smile as they muttered approvingly. Next would be Willa's turn. Folding her hands in her lap in an effort to seem calm, she alternated between studying the white polka dots on her navy blue dress and glimpsing at the judging in progress.

The judges read the sign identifying her entry as Apple Avocado Amazement. Three sets of eyebrows shot up, then squeezed together as foreheads furrowed upon examination of the entrée for eye appeal. Willa knew the greenish color, interrupted by beige slices of cooked apple and bits of maroon ham, was unique, but the topping of rat cheese and ten pats of melted butter made it look delicious and satisfying. Willa was confident that was exactly what they were writing on their little notepads.

Gingerly, Garrison dipped his fork into the casserole and served himself a small portion on one of the luncheon plates Willa had provided according to contest rules. At closer range, she was able to observe his refined features. A straight nose and lips that looked as though they'd have no problems issuing both commands and kind words set off expressive Mediterranean blue eyes. His hands, though strong, indicated by their manly smoothness that his work environment was indoors rather than in the rough elements of farm life.

As he tasted the casserole, Garrison seemed to be holding back a grimace. Willa flinched. How can that be? Don and Ron like my cooking just fine. Maybe the other judges will know what's good.

But when her dish evoked a similar response in the others, Willa felt her shoulders sag. They didn't even bother to take a second taste before moving on to the next dish. She knew she had lost.

Moments later, Dorothy's meatloaf won the blue ribbon. Dorothy rushed forward and thanked the judges, throwing more than one flirtatious glance Garrison's way. Seething at Dorothy's giddiness, Willa was in no mood to mingle among the judges and contestants. Instead, she snuck away, trying to convince herself she'd rather look at some of the other exhibits.

Only after she thought the bakeoff area would be empty did Willa return. She concentrated on packing her supplies in the picnic basket she had brought.

"So you're the one who made the Apple Avocado Amazement, huh?"

Willa jumped, startled by the unfamiliar male voice from behind her. Turning, she clasped a hand to her chest and met the unforgettable Mediterranean blue eyes of Garrison Gaines. "You scared me to death!" she blurted. Not an ideal way to begin a conversation.

"I'm sorry. Please forgive me." His glance flickered to her left hand. Willa discerned a pleased expression on his face when he noted she wore no wedding band. "Miss. . ." He let his voice trail off, obviously hoping she'd fill in the blank.

"I suppose I might as well tell you. Since everybody here knows everybody else and tends to each others' business, you'll find out eventually, anyway." Unwilling to look into his eyes lest his stare cause her to faint dead away, Willa grabbed a silver-plated fork and swiped it clean with a cotton dishtowel. "It's Johnston. Miss Willa Johnston." She rubbed the fork with more vigor than required, keeping her eyes upon her task. Willa noticed her voice had taken on a harsh edge. "Although a gentleman would have waited for a proper introduction."

"Your friend Dorothy didn't seem to mind introducing herself."

"Who says Dorothy's my friend?" Unable to resist temptation, she snapped, "I suppose my casserole would have won had I been as eager to meet you as she was." Her look met his.

"My feelings would be hurt if I thought you really believed that." An amused grin spread over his face.

"Nevertheless, I don't make a habit of introducing myself to strangers." Willa threw the fork into the basket as if the gesture would reinforce her statement.

"If I adopted that custom, I'd be alone forever, now wouldn't I?" he observed.

"No gentleman remains alone for long. Especially when he follows the rules."

"Rules left over from the last century." He leaned against the table, folding his arms. "Yes, the nineteenth century was a charming time. If I recall correctly what Miss Mahoney taught me in history class, this area was crawling with Indians. Some of those Indians were none too happy to see the settlers. Not to mention the other delights of the time." Lifting his right hand, he touched each finger and thumb with the index finger of his left hand as he ticked off a number of other disadvantages. "No electricity. No telephone. No indoor plumbing. No automobiles. And last but not least—no women's suffrage." He leaned toward her, so closely she could inhale the intoxicating scent of his aftershave lotion. "But gentlemen and ladies were always properly introduced."

Willa found herself unable to resist such confidence. "All right. You win." She tried to grimace, but instead a smile played on her lips. She noticed that he, too, wore no wedding band. She extended her right hand, grateful she had painted her nails with a fresh coat of Revlon polish the previous night. "Nice to meet you, Mr. Gaines."

His eyes widened as he gave her hand a firm grasp. "You know me?"

"I know your name is Garrison Gaines. You're from some little burg in Maryland. And you inherited the Old Gaines Place, so if I can put two and two together properly, that's where you live." She flashed him her best smile.

"So you know all about me, and I don't know a thing about you. That's not playing fair, is it?"

"Maybe not," she conceded.

"Then in the interest of fair play, won't you give me a chance to acquire some knowledge about you? Say, over dinner next Saturday?"

She hesitated.

"Surely you know enough about me."

Willa felt her heart beating. She hadn't been out on a real

date since she and Dirk had been an item. And that was too long ago. Should she accept? Surely Don and Ron would be thrilled to see her get back in circulation. Maybe they should meet Garrison first.

You're a grown woman. Take a chance.

"It's a date," she agreed aloud. "I'm easy to find. Look for the big yellow house on the corner of Massachusetts and Eleventh."

"You live alone in a big yellow house?"

"Nope. I live with my brothers. They're tough on any guy who shows the least bit of interest in me at all. Be ready to pass inspection." Willa kept her tone light, but her words about her protective brothers were all too true.

Her warning didn't seem to leave Garrison ruffled. He pulled a card out of his pocket and handed it to Willa. "Tell them they can check me out."

The cream-colored card was printed in script meant to represent strawberry icing. She read:

> *GOODIE GOODIE!*
> *You Have Lots to Gain with*
> *GAINES GOODIES*
> *Garrison Gaines*
> *Caterer*

"So, Prairie Center now has its first caterer." She was about to add, "That's just swell," when she realized he was gone.

Chapter 2

As he stood and shaved over his small white porcelain sink for the second time that day, Garrison thought about how much he regretted his impulsive decision to ask Willa for a date.

"What possessed me?" Then he remembered the way her big blue eyes gazed into his. How her lustrous blond hair framed her face, emphasizing rosy cheeks. . . .

Pain shot through his chin at the point where the razor dug in just a touch too deeply. Garrison flinched. "Ouch! That's what I get for daydreaming." His mood soured, Garrison applied a styptic pencil to the wound. Melting salt caused even worse agony, but the bleeding soon ceased.

Despite his resolve to concentrate on the task at hand, Garrison's thoughts wandered back to Willa. Not only was she a blond beautiful enough to put movie starlets to shame, but Willa also lacked affectation. He remembered his experience as a judge at the Prairie County Fair. He'd thrown inviting glances her way, but Willa had stood back as a horde of vipers descended upon him. What was the matter with these women?

You'd think they hadn't seen a man in five years. "Well," he chuckled, "maybe they haven't."

Out of all the women he might have asked out, why did he have to pick Willa Johnston? If he were a betting man, Garrison would have laid good money on the table that Willa's family had lived in Prairie Center for generations. She'd never want to leave the security of her hometown. Why couldn't he have found a nice girl who wanted to live on the East Coast?

Garrison sighed. He'd always known he had relatives out here in Kansas. They sent Christmas greetings every year. His family had even made the trip out West one summer. He remembered a sweet older lady and a few neighbor children who seemed nice enough, but once Garrison's family got back on the train to return to Maryland, he hadn't thought much about them or the Midwest. He certainly hadn't ever planned on living in Prairie Center.

As Garrison toweled off a few remaining specks of shaving cream from his newly clean-shaven face, a reflection holding a guilt-ridden expression stared back. "I've got to be fair to her," he told the mirrored man as he slapped on some bay rum aftershave. "I'll be the gentleman and keep my promise to take her to dinner. But there will be no second date."

❋

Willa was ready early for dinner with Garrison. A copy of Life magazine in hand, she sat in a burgundy-upholstered chair, an inexpensive reproduction of a Victorian style. She smoothed the back of her dress, styled suitably for a diminutive figure with decorative buttons from top to bottom. The matching belt showed off her small waist and fitted softly over hips she thought a little too ample. The cool cotton fabric was named Shy Pink, a sentiment that reflected her feelings well.

Willa had chosen her Sunday-best white shoes. She imagined this would be the last time she'd have a chance to wear them outside of church before the arrival of Labor Day demanded they be put away for the winter. She felt confident her small white hat, which would soon prove another Labor Day casualty, would take her to any Kansas City restaurant. She'd also tucked her short white gloves into her small white purse just in case he took her somewhere really elegant.

What had she been thinking to let such a smooth talker entice her into going out with him? And without a proper introduction! But the Second World War had changed what was once *de rigueur* in etiquette. In this day and age, relationships formed as effortlessly as a summer breeze lit upon chintz curtains and flowed just as easily—sometimes too easily, in Willa's opinion—into marriage. Unlike her best friend, Betty, Willa hadn't allowed herself to get caught in a whirlwind courtship before the war. A marriage that at the time had seemed oh-so-romantic had ended with Betty's premature widowhood and a little boy to rear alone.

Just as the onset of war resulted in a wave of weddings, so did its end. The love of some couples had survived long separations while military service beckoned. As soon as the service-men returned home, honorable discharge papers in hand, betrothed couples swarmed to churches and courthouses to fulfill postponed dreams of wedded bliss.

But not Willa. Her plight seemed even worse than Betty's. If only she had married her high school sweetheart, Dirk

Bridges, before he'd left for Europe! Perhaps now she would be like Betty, the mother of a little son, or maybe a tiny girl, with Dirk's gray eyes and stubbornness just as steely. If they had married before he shipped out, Dirk never would have felt free to marry a woman he met in France, leaving Willa with a broken heart.

"You should be thanking the Lord instead of moping about how he broke it off with you," Papa had told Willa when she received Dirk's good-bye letter. "Better to find out now that he's a scamp than after you're married." Sighing, he shook his head. "A man like that must not know the Lord at all. He could never make you happy, Daughter." Then he opened his Bible, its cover ragged from years of use, and read aloud Proverbs 28:25–26: " 'He that is of a proud heart stirreth up strife: but he that putteth his trust in the Lord shall be made fat. He that trusteth in his own heart is a fool: but whoso walketh wisely, he shall be delivered.' "

Willa simply nodded. Papa had been right, but Dirk's betrayal still hurt. For Papa's sake, she focused on the wisdom of his advice and the teachings of Scripture. From that moment forward she put on a good face, never letting on to anyone how deeply she had been wounded. How many nights she had cried in secret! How many times she had prayed to the Lord, begging to know why Dirk's rejection was His will. Why had her faithfulness to Dirk not been rewarded? Did the breakup mean that it was God's will for her never to marry? Willa knew in her heart that He would reveal His answer. But when?

Surely Garrison Gaines didn't personify God's response. Willa had fantasized about her future husband many times. He would be ingrained with all the best qualities of a Christian man. He would hold her, protect her, cherish her, and inspire her with kindness and encouragement. Garrison's glib confidence didn't seem to fit the bill. As for his appearance, she hadn't pictured the matinee idol looks of Garrison Gaines. She'd witnessed his effect on women at the Prairie County Fair. Who was she kidding? Even if she managed to snag him, how could she, just a plain, ordinary girl, hope to keep him?

She shook her head. No, Garrison couldn't be the man the Lord had in mind for her. Her glance caught the sturdy black telephone on the hall table. One call would solve her problem. Then again, backing out on the date this late would be the height of rudeness. Not to mention she might not be able to place a call on the party line. Mrs. Thompkins and Mrs. Williams would most likely be tying up the line, chatting away about their gout and arthritis. If she asked them to cut their talk short, they'd ask why. Then she could count on Mrs. Thompkins listening in on her call. The gossip wouldn't fade away for weeks.

Willa would keep her promise. She'd be polite and try her best to provide Garrison a pleasant dinner companion. But there would be no second date. She was sure of that.

Then why was she so jittery? The grandfather clock in the parlor gonged every fifteen minutes, reminding Willa that the appointed time neared. She tried to concentrate on her magazine, but every few minutes she would put it down to peer out the window and look for Garrison's car. She couldn't explain why she bothered, considering she had no idea what type of car Garrison drove. She imagined it was like most of the others in town—a pre-1941 jalopy. But no one fortunate enough to own any vehicle ever complained. During the war, automobile factories had been retooled to produce military vehicles. The effort had proven worth the sacrifice, but now that the conflict was over, everyone was ready to buy a car. Any old vehicle with an engine that ran would do. A new sedan or sporty model fresh off the assembly line might be spotted in a big city, but such a vehicle was a fantasy for most people living in rural Prairie County.

Willa sighed. She imagined Garrison drove a beat-up old truck since he needed extra cargo room to carry food and supplies for his catering business. Perhaps gallant Mr. Gaines drove a milk wagon that had seen its best days or a decrepit truck sold to him by a retired farmer or house painter. No matter. She could put up with riding in a rusty old Tin Lizzy, just to look into his sparkling blue eyes for one evening.

At that moment, she spotted a station wagon with wooden side panels slowly making its way up the street. Willa took in a breath so rapidly that a small whistle escaped her rounded lips. The car was beautiful, new, and shiny, the dream of any housewife with a load of kids.

Willa imagined the happiness of such a lucky woman until her gaze traveled to the top of the wagon. Her jaw dropped open as her hand clapped over her mouth in shock. A larger than life, four-layer white wedding cake, complete with an arch of white roses and a statue of a happy couple, sat proudly on top of the car. How could anyone drive over twenty miles an hour with such a monstrosity, much less through a tunnel? Why, it must be three feet tall! She laughed aloud.

"What's so funny, Sis?" Ron's voice came from the kitchen,

where he was assembling a model airplane.

Willa chuckled. "It's too hard to explain. You'll have to come see for yourself."

The sound of chair leg tips scraping against hardwood floors, followed by reluctant footsteps, told Willa that for the moment, her brother's curiosity was greater than his love of model planes. As soon as Ron was by her side, Willa pointed. "Isn't that a riot?"

Ron peered out of the window. He let out a snicker when he spotted the car. "I'd say something like that would get plenty of attention, all right. Maybe that's what it's all about." He leaned closer toward the window. "Looks like it's a fellow driving it. I guess if you're a girl, he wouldn't be too bad looking." Scrunching his nose, Ron let go of the curtain and stood back. He rocked on his feet. "I sure hope he's not thinking some girl would ride with him in that thing. She'd sure be a poor sap." The next moment, Ron's eyebrows furrowed. "Say, it looks like it's turning into our drive."

"Huh?" Willa turned her attention back toward the window. Her amusement evaporated as she watched the wagon pull in front of the house. For the first time, she noticed the sign for Garrison's catering business pasted on the side. She groaned aloud. "It's my date. Garrison Gaines." She extended her right hand to shake her brother's. "Nice to meet you, Ron. Just call me 'Poor Sap.' "

Chapter 3

Ron didn't bother to wait for Garrison's knock. He bounded out the front door and ran across the wide porch, down the steps, and across the lawn to meet Garrison. Should she wait before joining them? Mama had always said not to seem too eager. Making sure to walk slowly and with grace, Willa strode out to meet them.

"Get a load of this!" Ron pointed to the sign on the door. The letters, painted a shade of pink to mimic icing, proclaimed, You Have Lots to Gain with GAINES GOODIES. "You didn't tell me your date makes his living doing women's work."

Tightening her lips together, Willa breathed in such an agitated lungful of air that she felt her chest rise. Too embarrassed to stare Garrison straight in the eye, she gave her brother a warning look. "Nice evening, isn't it, Garrison? I see you've already met my brother. As you might have guessed, he's planning a career in foreign diplomacy."

"Aw, knock it off, Willa. I was just fooling around." Sufficiently convinced of Ron's chagrin, Willa made the introductions. To her relief, Garrison didn't seem to have been offended by Ron's remark.

"Nice meetin' you, Garry."

Garrison's lips tightened into a line as straight as a ruler.

Ron ignored Garrison's obvious warning that he didn't care for his name being shortened. "I'd better run," he told Willa. "I promised Sid I'd meet him later."

Willa watched her brother leave before she turned back to Garrison. This time her gaze met his. Her heart did an unexpected flip-flop when she studied those blue eyes again. She imagined herself swimming in water just that shade. Perhaps the Mediterranean Sea. She'd be wearing a beautiful swimsuit in a cool shade of aqua. Her strokes would be as smooth as those of Esther Williams, the mermaid of the silver screen.

Suddenly she remembered she should say something. "Um, don't mind Ron. He's full of himself. Thinks he won the war single-handedly, even though he wasn't old enough to serve until '44."

If Garrison noticed her prolonged stare or her awkwardness, he didn't give any indication. "So many of our soldiers were just kids when they were shipped out overseas. And they're still kids now." He shook his head. "They've seen more than they should have for their years."

"Just kids, huh?" Her mouth twisted into a wry grin. "What are you, a hundred?"

A pleasing chuckle arose from his throat. "Not quite. Although during the conflict, I felt that way sometimes. Even flying the plane when it felt like I was on top of the world, literally above it all." He paused, a flicker of remembrance darkening his features. "Perhaps especially when I was on a mission."

"So you were a flyboy. A glamour job." Willa knew her voice indicated that she was impressed.

"Not as glamorous as everyone says. I'm just like all the others who fought."

"You're right. You are just like all the others who fought for our freedom, Garrison. You're a true hero. And you always will be."

"Thanks for the vote of confidence, but I'm no hero." His gaze traveled skyward, as though he were remembering his fellow airmen. "I just did my part the best way I knew how. That's all."

"Maybe you can tell me all about it sometime."

"Maybe." He paused, silent in his own reflections. "Maybe not. I don't like to talk about it."

"I understand. Ron and Don are the same way." Willa forced herself to smile. She searched for a change of subject, then remembered the icing pink letters on his advertisement. "At least you're not shy about your business."

Garrison broke out into a winning smile, his white teeth gleaming in the evening sun. "You're right. I don't mind in the least. That cake has brought me a lot of business." He gave the wagon a fond pat. "Goodie Woodie and I have already traveled quite a few miles together. I brought her all the way out here from Maryland. I hope that trip was only the beginning of a long relationship."

Willa had stopped listening after Garrison told her the car's name. "Goodie Woodie?"

"A swell name for a swell car." A look of slight worry crossed his even features. "I know the wedding cake makes her a little unconventional, but she has to pull double duty as both my business and personal car. Even if I could afford a second car right now, I doubt I could find one. I only got Goodie Woodie because of a friend back home who works at a Ford dealership." He hesitated, a look of concern crossing his face. "You don't mind riding in her, do you?"

"No, no. Not at all." Willa knew her quick answer wasn't persuasive. But she could put up with anything for just one night.

A look of relief washed over him, making Willa glad she had agreed to ride in the unusual vehicle. She was just about to suggest they leave for dinner when Garrison looked toward the side yard. A trellis covered with climbing roses offered an entryway into the garden. "Those roses are absolutely gorgeous. Just like their owner."

Willa felt herself blush at his compliment. "If you think those are special, you should have seen my victory gardens. Not that I'm out of the habit of planting vegetables, mind you. I've already put up thirty quarts of string beans and twenty jars of sweet pickles. And I'm still expecting plenty of tomatoes yet." She tilted her head toward the back. "Would you like to see for yourself?"

"Sure!"

Willa led him through the side yard, conscious that her dress swished as she walked. She thought she felt Garrison's stare upon her, so she was surprised when a more familiar voice greeted her from behind.

"I guess I'm on my own for dinner tonight, huh, Willa?"

Willa turned to greet her older brother, Don. "What makes

you think that? I'll be glad to fix you something before we leave." She glanced at her date. "That is, if you're not in a hurry, Garrison."

"Not at all. The chef is flexible."

Where did he plan to take her to dinner? In a tiny town such as Prairie Center, no restauranteur presumed to be so egotistical as to use the term "chef." "Short-order cook" was more like it. A shiver of delight ran down Willa's spine. Surely he must have plans to take her to a stylish place in Kansas City!

"Let's say he's a personal friend of mine," Garrison said, answering her puzzled look.

"A man about town, then," Don joked.

"Really?" Garrison made a show of noticing his surroundings. From their vantage point, only four other houses, surrounded by generous yards, were visible. Their street was not a city boulevard, but a narrow lane that curved through the residential section. And it was no secret that they were near very few businesses. The village supported only the essentials—Prairie Center Pharmacy, Wilson's Grocers, County Dry Goods, Dr. Goodman's office, and Minerva's Diner. "Maybe. If you can call Prairie Center a town."

Folding his arms, Don bristled at the inference that his hometown was less than a bustling urban center. Hoping to salvage the conversation, Willa jumped in with introductions. Garrison displayed a disarming grin to show he was only joking. Don grinned back and extended his hand.

Garrison flashed his cerulean eyes at Willa. "If I stay around long enough, will I meet more brothers?"

"Nope. This is it. Don and Ron do a pretty good job of

watching out for me by themselves."

"You'd better believe it," Don concurred. "That means I want my sister home plenty early, Garrison."

Garrison's eyebrows shot up. "You've given a grown woman a curfew?"

"No, I'm giving you one."

"Don, you're the biggest joker," Willa observed.

"And you love me for it." Don smiled. "I guess I don't need to hold you kids up. If there's some roast beef left over, I'll make myself a sandwich."

"Are you sure you wouldn't rather have something hot?"

"Nope. I'm in a hurry anyway. I have a date of my own." He nodded to Garrison. "You take good care of my little sister. She's very special to us."

"I will," Garrison promised. As Don disappeared, Garrison observed, "I can tell he means what he says. I'd better be extra careful with you, Miss Johnston."

"You'd better be."

"Now that I've passed inspection, do I get to see the garden?"

"I haven't forgotten."

Garrison let out a low whistle as he studied the roses. Willa had planted more than a hundred bushes. Many were in full bloom, offering the eye a plethora of color.

"There must be a rose in just about every shade known to man here," Garrison speculated.

"I'm not sure I'd go quite that far, but I do enjoy variety." She touched a crimson bloom on a tall bush. "Mrs. Anthony Waterer. One of my favorites."

Following her lead, Garrison laid a hand on the deep green

foliage. He withdrew it just as quickly, bringing the offended finger to his lips. "Ouch!"

"I should have warned you. This breed has lots of thorns."

"I wonder if Mrs. Anthony Waterer was just as prickly."

"Let's hope not." Willa giggled. "Are you sure your hand's all right?"

"I think I'll recover." He extended his finger for her to inspect.

Willa took his strong hand in hers and lightly stroked where his forefinger had been pricked. "I think you're right. You'll pull through." To her surprise, she realized she really didn't want to release his hand. Having no excuse to prolong the pleasant contact, she let go and hurried to share the facts about a nearby tea rose. "Here's a Mrs. B. R. Cant, named for the wife of the hybridizer."

"Hybridizer?"

"Yes. Benjamin Cant developed this rose by combining other breeds. One of my old school chums sent me this plant from back East. She says hers are eight feet tall, but as you can see, I've had no such luck." Willa pointed to the three-foot-tall specimen with only a few silvery pink blooms.

"So you have friends back East?"

Willa was taken aback by the odd question since it had nothing to do with roses. His voice seemed to hold some hope that she did indeed have many friends on the East Coast. Perhaps he was searching for a ray of familiarity since he was new to the Midwest.

"She's the only one, really," Willa answered truthfully, even though she knew her answer was sure to disappoint him. "She met a serviceman from North Carolina, and they moved there after they married. Not an uncommon story in this day and age."

"And not in my parents' day, either. That's how Dad ended up in Maryland. He's a native of Prairie Center, you know—Ben Gaines. That's why Anita left the house to him. They grew up together. My grandfather, George Gaines, was her uncle."

"So why did your father leave?"

"Serving in the Great War took him to the East Coast. He met my mother there, and as they say, the rest is history."

"So he never came back?"

"Sure, for visits," Garrison explained. "But he didn't want to come back here to live in the old house after all that time. I'm sure Cousin Anita knew I'd end up with it. She always had a soft spot for me."

"So that's how you inherited the house. I was wondering how the son of a first cousin got so lucky."

His dark eyebrows rose. "I see I've been the subject of a bit of gossip."

"It's not gossip if it's true." She folded her hands and sent him a rueful smile. "Oh, all right. I admit it. We have been speculating about you. It's a small town, you know. And the old Gaines place is a landmark."

"In that case, I'll forgive you."

"I'm so glad the house is still in the Gaines family."

He nodded, swallowing visibly.

Why didn't he seem happy to be the new owner of such a beautiful old home? "I hope the renters didn't do much damage to the house. I didn't know them well, but they seemed nice enough."

Garrison shrugged. "I guess they were. They left the house in good condition considering its age."

Why did he seem so nonchalant about the house where he would be living? Garrison seemed to be hiding something, but what? Whatever it was, she could see from the dark look on his face that he had no plans to reveal his secret to her. At least not at this moment. She considered it best to return to the topic of roses. "Here's a Mrs. John Laing." Willa showed him a shrub with pink blossoms boasting a hint of lavender.

"Pretty. But are they all named after someone's wife?"

"Not all of them." She pointed to a delicate pink flower. "Here's a Ballerina."

"Looks more like a dogwood than a rose."

Willa studied the flower as though she were seeing it for the first time. "Come to think of it, you're right. It does look a bit like a pink dogwood."

"How do you manage to keep all these names straight?"

"I don't have any trouble at all. Each plant is as individual as a person."

"You obviously have great love for your flowers. No wonder you're so successful in growing them."

"I could be even more successful if. . ." She hesitated.

"If what?"

"You'll think I'm ridiculous."

"Try me."

Willa averted her eyes so she wouldn't have to see Garrison laugh at her dream. "I wouldn't mind having a hot house."

"What's so silly about that?"

"Oh, I don't know. I'm not used to thinking big, I suppose."

"Maybe one day you could own your own nursery," he suggested.

"My own nursery?" Willa didn't remember the last time she'd heard such an outrageous proposition. "Don't be silly. I would never dream of starting my own company. You're a businessman. You of all people should know it's a man's world."

"Perhaps. But the war showed us we might change that one day," Garrison observed as he led her to the station wagon.

"In the meantime, I'll be quite content to let you open the car door for me."

"And I'll be quite pleased to do so."

As she entered the station wagon, Willa wondered if she had been wise to leap from dodging Garrison's passes to jumping into his wagon. What must she look like, sitting inside a car with such an incredible rooftop decoration?

Maybe no one I know will see me, she thought, hoping her outward expression didn't reveal her embarrassment. She swallowed, then said in her most cheerful voice, "Let's go!"

As they rode through the neighborhood and down Main Street, Willa soon realized she would have no such luck. Everyone she'd ever met seemed to be outdoors.

As Goodie Woodie passed, two young children pointed and giggled. "Hi, Miss Johnston!"

Willa tried to ignore the heat flushing her face. Showing herself to be a good sport, she smiled and waved to the children. They moved their hands up and down wildly, as though she were Santa Claus himself.

"Who are they?" Garrison asked.

"Flora and Hattie. Twins from the Sunday school class."

"They're darling. About four years old?"

"As a matter of fact, yes." Willa indulged herself with one last glimpse of the towheaded cherubs. "I hardly expected you to notice the girls, much less be able to guess their age."

"Is that so? You think I'm the strong, silent type, eh? Maybe like Humphrey Bogart?"

"Not quite as tough as all that," she admitted.

"I guess I have a soft spot for little tykes. I have a niece and nephew back in Maryland. I miss them a lot."

Willa hadn't thought about Garrison in the context of a beloved uncle until that moment. Stealing a glance his way, she realized that beneath the ruggedly handsome exterior, he must have a tender side. Suddenly she could imagine him giving a little boy an encouraging pat on the back or smoothing a little girl's hair as she cried. Willa discovered she liked that image of Garrison.

A catcall rudely interrupted her daydream. A couple of hoodlums known to cause trouble in the local high school were having a laugh at Goodie Woodie's expense. Garrison's lips tensed.

"Don't mind them," Willa consoled him. "They're always looking for an excuse to make fun of people."

"Let's just hope they don't decide to vandalize the car. A machine like this isn't easy to hide, you know."

"Don't worry. They're more bark than bite." At that moment, Willa was actually glad to see someone else she knew. She waved vigorously. "Hello, Dorothy!"

Dorothy's eyes widened in question, followed by recognition, followed by the realization that Willa was sitting where

Dorothy wished she could be. Dorothy returned her greeting, but she looked none too happy. For the first time, Willa felt she had finally gotten one over on her rival.

Garrison looked amused. Knowing her feelings were strictly human and did nothing to glorify the Lord, Willa was grateful that Garrison chose not to question the source of her glee.

Not that he would have had much time to grill her. Two blocks later, he pulled the car over and parked on the edge of the Prairie Center Park. The term "park" was a bit grandiose for the tiny plot of land, but the Prairie County Garden Club took great pride in maintaining the little piece of shaded green paradise.

"This is it," said Garrison.

"This is what?"

"This is where we'll be eating."

"But I thought we were going to a restaurant."

"I could tell by the way you dressed." He looked sheepish. "I started to say something when I first saw you, but I didn't want to spoil the surprise. I know women like eating at fancy places, but why drive all the way into a stuffy, crowded place in Kansas City when we can eat in God's great outdoors?" Before she could ask anything more, Garrison hurried to the back end of the wagon and opened the door. From underneath a blanket, he retrieved a picnic basket. Holding it up to show Willa, he reminded her of a little kid who'd managed to pull one over on his mama.

Grinning from ear to ear, Garrison tapped the basket with his forefinger. "Besides, this is the best food in Prairie County."

"You don't say?"

"I cooked it myself," he informed her as he slammed the door shut.

"A great cook. And modest too."

Garrison opened Willa's door. "You said it! I'm quite a catch!"

Willa slid out of the car and tapped him on the shoulder. "Oh, you!"

As they both giggled, Garrison led her to a level spot and spread a pristine white tablecloth on the lush grass.

"What are you doing? You'll ruin your beautiful cloth!"

"Now don't you worry. That's what bleach is for."

"And he does laundry too!" Willa nodded as though she'd just agreed to buy a brand new washing machine.

"Much to my regret. I have to admit, I normally wouldn't bring you out here, but I didn't think it was a good idea for me to take you to my house where we'd be alone. Especially since you've got strapping brothers ready to defend your honor."

Willa could see from Garrison's expression that he was only half joking. Though she was a grown woman, Willa could hardly blame her brothers for wanting to protect her, especially after the way Dirk had treated her. Ron, being the youngest, was adept at letting troubles slide. Don was another matter. As the eldest of the three, he felt responsible for his siblings since both parents had gone home to the Lord. Papa had passed away only a little more than a year ago. At least he had seen both of his sons return home from the war safely.

While her brothers were physically whole, Willa knew that emotionally, Ron had a lot of growing up left to do. She felt in her heart he would keep close to the Lord. Don was another matter. She was troubled that Don seemed to want to do everything for himself. He didn't take solace in the Lord the way Willa could.

More troubling, Don was far more bitter about Dirk than Willa herself. Whenever she thought of Dirk, all Willa had to do was to remember how brutally the Lord was betrayed by one of his closest friends and disciples, Judas. For a mere thirty pieces of silver, Judas had handed Jesus over to the authorities, resulting in His crucifixion. How facile her troubles seemed in comparison! No wonder, since Jesus had said in the Gospel of Matthew, "For my yoke is easy, and my burden is light."

"So how do you like it?"

"Like it?" Jerked back into the present, Willa suddenly remembered she was picnicking with a new man. She forced herself to look at the food set on the cloth. Garrison had prepared an assortment of fresh fruits, a cut of beef cooked to medium rare perfection, a creamy potato salad, and bread that emitted the appealing aroma of yeast. "It looks delicious!"

"Of course. You don't think I run a catering business without knowing my way around the kitchen, do you?" He picked up a plain white plate made of thick china and spooned her a helping of each dish. "But the real test is the taste." He handed her the plate. "See what you think."

"Would you mind saying a word of grace first?" Willa asked.

"Of course not." A slight pink tinged his cheeks. "What was I thinking?" He bowed his head and led them in prayer.

Willa smiled. "Thank you, Garrison." She took a delicate bite of the potato salad, which proved to be as creamy in her mouth as it had looked on the plate. "Delicious!" As she tasted each morsel, she complimented the chef.

Willa could see she pleased Garrison with her unqualified approval. Together they enjoyed the rest of the sumptuous feast. Willa let her mind drift away from the past and enjoyed conversing in the present. Garrison proved easy company once he dropped his half-teasing manner and began to share his real thoughts and feelings with her. By the end of the meal, the stars were peeking out from the curtain of night, and Willa felt as though she had known Garrison for a lifetime.

If only it could have been like this with Dirk.

"You know," Garrison was saying, "I guess we'll have to see each other during the week from now on."

"Why?"

"All the weddings, you know. Would you believe I have every weekend booked for the next three months?"

With that, Willa broke into sobs.

Chapter 4

Now, now. It's not so bad." Garrison placed his hand in the small of her back to console her. "We can still see each other. After all, there are five weekdays and only two days on the weekends."

Willa didn't know whether to laugh or to sob even more. Garrison's overconfidence would be enough to turn off some women, but to Willa, it was part of his charm. At that moment, she knew she was anything but charming. An instant ago, she had been merrily chatting as though she had not a care in the world. And now here she was, sobbing so much that her shoulders were shaking. Garrison retrieved a crisp white handkerchief from his shirt pocket and handed it to her. How had she managed to embarrass herself so?

"You don't understand," Willa mumbled in between sniffles. She blew her nose. The indelicate sound caused her even further chagrin.

"Of course I do." He put his arm around her, but Willa took his hand in hers and gently removed it.

"No, you don't understand. No one does. But thank you for

trying." She rose halfway, letting her knees touch the tablecloth. Eager for any distraction, she began gathering the silverware. "Just let me help you put these things away. I need to go home." Following her own suggestion, she placed the dish in the basket with more care than needed.

Garrison joined her in the task, but not without wearing a quizzical expression. He sent a sympathetic glance her way several times. Pursed lips and questioning eyes revealed that he desperately wanted to say something, but Willa made sure to look unyielding when he seemed ready to speak. Sure, she'd made a friend in Garrison, but she wasn't ready to share her humiliation and utter heartbreak with him. Not now. Not tonight. Maybe not ever.

Later on the ride home, Willa didn't bother to look out the window to see if anyone noticed Goodie Woodie. Her mind was much too heavy. The concerns of only hours before—was her dress right, why did Ron have to insult her date—suddenly seemed trivial.

Continuing to be the gentleman, Garrison escorted her to the front door once they had reached the big yellow house. The living-room light was burning, indicating at least one of her brothers was already home. Under normal circumstances, Willa might have invited Garrison in for a tall glass of lemonade to offer cooling relief from the heat of the August night. Yet she found herself in no mood to display the minimum of good manners. Garrison paused expectantly for only a moment. Seeing that no invitation was forthcoming, he bid her a dejected farewell.

Willa remained on the porch and watched Goodie Woodie

depart. She had only made one promise to herself—to be a good dinner companion. She had failed miserably even at that small task. Anyone could see why Dirk hadn't wanted her. After tonight, she was sure Garrison never would, either. Sighing, she opened the door and slid into the house, making sure the hinge didn't squeak. She was in no humor to be grilled by her brothers. She didn't want to think about anything related to her date. All she wanted to do was to go to bed. In the morning after a sound slumber, things were bound to look better. As Scarlet O'Hara of Gone with the Wind fame would say, "Tomorrow is another day."

❋

Garrison put away the food that was left over from the disastrous picnic. The chore was accomplished by rote, not because he put any extra effort into it. He was too engrossed in thought. What had happened with Willa?

The time was early, barely past nine. He wasn't sleepy enough to call it a night. When he'd planned his little surprise, he'd figured the evening would last until well past ten. He had anticipated after the meal that Willa would invite him into her house for a glass of tea and a chat or to share her favorite radio program. Such an invitation hadn't happened, much to his disappointment.

Aimlessly he walked into the den, a cubbyhole in the back of the house beside the expansive kitchen. Though he hadn't occupied the place long, Garrison relished retreating to the comfort of his little corner of the world. The house hadn't been spruced up since it had been rented out years ago—as a favor to a family in need, for a dollar a year. Garrison was nevertheless grateful that the former occupants had left each window dressed in floral chintz. Though not to his taste, the curtains at least offered some privacy and relief from the sun.

A large radio occupied the part of the south wall that wasn't composed of windows. He could tell from a water stain on the hardwood floor that, at one time, the southern exposure was used to its full capacity to nourish thriving plants. Perhaps if he'd planned to stay more than a couple of months, Garrison would have bought one or two green things of his own, just to add life to the old place. For the moment, the radio was his only consolation. Yet his frame of mind left him in no humor to listen to a show. Not swing music, soap operas, or serials. He doubted even the Burns and Allen Radio Program could lift his spirits.

What had happened to Willa? She'd dressed for a big night out in Kansas City, but she hadn't sulked or pouted when she'd discovered he had other plans. In fact, during the meal, she'd chattered and laughed as though she were having a grand time. So why did she burst out into sobs when he told her he was busy for the next three months? His ego would have liked him to believe she was already so head over heels in love with him that the mere thought of their being apart made her go into a spasm, but he knew that simply wasn't the case. Something else had distressed her. But what?

Why did he waste his time worrying? After all, he'd be out of Prairie Center in fewer than six months. Because of Willa's outburst, he had missed his chance to tell her that he had only booked catering jobs for the next three months and had made no engagements after that. The income would allow him to buy what he needed to upgrade the house enough to appeal to prospective buyers. Once the work was done, he and Goodie Woodie would head back to Maryland.

He made a mental checklist of his "to do" list. The wood stove and icebox were out of date, but they still worked. He had no plans to replace either. The bathroom had a leaky faucet. A few floor planks were loose here and there. Garrison had no doubt he'd find other minor repairs to make as he readied the house to be shown to potential buyers. Thankfully, repairs should be easily accomplished on the weekdays he didn't have events to cater. The rest of the changes he planned for the six-bedroom house were cosmetic. A little paint here, a bit of polish there, and the property would be ready.

Garrison had no doubt the house would sell quickly. The surrounding farmland had been sold off in pieces some time ago, so now the three building lots the house occupied were more suited to living in the small community of Prairie Center than for grazing cattle. He knew its location was prime. On the edge of town, the house was still the most impressive home within walking distance of local businesses. Garrison had hired two seniors from Prairie County High School to do what he considered the hardest job, painting the exterior. He had chosen a fresh white, which would be set off by cranberry shutters and trim. His real estate agent had assured him that the color combination, while hardly original or daring, would boost appeal to most buyers.

He let out a sigh. Too bad he'd be leaving so soon. Willa was a nice girl, one he would make time for if he knew he was going to stay. Then again, maybe if she decided she liked him enough, she'd be willing to think about moving back East with him. Home to Maryland, the land of rolling hills, beaches, and crab cakes.

Garrison shook his head, willing his daydream to stop. What was he thinking? He'd somehow offended her so much that he doubted she'd want to see him again anyway. Besides, she was a sweet, genuine, hometown girl with deep family roots in Prairie Center. Why would she even consider leaving?

"It's no use dwelling on what can never be." Garrison sighed.

The clock on the fireplace mantle told him that the time had come for a local radio program he'd come to enjoy, Words of the Bible with Pastor Elworth Meadows. Pastor Meadows was surveying Genesis, teaching stories that Garrison already knew by heart. Even so, he was amazed that no matter how many times he revisited a passage, he took away something new.

Pastor Meadows instructed his listeners to turn to Genesis 24 and read:

> *"And it came to pass, before he had done speaking, that, behold, Rebekah came out, who was born to Bethuel, son of Milcah, the wife of Nahor, Abraham's brother, with her pitcher upon her shoulder. And the damsel was very fair to look upon, a virgin, neither had any man known her: and she went down to the well, and filled her pitcher, and came up. And the servant ran to meet her, and said, Let me, I pray thee, drink a little water of thy pitcher. And she said, Drink, my lord: and she hasted, and let down her pitcher upon her hand, and gave him drink. And when she had done giving him drink, she said, I will draw water for thy camels also, until they have done drinking."*

Garrison didn't hear the sermon. His mind wandered instead to Willa. No matter how many reasons he could think up as to why she would be opposed to a relationship with him, Garrison still felt a tugging at his heart. Could the Lord have sent him to Kansas in part to find the woman who would be his bride? And if He did, was Willa the one He had chosen?

Garrison prayed he would soon find out.

❇

Willa was just about to take the first sip of her big glass of cherry Coca-Cola at the drugstore counter when she spotted Garrison striding toward her seat. As much as she wanted to run away, she was helpless. He'd already seen her. It was too late to escape.

"I'll have what's she's having," Garrison instructed Rodney. Garrison took the stool next to Willa's and swiveled it in her direction. "How're things with you?"

Willa wished she could pretend she hadn't heard him, but she didn't see how she could. Besides, his curly black hair, smelling sweetly of Jervis hair tonic, gave him an appealingly boyish look. His smile was too endearing to resist. And those eyes! "The same, I guess." She took in a breath. *Might as well get the apology out of the way.* "About the other night. . ."

His hand swatted the air as if dismissing an annoying fly. "There's nothing to apologize for. If I had a nickel for every time I felt a little blue, I'd be a rich man."

Willa wanted to protest that she never should have been so rude and that Garrison had, in fact, done nothing to upset her. As she watched Rodney mixing Garrison's soda, she noticed he seemed a bit too interested in their conversation. Unwilling to speak further, she took another sip of her drink.

"I'm surprised to see you out this time of day," Garrison commented. "I thought you'd be at work. Maybe teaching school or something."

At that moment, Willa remembered that they never had gotten around to talking about her career. The conversation had flowed as though they'd known each other for years, so the usual getting-to-know-you chat never happened. "So I appear to be a schoolmarm, huh? Not sure I like that."

"Oh, not all of my teachers were so bad, if I remember right." He looked dreamily at the ceiling. "I seem to recall an English teacher, Miss Swanson. She was swell. And a good sport about the frogs we put in her desk."

Willa shook her head. "So you were a holy terror?"

"And not so good at English, either. But I seldom played hooky from her class. Even on beautiful days like this." He leaned toward her and grinned. "So why don't we take advantage of the day and go for a walk?"

"I have a feeling you won't take no for an answer."

"You have the right feeling." After he took a few sips of his soda, Garrison left a dime on the counter and strode along with Willa. She expected him to start asking questions as soon as they left the drugstore, but the walk to the park was spent in compatible silence. The warm, overcast day was perfect for a picnic. Most of the shopkeepers and clerks took advantage of good weather by eating lunch in the park, but since noon was well past, Garrison and Willa were able to find a bench where they could sit and talk privately.

"If you think you're going to find out what upset me the other night, think again," Willa told him. "As much as I enjoyed the picnic, that doesn't entitle you to know everything about me."

"Ah, a woman of mystery. But it would seem I am entitled to know if I did anything to upset you."

"You didn't."

"Do you mean that?"

"Yes."

"All right then. The subject is officially closed." Garrison folded his arms and began watching a couple pigeons flutter and chase a few crumbs someone had apparently spilled from a box of cookies earlier.

At that moment, Willa regretted she couldn't share everything with Garrison. She hardly knew him, but she somehow felt she could trust him with anything. Reticence held her back from sharing how Dirk had humiliated her. If she told him the story of the breakup, then Garrison might wonder why Dirk didn't want her. And if her high school sweetheart, a young man who supposedly knew her well, had dumped her, why should Garrison, a total stranger, want her as more than a dinner companion? At least that's what she imagined she would be thinking if she were in Garrison's shoes.

Contrary to Garrison's assumptions, Willa was hardly a woman of mystery. An act like that might intrigue a man for an evening or two, but his curiosity wouldn't last long. Perhaps sharing a lesser secret would be best.

"All right," she said aloud. "I'll tell you why I'm out this time of day, and it's enough to make anyone blue. I'm out because I no longer have a job. I was fired."

"Recently? As in yesterday?" he inquired.

Willa nodded.

"I'll bet I can guess why. A man returning from the war needed your job."

"Bingo. You probably don't know Mr. Henson. He's our local lawyer. I helped him with general office-type stuff. But as soon as his nephew came home from the war, I was history." Willa let out a resigned sigh. "Same thing happened to my girlfriends with their jobs."

He shrugged. "Seems reasonable to me. I'm sure most men have families to support."

"I suppose." Willa knew she didn't sound convinced. "It just doesn't seem fair, though. I did the job as well as any man."

"I don't doubt it. And you're right. It doesn't seem fair."

"You're just saying that to be nice." She folded her arms defensively.

"I'm nice, but not that nice." Garrison chuckled. He situated himself on his elbows, looking into the sky as though he were contemplating the shapes of the clouds. After remaining pensive for only a few moments, he sat upright and snapped his fingers. He leaned toward her. "Say, I have an idea! Why don't you work for me as my assistant?"

Willa laughed, remembering Garrison's pained expression when he tried her Apple Avocado Amazement. "That's a nice thought, but your job is preparing food that can take a blue ribbon at the county fair, remember? I don't think you and my cooking go too well together."

He gave her an indulgent smile. "I don't want you to cook. I want you to answer my phone, take care of my accounting, answer letters. You know. General office-type stuff." He winked.

Willa wasn't sure his offer was serious. "But what about all those poor former servicemen with families to support?"

"I doubt if they look anything as good as you." His countenance turned serious. "I admit I do have an ulterior motive. I'm hoping if you're my secretary, you might agree to sell me some of your flowers for decorations. I don't know of anyone else who can grow roses as beautiful as yours."

She gasped aloud, bringing a hand to her throat. "You really want to buy my flowers?"

"Why not? They're better than most professional florists could provide. You obviously have a knack for gardening."

Willa thought for a moment. Garrison was right. Maintaining the house for her brothers wasn't enough to keep her occupied all day. Even with volunteering at her church and weekly Bible study, she still had time to spare. Working outside the home would give her a little pocket money. And she could never ask for a job she'd enjoy more than working with flowers. *Why not take him up on his offer?*

She nodded once. "All right. I'll do it. When do I start?"

"How's tomorrow morning at nine sharp?"

"Nine sharp it is." Willa felt as though she were dreaming. To work for Garrison! In her heart, she knew there was another reason she wanted to take the job. To be near him.

That was a secret she would have to keep to herself.

Chapter 5

That's it. The last stroke of paint. We're done." Willa stepped back from the living-room wall, now painted a cool shade of gold. The color reminded Garrison of the sun shining on a pleasant spring day, much like the one they were enjoying at the moment.

"Hear hear! Let's have a round of applause for all of us hardworking painters!" Don, who'd been helping Garrison and Willa paint, clapped loudly.

"No matter what you decide to do with this room, Garrison, I think you'll enjoy this color," Willa observed.

Garrison didn't answer. A lump formed in his throat. He never thought he'd miss the old place, but now that the renovations were finally finished, he found himself reluctant to leave.

The house wasn't the only reason. Three seasons had passed since he'd first met Willa on a hot summer day. Now spring was in full flush, and the woman standing next to him had grown from an acquaintance to a true friend. As she'd promised, she'd shown up for work at nine sharp the morning after he offered her the job as his assistant. From there they had developed an easy friendship. Willa's beauty, both internal and external, hadn't gone unnoticed by Garrison. Because he planned to return to his home state one day, he didn't dare let on that he'd like a deeper relationship with Willa. In spite of the temptation she offered, Garrison had been careful to maintain a close distance.

Guilt pangs had shot through his conscience as he watched Willa paint his house, a job that definitely blurred the line between the professional and personal. He hadn't planned on her taking up a paintbrush, but she'd thrown herself into the task with a cheery demeanor and recruited her brother to boot. Moving the brush up and down in even strokes seemed to relax her. Willa was obviously pleased with the tangible rewards of her work. She'd helped him select stylish yet tasteful hues for each room. Every space looked fresh, ready for new occupants. If only. . .

Willa interrupted his musings. "I've got roast beef hash at home in the icebox."

"Sounds like a winner," Don said. "Let me be the first to wash up. I'm starved."

Garrison chuckled as he watched Don depart. "Willa, you're always prepared. You remind me of Rosalind Russell in His Girl Friday."

"Oh do I?" Tilting her head, she placed a dainty hand on each hip. "I'll take that as a compliment."

"Naturally. You're always one step ahead of me." Garrison swallowed. What would he do without Willa? At that moment, he realized what he'd been trying to deny for months. He didn't want to go back to Maryland any longer, even though that's where his family and old friends were. A job was no problem.

He'd been promised a chef's position at a friend's restaurant in Baltimore, a city famous for seafood. Garrison was a natural at creating melt-in-your-mouth crab cakes and succulent, buttery lobster tail. He hadn't seen a mussel or crustacean since he left the East Coast. There was nary a Virginia ham in all of Kansas, as far as he could tell. All the Midwesterners he'd met wanted beef. Beef, beef, and more beef. Rare, medium, well done. With or without gravy. Any kind of meat would do, as long as it came from a cow.

His thoughts wandered to the ocean, its lapping waves making soothing sounds as they ran upon the sand. How he missed lying on the beach, building sand castles, and letting the sun's intense rays warm his body. He sighed.

"A penny for your thoughts," Willa offered.

"Huh? You heard me?"

"I heard the most mournful sigh. Are you thinking about Maryland again?"

"Yes. I do miss it."

"We are in the twentieth century. There are planes, you know," she reminded him.

"Are you suggesting I should take one?"

"As long as you don't stay forever."

As soon as the words were out of her mouth, Willa's beautiful face turned the most becoming shade of pink. She turned away from him and pretended to be engrossed once more in putting away the leftover paint.

Unwilling to pry, Garrison didn't press Willa about her feelings. Aside from her last remark, which he could tell hadn't been planned, Willa had done little to indicate she was interested in him beyond the easy camaraderie that developed through their work relationship. Could he have been blind all this time? Could Willa possibly look at him as more than a friend?

Don poked his head in the doorway. "Ready to go?"

"I am," Willa answered. "Garrison, you will be having dinner with us, won't you?"

"Sure he's eating with us," Don interjected. "He's got to drive us home anyway. He might as well stay."

"As if you don't see enough of me already. What with Willa working for me every weekday, and us being in the same Sunday school class. . ."

"Trust me, Don would tell you if he didn't want you around. Isn't that right, brother dear?"

"That's right," Don agreed.

"Besides," Willa added, "I've already looked in your icebox. I know all you've got in there is a bottle of soda pop."

"All right. You win," Garrison conceded. "That's the best offer I've had all day. I'll be out as soon as I wash up."

After Garrison washed up, he met Willa at the car. "I can't believe it," he said as he opened the door on her side of the car.

"Can't believe what?"

"How you've gotten attached to Goodie Woodie." Before she could answer, he ambled around to the driver's side and slid in the seat beside her.

"What makes you think I've gotten attached?"

"You don't complain about her anymore."

"I never thought I did," she protested.

Garrison grinned. "Not in so many words. But I remember the look of horror on your face when you first saw her. And I remember how embarrassed you were when people recognized you. I think you wished the floorboard would develop a hole so you could slink through it and escape through a manhole in the street."

She laughed. "I was that bad, huh?"

"Yes, she was," Don piped up from the backseat.

"Enough of that, or you won't get any hash," Willa teased.

"That's all right. She takes a little getting used to," Garrison admitted.

"Which one?" Don asked. "The car or my sister?"

"Very funny. You're a regular Bob Hope." Willa shook her head. "I have to admit, I kind of like riding around in her now. Everybody knows us, and they always wave."

"She is a bit conspicuous," Garrison noted as he parked in front of Willa's house. He peered into the side yard as he set the parking brake. "I see the roses have begun to bloom."

"Yes, the first few buds have made an appearance. I don't get as many blooms from the ones I grow outdoors as I do from my plants in your hot house, though. I guess I've gotten spoiled. The weather isn't so reliable."

Garrison thought back to when he'd first agreed to put up a small hot house on his property for Willa to grow flowers for winter events. Even though he'd told himself he wouldn't be there to enjoy it long, he figured the investment would increase the property's value. Since it was erected, Willa had expanded her expertise to include orchids and other exotic blooms. Willa's flowers had soon come into demand for events not even related to Gaines Goodies. Garrison only hoped the new owners of the house would allow Willa to use the hot house for her business.

"Maybe the weather isn't always perfect, but you still manage to coax blooms from the most difficult breeds," Don told his sister as they exited the station wagon.

Willa shot her brother a look of thanks before turning her attention to Garrison. "Speaking of difficult breeds, I want to show you the blooms on one of my rose plants. They're lilac pink. See if you think they'd be any good for the Brewster wedding."

"While you two are talking flowers, I'll go in and set the table for supper," said Don. "But don't take all day. I'm hungry!"

"We'll try not to," Willa answered.

Garrison seemed doubtful about Willa's choice in flowers. "I think the bride would really like blue roses. Will she be satisfied with lilac?" he wondered aloud as they walked to the garden.

"She'll probably have to be. There really aren't any blue roses. Some breeders wish they could come up with a rose that is truly blue, but I don't see how they ever will because the blue color pigment isn't present." She led him near the middle of the garden, where a shrub with round blooms waited. "Here she is. One of the best old roses. The Reine Victoria."

Garrison let out a whistle. "Beautiful."

"I think I'll suggest that we mix these with white in her bouquet, and yellow for the bridesmaids' bouquets, to match their dresses."

He nodded. "Sounds great. I don't think you'll have much trouble convincing her." Garrison studied the lilac blooms. "Why don't you enter one of these specimens in the fair this year?"

"The fair?" Willa shrugged. "Oh, I don't know. Do you really think it would stand a chance of winning anything?"

"Are you joking? Everyone knows you grow the most beautiful flowers anywhere around. I think they're even more popular than my cooking, sometimes."

"I don't think so. But thanks."

As she contemplated his suggestion, Garrison noticed for the hundredth time how the golden streaks in her yellow hair caught the sun, making the strands sparkle like a multifaceted diamond solitaire.

"You know, Garrison," Willa said, obviously oblivious to his thoughts, "if it hadn't been for you, I never would have considered selling my flowers. You gave me the confidence I needed."

"I don't take any credit for that. You did everything on your own. Although I might fill out the form for you to enter some of these in the fair, just to make sure you don't conveniently forget."

"But I'm going to enter the cooking contest again this year. I'll be busy enough with that."

Garrison tried not to grimace. "Uh, is your entry anything like last year's?"

"Nope." She shook her head. "This year it will be either a fruit salad or a beef dish."

"So why do you want to enter the cooking contest?"

Willa's blue eyes widened as if to say he was crazy for asking a question with such an apparent answer. "Because Mother always entered, of course. She won first place many years."

"So?"

"What do you mean, so?" Willa's voice had taken on a defensive tone.

"I think it's wonderful that your mother's cooking was recognized with blue ribbons." Garrison tried to speak softly. "But does that mean you have to enter the cooking contest? Your talents lie in gardening. Why not make the most of that instead?"

"But Mrs. Sours always takes first place in Rose Specimens."

"So?" he challenged her again. "Give her some competition."

"Oh, I don't know. Winning a blue ribbon every year means so much to her. Besides, she was my first-grade teacher. If I enter against her, everyone would think I'd gotten too big for my britches."

Garrison laughed aloud. "You take the cake, Willa. Have you looked in the mirror lately? You're not a little girl anymore."

Willa flushed, her cheeks turning a most flattering crimson. "I know, but my brothers would be terribly disappointed if I didn't enter the bakeoff. And anyway, I've already started looking through Mother's old recipes. Maybe I can duplicate her chocolate mousse."

"That's quite ambitious. Chocolate mousse is more difficult than you might imagine."

"Really?" Willa asked. "How bad can it be? It's just melting a little chocolate, whipping some cream, pop it in the icebox, and voila!"

Garrison tried not to laugh. "How about I teach you how to make it? I'll even let you use my recipe, as long as you promise not to share it with anyone else."

"Really? You'd do that? For me?"

"I certainly wouldn't do it for anyone else. Except perhaps, for my own mother."

"This is wonderful! I can make individual dishes for the next wedding rehearsal dinner we've booked. I know the Whitneys will be impressed."

"I'm sure they will be. But please let me supervise the process."

"Oh, I don't need supervision. Didn't you just say I'm a big girl now?" Her voice grew faster. "After everyone tries the mousse, it'll be a cinch to win the blue ribbon at the fair!" The excitement in her eyes showed she meant what she said.

"I don't know."

Willa wasn't paying any attention to reason. Her hands were clasped, and she was bobbing up and down on her toes as though she'd just won a million-dollar sweepstakes. "Don and Ron will be so proud! What a wonderful tribute to Mother!"

Garrison hated to burst her excitement, but he knew she'd have to face facts if she hoped not to embarrass herself in front of everyone at the fair. "But wouldn't your mother be even more proud of you if you forged your own identity? You have a special talent with flowers, especially roses, Willa. Why not share that with the world?"

"I don't know. . . ."

"Be a woman in your own right. The beautiful woman you are."

Willa didn't answer except to divert her attention to a gorgeous red rosebud nearby. Placing her hand lovingly underneath the cherry-colored bloom, she was gorgeous enough to grace the pages of Photoplay.

"I have something for you. Wait right here." After hurrying to the car, he retrieved a plant wrapped loosely in tissue paper.

"This isn't another picnic, is it?" she asked as he approached her in the garden.

"Uh uh." He shook his head and handed her the object.

Searching under the paper, Willa discovered an exquisite rose plant with a coveted bloom, a splendid yellow rose edged in pink. She gasped in delight. "A Peace rose! I've wanted one of these ever since it was introduced last year! How did you manage to get this?"

"It wasn't easy. Apparently, every gardener in America wants one to remember the end of the war."

"So do I." Willa touched a bloom. Garrison could feel her love for the petal he knew to be velvety soft. She looked back at him, her eyes glowing with delight. "I know just where to plant this." She tilted her head toward a corner. "Right in front of my bedroom window, so I can look at it every day when I wake up and every night before I go to bed." Sighing happily, she set the plant on the ground. Before Garrison realized her intent, she drew near him, closely enough that their faces almost touched. Tenderly, she rested her head on his shoulder and wrapped her arms around his waist. "Thank you, Garrison," she murmured into his chest.

Garrison wrapped his arms around her in return, reveling in her feminine softness. "I didn't get a reception this warm when I built the hot house."

"The hot house was for business. But the rose is for me."

"Yes, it is." He had imagined her warm body next to his ever since they first met. Yet the fantasies proved only a mere shadow of reality. He was close enough to smell her sweet hair, the light tea rose perfume she wore. Garrison broke away just enough to look into her eyes, the big blue eyes he had fallen in love with. When he kissed her lips, she didn't resist.

Chapter 6

"Congratulations, Willa! The mousse looks perfect!" Studying the frothy chocolate mountains, all chilled in individual serving dishes, Garrison applauded.

Folding her arms victoriously, Willa nodded once. "See? I told you there was no need to supervise me. I can be trusted in the kitchen, after all."

"I stand corrected." His boyish grin was her reward. "I'm sure the mousse tastes even better than it looks. It's certain to be the perfect ending to the wedding rehearsal dinner."

"Of course! It's chocolate, isn't it?"

Garrison laughed, but doubt clouded his blue eyes. "You have tasted it, right?"

She shook her head. "No. But what could go wrong? I didn't even have to turn on the oven. It's not like a soufflé that could collapse while it bakes."

"True. But you'd be surprised at what can go wrong in the kitchen."

"You worry too much." Willa rubbed her stomach and grinned like she'd seen her brother Ron do when he got to scrape cake batter out of the bowl. "And I did try a little when I scraped out the bowl, just before I put it in the icebox to set. It tasted fine then."

"I'm sure it did. But the recipe I gave you was pretty complicated. It would have been a good idea to try it after you chilled it, just in case."

"Well, I did make two extra portions for us to try before dinner, but. . ."

"I know. The bride's mother called at the last minute and asked if we could add two more guests. Thankfully, I had prepared extra beef for just such an emergency." He eyed one of the dishes of mousse as though he wished he could devour it then and there. "Next time, make four extra servings, won't you?"

"That's a promise." As she studied the dishes of mousse, Willa nearly jumped with delirious happiness. Nothing could ruin this night. "Oh, Garrison, I'm so thrilled! Now everyone who thought I couldn't as much as boil water will know how wrong they were!"

At that moment Thomas, a high school senior who Garrison had hired as an extra hand, scurried in with a stack of dirty dishes. "They've been talking about your decorations all night, Miss Johnston. Your roses sure are swell. The place looks more like the Ritz than the church fellowship hall."

"Really?" Willa felt her face flush with pride. "Everyone likes the flowers?"

Thomas nodded. "I overheard Mrs. Benton say she'd like to hire you and Mr. Gaines for her daughter's wedding in July." As he shot a glance toward Garrison, Thomas's lips pursed into a disappointed line. "Too bad you won't be able to take her up on it, Mr. Gaines."

Why did Thomas make such a remark? Willa realized that Garrison must have already made vacation plans for the summer. As much as she didn't want to interfere, she knew she had to advise him against turning down such a lucrative job. "Garrison, if I were you, I'd rearrange my schedule around that wedding if she wants us for it. Everybody in town will be there, and lots of out-of-towners too. At least five hundred people. You don't want to pass up the chance to cater a big affair like that!"

"Oh, he'll be long gone by then," Thomas noted as he ran water over the dishes in the sink.

"Huh?" Willa's head snapped in Thomas's direction. "What do you mean, long gone?"

"Nothing," Garrison interrupted.

Thomas ignored Garrison's warning look. "Don't you know? Mr. Gaines is going back to Maryland. We'll be out of a job pretty soon. Good thing I'm going to college next semester." Shaking his head, Thomas returned to his chore.

"Maryland? What's this all about?" After setting a dish of mousse on the counter, Willa folded her arms and stared into Garrison's eyes.

"I should have told you earlier, I suppose," Garrison confessed, a sheepish look crossing his face.

"So it's true? You're going back to Maryland?"

"I got an offer on the house. I haven't gotten back to them yet, but they're willing to pay my asking price. I'd be a fool not to accept."

So he was selling the house! Willa could hardly believe what she was hearing. Suddenly her stomach felt as though it were about to hit the floor. "I thought we were painting the house so you could live there. You didn't tell me you were planning to sell it." Despite her best efforts to remain calm, she heard her voice rise in pitch and volume.

"I didn't know you hadn't said anything to Miss Johnston," Thomas called over from the sink. "Sorry I spilled the beans."

"Go and make sure everyone's water glass is filled." Garrison's tone was curt. After shaking excess water from his hands, Thomas quickly disappeared to tend to his new assignment.

"How could you do this? How could you lead me to believe—" Willa fought back her tears.

"I was going to tell you. . . ."

"When?"

Before Garrison could answer, the kitchen door swung open. Thomas, holding a half-empty pitcher, hurried over to Willa. "I hate to be the one to bring even more bad news, Miss Johnston, but I thought you should know that Mr. Bridges is out there."

"Oh." Her former fiancé. Willa barely recognized the weak voice that came out of her mouth.

"He's with his wife."

So Dirk and his wife were here. She hadn't seen their names on the guest list. Maybe he and his wife were the last-minute guests. Willa's heart did a funny flip-flop. The emotion was not the giddy happiness she felt around Garrison, but a tense, dejected feeling. "Are you sure?"

He nodded. "I know Mr. Bridges. Me and my buddies see him every weekend at Barney's Pool Hall in Kansas City."

"Really? He never used to play pool."

"He does now. He's pretty good at it too." Willa's face must have shown her distress, as Thomas turned serious. "Do you want me to serve dessert at their table?"

"No, that's all right." Willa shook her head so hard her hairpins nearly jiggled loose. "I can serve them."

"Yes, Ma'am." The young man exited.

Garrison's brows furrowed. "I don't understand. Why should you be worried about seeing Dirk Bridges?" He flashed her a wry grin. "He didn't hustle you at pool, did he?"

"If only it were that simple." Chagrined, Willa set her gaze upon the floor tile. "It's nothing."

"Don't give me that. What did this man do to you?" Garrison's tone had become edgy.

Willa looked back into his face, the face she had grown to love. "So you'd like to defend my honor?"

"If it needs defending, yes. I won't have any man insulting you."

She laughed. "I wish you had been around years ago. Maybe I wouldn't have gotten engaged to Dirk in the first place."

Garrison's mouth dropped opened. "Engaged?"

"Unfortunately, yes. He was ready to leave for his army basic training when we agreed to marry after the war. But instead, he went to France and found someone else." In that instant, Willa realized that when she told Garrison about the broken promise, she felt as though she were talking about someone else. Perhaps Garrison had healed her heart after all—but was it only to break again?

"How did Thomas know about your engagement?" Garrison asked. "He must have been only a sophomore in high school when the war ended."

"I know. But word gets around. Especially when somebody gets dumped."

"I take it you haven't seen him since?"

"No."

Garrison's eyes softened with sympathy. "Look, I wanted you to serve the dessert so you could enjoy the glory. But now I'm not so sure that's a good idea. Why don't you let me serve it?"

"No. I've avoided Dirk this long. I've got to face him sometime. It might as well be when I'm serving an unforgettable dessert."

"All right, then." Garrison sent her a determined nod. He balled his hand into a fist and gently tapped her on the shoulder. "That's the spirit! Let him see what he's missing."

"Yeah. Let him see what he's missing." Willa was grateful that Garrison didn't notice the lack of enthusiasm in her voice as he became engrossed in perking a fresh pot of coffee. She didn't know how much longer she could act as though her emotions were as relaxed as a hound dog snoozing on the front porch. First, Garrison broke the news he was leaving for good. Then Dirk showed up for the dinner. How many more rotten announcements could she take in an evening?

"Lord," she prayed silently, "when You deliver bad news, You really throw a one-two punch, don't You? Please, give me the strength to get back on my feet and come out fighting like a champ!"

Willa felt a consoling hand on her shoulder. "I just got a peek at the old flame and his wife," Garrison whispered.

"You did?" She wanted to ask Garrison if Dirk had changed,

but how would he know? Besides, none of that mattered now. Instead, she lifted her face so that her eyes met his. "What does she look like, Garrison?"

"She looks like the type of cheap, flashy woman that gets a man's notice very quickly." He touched her chin, letting it rest on his fingertips. The blue eyes she loved so much penetrated hers with their intensity. "But it takes someone special to hold a man's attention." Garrison let go of her chin and embraced her protectively. She felt safe in his arms, as though Dirk or no one else could ever hurt her again. "He was crazy to let you get away."

To Willa's dismay, he broke the embrace. Her reward was to see a longing look cover his face. A yearning expression that she hadn't seen on any man's countenance for a long time. Far too long.

At that moment, Willa realized she didn't seek revenge against Dirk. Suddenly, his rejection seemed no more important than yesterday's news. Garrison was the man she loved. The man she had loved from the first moment they met at the Prairie County Fair. But he was leaving. The idea was more than she could bear. But bear it she would. For now, she had a rehearsal dinner to cater. She could think about her failures after she got through this evening.

"I–I've got to get going, Garrison. They're waiting."

Rolling a dessert cart laden with dishes of mousse, Willa hoped no one would notice her as she transported the cargo to the head table, which was to be served first. Most of the guests were too involved in their own conversations to pay attention to Willa, although friends and acquaintances greeted her pleasantly. Many of them complimented the white, deep pink, and pale purple roses she had used to decorate the fellowship hall. Since the bridesmaids would be wearing lavender dresses with burgundy sashes for the ceremony, she planned to use the same variety of flowers in the church sanctuary the following afternoon. She felt herself beaming as compliments about the fresh, full blooms and stunning colors were repeated again and again. Even expert gardener Mrs. Sours commended her efforts in growing the flowers and her talents in arranging them.

Though she wasn't surprised to receive some good words about her roses, Willa was even more pleased when people oohed and ahhed over how delicious the creamy mousse appeared. Unwilling to give the impression they were too eager to consume food at such a formal occasion, no one dug into the treat too quickly. However, Willa could see that everyone looked forward to topping the night off with delectable chocolate.

Willa's confidence soared so that she almost forgot she had to face Dirk. She moved as slowly as she could, prolonging some conversations beyond their natural ending. She even put up with Dorothy, who made sure to let her know her new beau was the member of a prestigious family who lived in Kansas City's Ward Park. Anything to delay confronting Dirk.

Despite her best efforts to dawdle, all too soon Willa was approaching Dirk's seat. Soon she would be forced to serve him. Willa's heart started pounding. For a moment, she wished she had taken Thomas up on his offer to serve dessert in her stead. Even letting Garrison take her duty seemed a better option. But it was too late.

As she got within earshot of his conversation, she could hear her former fiancé carrying on an animated conversation about automobile engines with the man across the table. Maybe Dirk would be so consumed by his passion for eight-cylinder internal combustion engines that he wouldn't bother to look up when she served his dessert. If he tried to acknowledge her, Willa had already decided she would turn her head and pretend she hadn't heard.

Maybe that wasn't the right thing to do. Some might even call it a lie. Perhaps avoiding his greeting would be a lie and even the coward's way out. At the moment, she felt too helpless and tongue-tied to talk to him as though nothing had ever happened. She just couldn't. Willa prayed the Lord would understand. Surely He knew her distress!

Of course He does! Her conscience brought to mind the Savior's comforting words in the twelfth chapter of Luke: "Even the very hairs of your head are all numbered. Fear not therefore: ye are of more value than many sparrows."

Willa kept repeating this verse in her head as she got closer to Dirk. Still, her hand shook as she placed Dirk's dessert in front of him. To her dismay, being so near the muscular blond made her stomach feel as though it were contorting into a thousand knots. Now that she was close, Willa could see that Dirk looked better wearing a stylish new suit than he had in his army uniform. Yet no amount of comely looks could make up for how he had broken his promise to marry her. Willa thought about the token he had given her, his pledge that he would return from the war and make her his wife. After he broke off with her, Dirk had said she could keep the ring, but Willa had returned it. The little diamond that once held so much meaning had become nothing more than a sterile block of stone.

Willa stole a look at the new Mrs. Dirk Bridges. The diamond she sported looked familiar. Too familiar. A shocked Willa guessed that Dirk had simply given his new wife her old engagement ring.

How could he give her the same ring? And for what? A betrothal of a month or two, at most? Perhaps not even that long. Perhaps they were engaged only a few days before they hurried to the altar—or a French courthouse, more likely. How could such a whirlwind courtship compare to the years we spent together, the years when everyone in town was certain we would one day marry?

Once her gaze left the wife's ring finger, Willa observed the woman herself. Her hair was bleached almost white, its natural dull brown evident by the roots. Rouge and lip color were applied with a heavy hand although, Willa had to admit, without flaw. The Frenchwoman was dressed fashionably in a bright red off-the-shoulder evening dress, a cut much too daring for Willa to consider wearing. She supposed she looked like a frump in comparison.

Willa's hand was still shaking as she set the mousse in front of Dirk's wife. She prayed the woman didn't notice, but her prayer wasn't answered in the way Willa would have liked.

"So, Dirk, ees zis the girl who thought she was engaged to you before zee war?" she asked.

Guests within hearing range shifted in their seats. Though they pretended not to be interested in the exchange, Willa could tell they were listening to every word.

Dirk simply stared at the chocolate confection. Willa could tell from his mortified expression that he wished he could fall face first into it rather than answer his wife.

"Zis must be her. I know her from zee picture you showed me." The new Mrs. Bridges assessed Willa from the tip of her blond hair to the open toe on her navy blue heeled sandal. "I must say zee picture flattered her."

"Good evening, Willa. Nice to see you again," Dirk muttered, barely allowing his gaze to rest on her face.

Willa wanted to scream, "Nice to see you? You have some nerve!" Instead, she threw her shoulders back so she stood at her full height. "Good evening, Dirk."

"So zis is zee girl!" The Frenchwoman's dark, penciled eyebrows rose as her red lips puckered. She looked as though she was trying to refrain from bursting into laughter. She turned her attention to her husband. "Vhat ees zee matter? You are not afraid to introduce us, no?"

"Of course not." Dirk could barely contain his emotions—obviously a mixture of embarrassment and anger. "This is Willa Johnston. Willa, this is Nanette Bridges."

"Hees wife," Nanette said pointedly.

Willa only managed a nod. "Nice to meet you," was more than she could muster. Nanette was so overtly thrilled by the chance to rub her victory in Willa's face that she couldn't contain her glee. Or was she simply insecure? Willa realized that perhaps Nanette still viewed her as competition. But why? She had made no effort to contact Dirk since he had written the good-bye letter that bore a French postmark. Dirk had made his decision and had not indicated to Willa that he had any regrets. Or was that a hint of remorse she caught in Dirk's eyes? No matter. He had chosen Nanette. Willa wouldn't want

Dirk now even if he begged. Breaking up a marriage, no matter how ill advised, surely wasn't God's plan for Willa.

Willa's thoughts were interrupted by the voice of a nearby guest. "What's this?"

"Is your dessert soupy?" whispered another.

"Soupy doesn't begin to describe it. Liquid is more like it."

Horrified, Willa watched as one guest after another dipped a spoon into the mousse, only to discover that, somehow, the dessert had not chilled into the expected frothy cloud of chocolate. Dorothy's face wore a look of amusement mixed with disgust. She whispered something into her suitor's ear.

Willa inwardly groaned and surveyed the room in hopes that the few guests at Dirk's table were the only ones whose desserts had proven disastrous. Maybe the rest of the guests were enjoying a properly prepared dessert. Her hopes were crushed when she saw the puzzled looks, grimaces, and questioning expressions on the faces of the every other guest present. Every single dessert was apparently a flop.

Willa felt her mouth drop open in despair. What could have happened? If only she'd listened to Garrison. If only she had tasted one of the desserts before serving a disaster to a whole room full of dinner guests! Or better yet, if only she had let him help her, as he had suggested. Now she had made a fool of herself and of Garrison!

"Vhat ees this?" Nanette wondered aloud. "Zee dessert is not up to, how you say—up to par?" Nanette picked up her dessert spoon and stabbed the top of the mousse. Underneath the perfect top, the concoction was nearly liquid. "Zis is not like any mousse I have been served in Paree." She turned her attention to Willa. "Ees zis how you Americans prepare a mousse? Or have you not enough electreecity to operate your icebox?"

Not knowing what else to do, Willa pretended to be too occupied with picking up the next dessert from the cart to notice her comments.

"Perhaps you could take a few lessons from someone who knows her vay around zee kitchen?" Nanette mocked in a voice too loud for anyone nearby to ignore.

"That's enough," Dirk hissed.

Dirk's admonition was too little, too late. Willa felt tears rush to her eyes.

She heard Thomas whispering into her ear. "Is everything all right? Do you want me to get Garrison?"

Willa shook her head.

"Garrison? Ees zat zee caterer? *Oui, Garçon,* I would like to see zee caterer." Nanette swiveled in her chair, her hand airborne in an expressive gesture. Before Willa could stop what was happening, Nanette's fingers hit the side of the dish Willa held. The chilly mousse tipped toward the woman. Willa made a swipe to catch the dessert, but her efforts were futile. The brown soup, generous dollop of whipped cream, and frothy chocolate topping landed on Nanette's upswept coif. The half-empty dish hit the back of the chair, splattering more liquid on her dress, before hitting the wood floor and exploding into pieces.

Willa gasped. "I'm so sorry! Are you all right?"

Nanette rose so quickly that the wooden folding chair in which she sat toppled to the floor behind her, echoing throughout the hall. She touched her blood-red fingernails to her hair, trying to smooth the curls back into place in spite of the mess the chocolate had made of her coif. With sticky sweetness covering her hands, she shook them out, splattering the floor and white tablecloth with brown specks.

In spite of the fact that Nanette had speckled Willa's dress and shoes with mousse in her fury, Willa placed her fingertips lightly on Nanette's shoulder in a conciliatory gesture. "Let me help you."

Nanette swatted Willa's hand away. "You do not dare to touch me! Have you not done enough damage already?" She surveyed her frock. "Just look at zis dress! I'll have you to know zis was very expensive. I'll make sure you reimburse me every penny, you, you!" Nanette stomped her feet. "How you say—incompetent fool!"

"Nanette!" Dirk intervened.

"Dirk, do somezing. Make her comprehend zat she shall pay for zis!"

"It's only a dress. Sit down."

As Willa returned Nanette's chair to its upright position, she heard the guests' reactions. Some chuckled. Others whispered. Still others' tones indicated their stunned amazement.

Willa couldn't remember a time she'd been more humiliated. The whole town, the whole county was laughing at her. And she couldn't blame anyone but herself.

Abandoning the serving cart, Willa ran through the back door of the dining area, through the kitchen, and out through the screen door, nearly tripping on the back steps. The spring night smacked her with brisk air, but Willa ignored her shivering body. She was too busy trying to escape. She had ruined everything. Garrison would never forgive her!

Chapter 7

Willa didn't remember the walk home from the church. All she could do was to hurry past familiar houses and streets she'd known all her life. Falling tears blurred her vision. Occasionally a car would honk its horn. Willa waved but tried not to look at anyone. She didn't want anyone in the friendly little town to stop and offer her a ride home. Anyone who did would notice she was upset and start asking questions. Her humiliation was too deep to share, even with lifelong friends.

Ron was in the kitchen, snacking on cookies and milk, when she ran through the back door. He looked at his watch. "Say, isn't it a little early yet, Sis? Everything went all right, didn't it?"

Willa gave him a quick nod.

"What's the matter, Sis? Why did you come in through the back?" He peered out the front door. "Didn't Garrison bring you home?"

Willa shook her head.

"Say, you two didn't have a spat, did you?"

"Not exactly."

"Then what?"

"I don't feel like talking about it." Willa rushed out of the kitchen, through the dining room, into the security of her bedroom, and shut the door behind her. Sitting on her bed, she wept. "Dear Lord," she prayed, "why am I so clumsy? How did I manage to ruin the most important night of my life?"

Willa waited for an answer, but none seemed forthcoming. She kicked off her navy sandals and rolled over on the bed, letting her face bury itself in her pillow. Too distressed to think, she fell into a fitful sleep.

"Sis! Wake up!" Ron shook her shoulder.

"Wha—" Willa realized she felt a sick feeling in the pit of her stomach. She wondered why, until she remembered what had transpired that evening. Looking toward the window, she could see through the crack between the curtain and sill that it was still dark.

"What time is it?"

"A little after ten."

Good. Maybe she could get a few more hours of sleep before she had to face reality. "Leave me alone."

He shook her again. "Get up. Garrison's here."

She shook her head. She wasn't ready to face him. Not yet. "Tell him I'm not home."

"Don't be silly, Willa. Get up and go see him."

"No." She turned on her side, away from Ron.

"Look, I don't know what happened, but you've got to see him sometime."

"No. Tell him to go back to Maryland. I don't want to see him ever again."

"But I want to see you," Garrison's voice interrupted.

Willa looked in the direction of his voice. Garrison was standing in the entrance of her room. Her heart betrayed her by leaping for joy. At that moment, Willa realized her eyes must be puffy and red from crying. She was still in her clothes. Certainly they were wrinkled and crumpled. Perhaps he was headed back to Maryland, but she had enough pride that she didn't want him to see her like this!

"I can see I have no choice," she agreed grumpily. "But will you give a girl a minute to freshen up?"

Garrison disappeared into the parlor almost before her request was out of her mouth.

Ron rolled his eyes. "I hope you settle your tiff soon. I liked you better when you weren't moping around."

Seeing her image in the large, round vanity mirror, Willa had to agree. "Go and talk to him while I freshen my lipstick, will you?"

As he went to comply, she patted around her eyes with a bit of loose translucent face powder to conceal red in the wrong places. Quickly she touched her lips with a dab of lipstick to add color in the right place. After running a comb through her hair, she smoothed her dress into place, satisfied she looked as good as a girl could look this late in the evening.

She knew she needed to ask Garrison's forgiveness, but she wished he'd waited until she was ready. Well, she reasoned, all she could do now was to stand straight and keep her head held high. After all, he had reason to ask her forgiveness too. The nerve of him, accepting her help in fixing up the house when he planned to move all the time!

Willa had worked herself up into a subdued fury by the time she stepped into the parlor. No matter what he had to say, no matter what accusations he might make, she was ready for him. She was ready to face the angry glint in his eye, the darkness in his face.

To her surprise, the Garrison waiting for her wasn't in the foul mood she anticipated. Instead, he paced the floor aimlessly while holding a nearly full glass of lemonade. He wore an expression of worry compounded with anticipation, reminding her of an expectant father waiting for his wife to deliver a baby rather than a man enraged that an event he catered had just been ruined.

As soon as he noticed her, Garrison set down the glass and rushed toward her. He put a hand on each of her shoulders. "Willa, I got here as fast as I could. I would have been here sooner, but I had to clean up." His eyes were wide with anxiety, his mouth slack with worry. "I'm sorry. You must think I'm terrible for not coming to your rescue."

"Coming to my rescue? But I'm the one who ruined your dinner. I never should have insisted on making the dessert. I–I'm sorry." She looked down at her feet in a display of genuine shame. How did he manage to make her behave this way? She had entered the room looking for an apology, and instead, she had rushed to explain herself to him.

"There will be other dinners."

Remembering why she was infuriated, Willa stared into his face. "Is that so?"

"Of course." He began ticking off names on his fingers. "There's the Smith party, the Williams birthday, the Bennett wedding—and that only takes me until the end of this month."

"And then you're leaving." Willa kept her voice flat, fighting every urge not to plead with him not to go. How would she ever be happy without him being nearby?

As her words registered, pain clearly marked his face. "I can make a provision in the contract that you are to have use of the hot house. You might have to pay them a little bit of rent each month, of course. But at least then you won't have to worry about being in business with me anymore. You can grow and sell your flowers. Maybe open your own florist shop on Main Street. I know your store would thrive." His monotone belied the excitement his words should have generated.

"But that's not what I want."

"It isn't?"

"No, at least I don't want a business to be my whole life. I realize now that it wasn't being in business that made me happy. It was being in business with you."

His Mediterranean blue eyes were intent on hers, reminding Willa of the day she fell in love with Garrison. "When I first came out here, I wanted to hightail it out as soon as I could. I never dreamed I'd meet someone like you, Willa."

"But I know how much you want to go back East, Garrison. Back to your beaches and oceanside. I understand. Really, I do." Willa only hoped her protest was convincing enough to set him free. She would never ask him to give up the life he really wanted just to stay in the Midwest with her. She would somehow do without hearing his voice, working by his side, sharing a hymnal each Sunday, observing again and again his handsome looks. She loved him enough to give up being with him should he be happier somewhere else.

Willa focused on her shoes, praying tears wouldn't fall. She didn't want Garrison's pity. She couldn't stand that.

"Do you really think I could choose the ocean over you?"

Surprised, she looked up into his eyes. Though Willa had never seen an ocean, she imagined no body of water could be more beautiful than his eyes. "What are you saying?"

"I'm saying I'd like to stay here. Right here in Kansas. If you'll agree to stay by my side. As my wife."

Willa's heart began beating faster than she'd ever felt it beat before. "Do you really mean that, Garrison?"

"Let me show you how much." Stepping back from her, he reached into his coat pocket and took out some papers.

"What's that?"

"The contract to sell the house. I haven't made any promises to the potential buyers. But after tonight, I've made up my mind. I'm staying here in Kansas." Garrison ripped the papers in half.

Willa gasped.

"So what will it be, Willa? Will I be staying here all by my lonesome in that big old house? Or will you be Mrs. Garrison Gaines?"

"Even after tonight?"

"Especially after tonight. I'll eat chocolate soup every night of my life if I get to spend it with you."

"Then I think you know the answer." Willa fell into his embrace. "I only have one condition."

His eyebrows rose. "And what's that?"

"I'm not so fond of chocolate soup, myself. So would you mind doing the cooking?"

He broke out into the smile she had always loved. "It's a deal. The best deal I ever made."

"Then I'm yours. Forever."

Their lips met, melting together in a kiss they knew was only the beginning of a life full of love and happiness, with many more kisses to come.

TAMELA HANCOCK MURRAY

Tamela is a Virginia native who is blessed with a wonderful husband and two daughters. When not shuttling her daughters to and from their many activities, she enjoys writing both contemporary and historical Christian romances. Her cooking skills have improved considerably since serving her husband raw scalloped potatoes and burned chicken as a newlywed.

A Change of Heart

by Christine Lynxwiler

Dedication

To my daddy, H.B. Pearle,
whose unwavering confidence in me
has always made me believe I could do anything,
and to my mama, Ermyl McFadden Pearle,
who continues to teach us all by example
what it means to love sacrificially.
I love and appreciate you both,
more than words can express.

Thanks, as always, to my own hero, Kevin,
and our two precious daughters, Kristianna and Kaleigh.
God has blessed me beyond measure.

How excellent is thy lovingkindness,
O God! therefore the children of men
put their trust under the shadow of thy wings.
PSALM 36:7

Chapter 1

Beth Whitrock gently bounced her crying nephew and glanced around the empty Prairie County fairgrounds. Two weeks from now it would be a beehive of activity, but today, except for the parents and babies standing in line with her for the baby contest rehearsal, the area was deserted.

"So they roped you into baby-sitting, huh?"

She swung around to confront the masculine voice. Intense blue eyes sparkled in a tan face split by a lopsided grin.

"Yep." She shifted the fussing baby to the other hip and tried to evaluate the man. A bit forward for a stranger, but there was something so appealing—so familiar—in that smile. She started to turn back around toward the front of the line, but a hand on her shoulder stopped her.

"You do remember me, don't you?" His voice poured like rich honey, and Beth took such pleasure in hearing it that his words almost didn't register. When they did, she looked again at the familiar blue eyes and the wavy dark brown hair. Of course.

"Zach Gaines. How could I not remember you? You've changed, that's all. Grown up." Her sister, Lacey, had mentioned

Beth's childhood pal Zach was now one of her and Rob's closest friends. Suddenly Beth remembered hearing his wife had died. She was flustered but felt compelled to mention it. "I'm sorry about your wife. I know that must have been hard."

"Yes, it was. Thanks." He spoke as one used to receiving such condolences and taking little comfort from them. Looking around, he turned his gaze back to her. Apparently missing Drew's older sister, he asked, "Just you and little Drew today?"

"I dropped Hannah off at softball practice on the way here." Drew's whining grew louder. Embarrassed by her inability to soothe him, Beth ruefully acknowledged her fourteen-month-old nephew was actually reaching for Zach.

"Hey, Buddy. Come see Uncle Zach."

A quiet sigh of relief escaped Beth's lips as she surrendered the squirming child. She loved her niece and nephew, but after one day of baby-sitting, she'd come to the humiliating conclusion she was a failure. What had her sister been thinking, to leave her two children alone with their inept aunt for three weeks?

A niggling memory of the conversation with Lacey caused her to turn her attention back to the man holding Drew. "Didn't I hear your folks moved to Florida?"

"Yes. Remember my older sister, Judy?"

She nodded.

"When Mom and Dad retired, she took over the catering business and moved it into her own house."

Beth suddenly remembered the whole conversation with her sister, but just to verify, she asked, "Who's living in their house now?"

"The kids and I moved into it a couple of years ago." He

smiled as he reached to unfold chubby little fingers away from the death grip the baby had on his ear.

Realization dawned. Living in the old Gaines place about a mile down the road, Zach was now Lacey and Rob's next-door neighbor. Every note in the house said, "Call our neighbor if you have any trouble. He's available twenty-four hours a day"—followed by his phone number.

Scoffing at her sister's obvious matchmaking attempts, Beth had determined not to call unless the house was on fire. She'd assumed it was someone in the subdivision a couple miles the other way. Why hadn't Lacey mentioned it was Zach Gaines she was trying to fix her up with?

Lowering her gaze to the adorable child asleep in a stroller in front of Zach, Beth smiled. "Is this your little girl?"

"Yes. . .Cassidy. She's two." Love shone on his face as he looked at the sleeping toddler.

"She's beautiful." Beth knew why Lacey hadn't mentioned her "available" neighbor was Zach Gaines. She knew very well Beth was awkward with kids and committed to her career, therefore she didn't go for men who had children. No matter how nice. . .or that since high school he'd gone from cute to gorgeous.

"Thanks."

"You're wel—" The chime of her little cell phone stopped Beth in midword, and she flashed Zach a rueful grin. "—Come." When she flipped open the tiny receiver and began to talk, the scowl on Zach's face startled her.

Her assistant's voice rattled in her ear, but Beth could barely comprehend her questions. Swinging around to avoid his frown, Beth hurried to answer the girl's questions and ended the connection.

When she turned back to Zach, she smiled. "Sorry about that. Trying to keep up with my work from Lacey's home is turning out to be quite a challenge."

"I understand." He handed Drew back to her and gripped the handles of Cassidy's stroller. "I don't think Cass is going to wake up to go through the practice run. I'd better go tell Mrs. Duncan." With a frosty half-smile that didn't reach his eyes, he said, "If you'll excuse us."

She nodded, and he was gone. For the second time that day, Beth questioned her sister's judgment. She couldn't seriously want to fix Beth up with such a moody man.

❋

Zach listened with half an ear to the excited chatter of his eight-year-old twins, Jeremy and Jessa, as he unlocked the door of the big, whitewashed house. Cassidy, refreshed from her nap, toddled up and down the length of the porch.

"Mmm. . .something smells great, Dad." Jessa ducked under his arm and ran toward the stairs. "Be down in a minute," she called over her shoulder. "I've got to put our 4-H stuff away."

Pausing in the doorway, Zach looked at Jeremy. "Make you a deal, Son. You bring your little sister in, and I'll put supper on the table."

"Got her."

Zach hurried into the kitchen and retrieved the roast and vegetables from the oven. He'd put it on to cook before dropping the twins off and going to the rehearsal for the Most Beautiful Baby Contest.

As he thought of the rehearsal, Beth Whitrock's heart-shaped face popped into his mind. Her thick curly auburn hair and emerald green eyes had captured his attention long before kindergarten, and her sweet personality had held it. Since they were neighbors, their childhood friendship had blossomed and had actually survived all the way through junior high.

Then had come high school, and everything had changed. A gawky newspaper reporter, he'd had little in common with the homecoming queen. He never dreamed she'd come back to town; and when her sister had mentioned her impending arrival, he felt maybe, finally he had a chance.

Today when he'd met her, not as Zach Gaines With Too Many Brains, as his friends had jokingly called him then, but as Zachary Gaines, syndicated newspaper columnist, he'd thought the playing field had been evened and maybe a happy ending was in sight. Until she answered that irritating cell phone. Another career woman. . .the last thing he needed.

Setting the steaming roast on a trivet, Zach thought of Claire. She'd been so ambitious. And look what it had cost them. Their future. . .their family. He reached for the plates and snagged four forks from the silverware drawer.

Claire hadn't given the family a thought when she'd gone back to work early after Cassidy's birth. Foregoing the law firm's standard six-week maternity leave, a month after the delivery she'd resumed her grueling schedule. He didn't know why he'd been so shocked and disbelieving when the policeman told him she had fallen asleep at the wheel and crashed into a tree. It had taken the full two years since her death for him to forgive her. With God's help, he had, but he still keenly felt the full responsibility of his children.

Shaking his head, as if he could physically force both the memory of his wife and the image of Beth from his mind, he called, "Supper's ready. Come on, guys."

Bounding footsteps resounded on the hardwood floors, and the beaming faces of his children soothed his troubled thoughts. He thanked God again that he had been able to syndicate his column after Claire's death and work from home. Moving to the old family home had been a logical choice, once he was freed from his desk at the Wichita paper. The abundance of fresh air and sunshine, along with time, had helped mend the children's wounded hearts.

"Jeremy, would you like to thank God for the food?"

"Sure." The boy's head bowed, and he clasped his hands together. "Dear God, thank You for this food. Please help it to make us healthy and strong. And God? Please keep Freckles and Bugs healthy too. In Jesus' name, Amen."

"Are the rabbits sick, Jeremy?" Zach frowned as he prayed a silent prayer asking God to protect his kids from any more loss.

"No, they're fine." Jeremy glanced to his sister as if for confirmation.

"We just want them to be perfect for the fair. They have to be if they're both going to win a blue ribbon." Jessa filled her plate as she spoke and shot her brother a warning look.

Something was up. But Zach knew his twins well enough to know they would tell him when they were ready.

"How'd rehearsal go, Cass?" Jessa's change of subject confirmed his suspicions.

At Cassidy's puzzled look, Zach explained. "She fell asleep and didn't wake until we pulled in to pick you up from your meeting. So her first run-through was a bust. Next week, we'll try to nap before the rehearsal." Maybe a nap would keep him from being rude to Beth again. He was sorry for how he'd acted. She had every right to pursue a career. How she lived her life shouldn't matter to him.

But he had a promise to keep. Rob and Lacey had asked him to check in on her and make sure everything was okay. After his behavior at the fairgrounds, she'd probably slam the door in his face.

Looking at the huge amount of roast and vegetables still in the dish, he realized he had the perfect excuse to see her and try to set things right. "Let's go for a ride after we finish eating, kiddos. We need to check in on a neighbor."

"Why, Dad?" Jeremy asked.

"We're commanded to love our neighbor, remember, Buddy?" He smiled at the irony of the wording of that verse in light of his old feelings for Beth. "And of course, our neighbor is everyone in the world, right?" He smiled at his son's almost empty plate and handed him a paper towel to wipe the roast juice from his chin. Zach's cooking never went to waste with the twins around. "Aunt Lacey's sister is taking care of Drew and Hannah while they're gone, and I thought we'd take them the rest of the food."

"Doesn't she know how to cook?" Jessa piped up.

Remembering Beth's inexperienced handling of the cranky baby, Zach smiled. "I don't think she's used to kids. I imagine she needs all the help she can get. Now, finish up and let's go."

✻

"I'll get it," Hannah yelled. "Must be pizza."

"No!" Beth ran from the baby's room, holding Drew. "Hannah, I haven't ordered the pizza yet. I was going to when I finished changing Drew's diaper."

"Oh." Hannah's voice drifted down the hall. "It's just Uncle Zach and the kids."

Beth froze in the doorway of the living room as Hannah ushered Zach and three children in.

"That smells great. Is it for us?" Hannah stood on tiptoes and peeked into the covered dish Zach held in his hands.

"Well, yes, as a matter of fact, it is." With a sheepish half-grin at Beth, Zach said, "Consider it a peace offering." His pleading eyes mesmerized her, and she couldn't bring herself to look away.

She heard Hannah say something to the kids who'd accompanied Zach. When the front door closed behind all the children except Drew, she found her tongue. "Will they be okay out there?"

"Oh, yeah. They're good kids. Jeremy, Jess, and Hannah will all keep an eye on Cassidy. But Drew, there, looks like he has a little problem." His grin grew broader.

Beth looked down at the baby's disposable diaper. One tab was attached but the other hung unfastened. She felt her face grow hot as she gently settled Drew on the couch and finished the job. Humiliated by her ineptness, she kept her attention fixed on the trains and fire trucks that covered the soft cotton onesie.

"Beth?" Zach's voice forced her gaze up to meet his. "It's

great to see you again. I'm sorry for how I acted earlier. I was a jerk." He glanced down at the dish in his hands and shuffled from one foot to the other. "So, this really is a peace offering. I made roast and vegetables, and I was hoping you hadn't eaten."

"No, we haven't. Thank you very much." Beth situated Drew on the floor with some colored blocks and beads and took the dish and placed it on the kitchen counter. When she returned to the living room, she crossed to look out the bay window at the children playing tag. "Your children are beautiful. I can see why you entered Cassidy in the contest."

Chagrin flashed across his face. "The contest was the twins' idea. Jeremy and Jessa have 4-H entries in the fair, and they didn't want their little sister to feel left out. She loves to play dress-up."

"How sweet." Feeling awkward, Beth noticed Drew had toddled over and retrieved a book from the bookcase.

Before she could move, Zach was beside the baby, gently replacing the book with chewing beads. "Here, Buddy, you don't want to ruin your dinner by eating that book." Holding the novel with two fingers, he gingerly wiped it dry on his jeans leg, then handed it to Beth with a chuckle. "Guess it was a story he could really sink his teeth into."

"It's good to know some things never change. Your jokes are as corny as ever." She smiled and slid the book back into its place on the shelf. Sitting down beside Drew on the floor, she ran her hand gently over his fuzzy white head. "I don't know why Lacey entered Drew in the contest." Realizing how that sounded, she rushed on, "I mean, he's beautiful too, but at his age I'm not sure what he'll gain from the experience."

"I'm afraid it may be my fault. I mentioned Cassidy was going to be in it, and your sister asked to make a copy of the entry form." He sank down onto the braided rug beside Beth, leaning back against the couch. "She was very excited. She must have forgotten they'd be out of town."

Not likely, Beth thought. They'd had the reservations for almost a year, and Lacey had called her sister at the travel agency every month to add more details to her plans. No way she'd forgotten.

As Beth looked at the relaxed positions she and Zach were in, she had to admire her sister's wiles. Their easy companionship reminded her of a typical day after junior high school when they would study together over a plate of cookies.

"Why do I suddenly crave chocolate chip cookies?" Zach asked, the twinkle in his eye affirming that he remembered too.

"Well, you'll have to make them. Yours always turned out better than mine," she reminded him.

"You know, it took me years to realize that you bragged on mine to get out of doing the work yourself. And now here I am, about to fall for it again." He pushed himself to his feet and reached a long arm down to help her up. When his large hand enfolded her tiny one, he gave a powerful yank, and she laughed as the momentum of his pull threw her past him. "The only thing is. . .now I have a little army of munchkins to help me."

Beth picked up Drew as Zach stepped to the door and called the children in. At the words "chocolate chip cookies," they came running. Beth sat Drew in the playpen in the kitchen and watched in awe as a patient Zach gave each child a job, even allowing Cassidy a turn at stirring. While Zach carefully set their creations in the oven, they stayed back and watched with wide-eyed anticipation, then scooted out the door.

"What's my job?" Beth asked playfully.

Zach turned from where he was setting the timer and grinned. "Your job, little lady, is to do the washing up, of course."

"Washing up?" She put on her worst Southern drawl and batted her eyelashes for all she was worth. "You obviously don't know what an important businesswoman I am. I'll have you know at work I even have an assistant of my very own who gets my coffee for me." Her teasing smile faltered when Zach's eyebrows knitted together and a frown replaced the grin from minutes before.

He turned on the faucet, squirted in some dishwashing detergent, and grabbed the mixing bowl off the counter. He attacked it with a vengeance, and the silence grew thick as Beth tried to figure out what had caused his sudden change in attitude.

"Zach, I was just kidding. I don't mind washing up."

"Neither do I." His answer was polite but cool. Even when she placed the beaters in his sinkful of soapy water and began to put away the ingredients on the counter, he didn't say anything else. When the timer went off, he retrieved the cookies from the stove.

Looking at the cookies, still soft and gooey, she gasped. "Aha! I remember now! Your secret to great cookies. You told me one day, but I'd forgotten until just now." He didn't acknowledge her words, but she continued, "Take them out a few minutes early and let them stay on the hot pan until they cool." She slapped the heel of her hand against her forehead. "I could have been making them all along."

Just then the kitchen door opened, and the children came rushing back in. "Are the cookies ready?" Jeremy asked.

Beth waited to see if Zach's sudden sour mood extended to his son.

"Two more minutes." Zach's easy grin was back, and Beth wondered again at his moodiness. He hadn't been moody when they were young, but then again, he had ignored her during most of high school.

When the children pronounced the cookies cooled, Zach dried his hands on a dishtowel and, using a spatula, carefully lifted the cookies onto two paper plates.

"Now," he said when he'd finished, "we have to get home so you guys can get your chores done." Holding his hand up, he continued, "No arguments. Miss Beth and Hannah haven't even eaten yet. We'll leave them some cookies for their dessert and take some with us."

Leaving Hannah doling out the roast and vegetables onto plates for the two of them, Beth followed Zach as he ushered the twins and Cassidy to the door with their plate of cookies. The children yelled good-bye and rushed out. Zach turned to meet Beth's eyes for the first time since his unexplained displeasure in the kitchen. The plaintive expression she saw there confused her, and that feeling only increased when he spoke. "I'm sorry. I came to make things better and probably just ended up making them worse."

She wasn't sure what to say to that, so she said nothing.

"See you later."

"Thanks for the food."

When she closed the door behind him, Beth leaned against the smooth oak, her hot face soaking up the coolness of the wood. If she didn't know better, she'd think her working bothered Zach, but he'd never been chauvinistic. So what was it she kept doing to upset Zachary Gaines?

Chapter 2

Zach looked up from the computer screen and put his hand to the back of his aching neck. He was getting too old for such a small amount of sleep. Beth Whitrock had invaded his brain, and he had to get her out. At three in the morning, after hours of tossing and turning, he'd sat up in bed and prayed for God to give him the strength to resist her. But peaceful sleep had still eluded him.

Like insomnia, writer's block was something he wasn't familiar with. . .the words always seemed to just come. From his life, or other people's, fresh ideas were always there just waiting to be used. But since finally leaving his bed at six this morning, he'd had five false starts already, and he was no closer to getting a column out than when he had put Cass down for her nap thirty minutes ago. He picked up a cookie and dipped it in his milk. When it stopped dripping, he popped it in his mouth.

"Hmm. . .secret to great chocolate chip cookies revealed," Zach mused. A smile tugged at his lips as his fingers flew over the keyboard. An hour later, the humor-laced story of two nameless junior high kids and their contest for the perfect cookie covered the page. With a sigh of satisfaction, he e-mailed it to his editor just as Cassidy sleepily toddled into the room.

He picked up his daughter and buried his face in her curls, breathing in the sweet smell of baby shampoo. His children were so precious to him, and he couldn't let anything jeopardize their well-being. He had begun to think in the last few months that he might remarry someday. But his main criteria in choosing a mate would be someone who would be a good mother and put the children ahead of her own needs. Now if his treacherous heart would just remember that when he was around Beth.

❋

Beth squinted at the morning sun shining across her face. Something smelled delicious. Rolling over, she peered at the clock. She'd overslept. Memories of walking the floor last night with a teething Drew came rushing back. Apparently she'd forgotten to set the alarm. They'd be late for church.

She grabbed her pink terrycloth robe, and cinching the belt tightly around her waist, she flew down the hall to the kitchen. In amazement, she stared at her nightgown-clad niece serenely buttering toaster pastries.

"Hannah! How long have you been up?"

"Not too long." The girl ducked her head. "I wanted to surprise you with breakfast. It's been so much fun having you here. Are you mad?"

"Mad? No, of course not. This is the sweetest thing anyone has done for me in ages." She crossed the kitchen and enfolded Hannah in a hug. Dropping a kiss on the top of her niece's head, she smiled and slid onto a bar stool, patting the one next to her. Hannah sat down, and Beth bowed to thank God for the food. Just as she opened her mouth to speak, a small hand slipped into hers, and she squeezed it tightly.

"Dear God, thank You for giving me this time with Hannah and Drew. You know how much I love them. Thank You this morning especially for Hannah's kindness in preparing breakfast. Bless the food to the nourishment of our bodies as we eat. In Jesus' name, Amen."

Hannah's eyes sparkled as they unclasped hands. "I love you, Aunt Beth."

"I love you too, Honey."

The baby monitor on the counter lit up suddenly as fussy cries emitted from the speaker. "Uh-oh, sounds like trouble." Hannah grinned.

"I'll go get him." Beth wrapped a napkin around her pastry. "I'll take this with me. Would it be pushing it to ask you to clean the counter off when you get done?"

"No problem."

Thirty minutes later, Beth balanced a half-dressed Drew with one arm and snagged a tiny brown loafer from under the edge of the couch. With a rueful smile, she thought of her normal Sunday mornings. She usually rose early and made herself a big cup of French vanilla cappuccino, which she would take out on the deck of the townhouse she rented in Atlanta. There she would sit for an hour in prayer and meditation, sometimes reading Scripture, sometimes just communing with God. Then she would enjoy a leisurely bath and calmly dress for church.

This morning Hannah had picked out her own church

clothes and helped Beth choose something suitable for Drew. While Hannah ran down the diaper bag checklist, Beth had gone on a quest for Drew's missing shoe. She quickly slipped it on the baby and hurried back to her room, where she gently placed Drew on the bed and threw on a dress. When her hose and shoes were on, she ran a brush through her tangled curls and started out the bedroom door.

"Oops." She turned around and scooped up Drew. "Sorry about that. I knew I was forgetting something." His answering gurgle eased the tension of her hectic rushing. "You know I could never forget you, Sweetheart," she said, hurrying down the hall to peck on Hannah's door. "You almost ready?"

Her niece emerged, wearing a red shirt and denim jumper. The black clogs set the outfit off to perfection. Beth had spent the morning in awe of Hannah's maturity. When Lacey had begged her to stay with the kids, Beth had envisioned three weeks of being at the beck and call of two demanding children. She'd even suggested Lacey ask their own mother to do it, since she only lived down the road, but her sister's travel time had coincided with their mom and dad's annual vacation.

Drew have proven to need constant attention, while twelve-year-old Hannah was actually more help than she was trouble. And both of them were sources of such great pleasure.

A short while later, Beth and Hannah slipped into the crowded church building. Hannah led the way to the nursery, explaining as they walked that, while Drew was teething, Lacey left him with the nursery grandmother during the entire service. Beth had definite misgivings about deserting Drew, but her fears were relieved when the elderly woman's eyes lit up as soon as she saw the baby.

Drew reached for her, so Beth kissed his fuzzy head and passed him into the waiting arms. After Hannah hung the diaper bag on a peg, they made their way out to find a seat. It wasn't until Beth met Zach Gaines's amused blue eyes that she realized where Hannah had been leading her.

"This is where we always sit." Hannah motioned to the pew Zach and his family already occupied.

Beth couldn't argue since Hannah had already taken a place on the other side of the twins, leaving an empty spot next to Zach. Sliding in, Beth flashed him an apologetic smile. "Kids." Their last meeting had ended so badly, and she still had no idea why. She wanted to be sure that he didn't think she had connived to sit by him.

"Yep. Can't live with 'em, can't live without 'em." His soft voice sounded friendly enough.

Beth struggled to keep her mind centered on the Bible lesson, especially after the children had gone to their respective classes, leaving her and Zach alone on the pew. Since she had taken the empty place next to the aisle, she couldn't scoot away from him, and he showed no signs of moving.

After class was over, the children filed back into the auditorium. Beth watched Zach as he looked over each child's take-home paper, exclaiming at their artwork or correct answers. She excused herself to check on Drew and slipped back into her seat just as the first song began.

As the preacher spoke on "leaning not on your own understanding, but trusting in the Lord with all your heart," Beth thought of her own busy life. She trusted God, but so far her life had gone according to her own plan. Her job was great. Her boss, though a little demanding—okay, a lot demanding—rewarded her for her hard work with money and benefits that made it easy to take care of her financial needs. She was close to being able to buy into a partnership with Bob. She loved her work—helping others make the most of their travel. Then why was there such an unexplained longing in her heart?

Her life in Atlanta, which had once seemed so peaceful, now appeared dull. She'd avoided children in the past because she always felt awkward with them, especially compared to Lacey, who had been a natural born baby-sitter when they were growing up. Looking back at what a wonderful time she'd had with Lacey's children during the past week, she thought how ridiculous that reasoning had been.

When worship was over, Hannah and Jessa bounced over to the adults. "Can we go eat at the Country Kettle?" Jessa asked.

Hannah looked to Zach as if for backup, then chimed in. "Please. We go there every Sunday, don't we, Uncle Zach?"

"Well, not every Sunday, but yes, most Sundays." His conspiratorial grin caused Beth's heart to flip-flop. "Kids eat free," he added in a pseudo-whisper. "Rob and Lacey and I consider that to be a good deal."

Surprised but pleased that he wanted to go to lunch with her after his bizarre behavior at their last meeting, Beth nodded. "That sounds great."

❇

Laughter resounded around the table as Zach regaled the kids with stories from his and Beth's childhood. He told of the time Beth had blown a huge bubble and gotten gum in her pigtail.

Zach had sneaked into his mother's sewing room and gotten the scissors. Safely back in the clubhouse, he'd played barber for the first and last time.

"Barber? He held my pigtail straight out and cut it off right below the rubber band. I thought my mom was going to have a heart attack." Beth wiped the tears of laughter from her eyes.

"Yeah, but you didn't rat on me. You took all the blame yourself."

"Well, if we'd both gotten grounded, who would have slipped me all those cookies?"

When the waiter brought the check, Beth grabbed it. Zach glowered at her.

"Hey. You brought supper to me the other night. This is as close as you'll get to being repaid."

"I invited you."

"No, actually, Hannah did. Besides, I'm a working girl with my very own bank account. I can handle it."

Zach's hand froze in midair. "Of course. I forgot. You probably make more money than I do."

"I wouldn't go that far. I have a good job, but I'm not famous." She grinned to take the sting out of her victory over the check.

"Power and fame—they both have their price." Zach spoke quietly but turned away. Beth shivered from the sudden chill in his demeanor.

Driving home a few minutes later, Beth thought about the abrupt change in Zach's attitude. She was sure it had something to do with her career. Probably Zach's late wife had not worked outside the home and now he measured all women to her standard. Beth thought being a stay-at-home mom was a magnificent choice, but as long as the children and family came first, she also believed a career was an option.

Whether she was right about the reason for his swift mood swings, one thing was clear. Despite Zach's lighthearted reminiscing, he wasn't the same easygoing guy she remembered; and though she cherished the memories, she had no time to contend with a cantankerous man. Even if he did have melt-your-heart blue eyes.

Chapter 3

Horrified, Beth looked from the shiny handle in her hand to the small fountain of water spewing out of the gaping hole on the kitchen faucet. "Hannah!" She frantically scavenged through the drawers to the right of the sink. Grabbing a handful of dishtowels, she screamed again, "Hannah! Come here!"

"Yeah, Aunt Beth, what's wrong?" Hannah came to a sliding stop when she entered the kitchen door. "Oh, no! What happened?"

"I don't know." Beth fought back the tears. "I just turned the water on, but when I pushed the handle toward hot, it fell off in my hand." She struggled to keep the panic from her voice. "Hand me a pan, Sweetie. Let's see if we can do something about this."

Hannah grabbed a stainless steel pan from the hooks above the stove and shoved it into her aunt's waiting hands. Beth murmured her thanks and gave her frightened niece what she hoped was a reassuring smile. She moved the rags and put the pan over the spurt of water. With a grimace, she realized all that was doing was forcing the water straight back down. Down to the top of the sink, where a steady river ran down the cabinet to the ceramic tile floor.

"Great," she grumbled, "what do I do now?" Just then her eyes lit on Lacey's hot pink note on the front of the refrigerator. "In case of trouble, call our neighbor. He's available twenty-four hours a day." Oh, brother. Or in this case, oh, sister. What had Lacey done? Had she booby-trapped the house to force Beth into seeing Zach? Surely even a meddling, matchmaking sister couldn't have counted on him showing up with a pot roast last Thursday night or inviting them to the Country Kettle the day before yesterday. Or could she have?

Resorting back to applying pressure with the dishrags, Beth sent up a silent prayer, then twisted her head around to look at Hannah. "Can you bring me the phone book and the cordless phone?"

"Sure, but you don't need a phone book. Uncle Zach's number is right there on the fridge."

Like mother, like daughter. "Yes, Dear," Beth said, struggling to relax her clenched jaw, "but I'm going to call a plumber."

Three fruitless phone calls later, Beth stared in horror at the pile of bath towels Hannah had brought from the bathroom to sop up the never-ending supply of water. Through tears, she read the numbers on Lacey's note and punched them in with sharp, angry jabs. When he answered on the first ring, she fought back sobs of gratitude.

"Zach? This is Beth. Uh. . .I was turning the water to hot in the kitchen and the handle came off in my hand. Water's spurting like crazy—"

"I'll be right there."

Beth stared at the receiver as the dial tone reverberated in her ear. Why hadn't she done that in the first place? Judging from the puzzled look on Hannah's face, the twelve year old was wondering the same thing. "Would you go make sure Drew is still sleeping, please? Thanks for the help. Hopefully, I can handle it until your uncle Zach gets here."

Five minutes later, Beth noticed the trickle of water from under the rags seemed to have slowed. She cautiously lifted them and sagged with relief. Apparently, Zach had turned the water off out at the road. Which meant he would probably be here to assess the damage any minute. Most of the damage was to her clothes, she thought, as she raced up the stairs to change.

She replaced her soggy shirt and sweatpants with a crisp green cotton top and indigo jeans. A glance in the mirror made her wish her hair could be fixed so quickly. The mist of water had kicked her curls into high gear, and she looked like an old, longhaired Shirley Temple minus the cute. Picking out the curls a little with her fingers, she gave the mirror a shrug. Who was she trying to impress, anyway?

She found Zach in the kitchen, staring in consternation at the handle in his hand. When he heard her footsteps, he turned around. The admiring glance in his eyes soothed her bad hair day grumpies, and she smiled.

"It's really strange. It looks like this screw just worked its way loose. It would have been wobbly for awhile, though, and Rob is so particular about things like this. . . ." He turned back to the sink and pulled a wrench from the small toolbox on the counter. In less than a minute, he sang out, "As good as new."

She watched his gaze scan the piles of towel and puddles of water on the floor. His eyes grew wide, and she bit back a laugh. It did look bad.

"Don't worry. I won't make you help me clean it up." She reached to spread the driest towels around to sop up the worst of the puddles.

"I don't see how it got so bad so fast. Didn't you call me immediately?" He moved over to help her, and she found the nearness disconcerting.

"Well, after trying a few things myself and calling three plumbers. . ."

"Bethie, when did you stop trusting me to get you out of jams?" His tender voice sounded very close to her ear.

She spun to face him, surprised by a tiny niggle of hurt from the past. Years of honesty forced the words from her mouth. "Maybe when you wigged out on me right before the big English test? Remember? The one you were supposed to be helping me pass?"

"Wigged out on you?" Disbelief tinged his voice, and his blue eyes held her captive. "You're the one who didn't want to be seen with me." He chuckled slightly. "Not that I blamed you. In fact, I decided to make it easy for you."

"Why would you think I didn't want to be seen with you, Zach?" Beth asked, amazed at how important something that had happened fifteen years ago had suddenly become.

"Why would a member of the homecoming court want to be seen with a nerdy newspaper reporter? Besides, I heard what you said that day we were studying at the Dairy Bar." He smiled as if to show her that he knew how ridiculous this conversation was, but he continued. "I came out of the bathroom just as Tina Thompson asked you who you were there with. Your face turned several shades of red, Beth. And then you said, 'Nobody.' "

Beth opened her mouth to deny it but shut it again as she remembered how the girls had teased her about her English grade. She'd never been embarrassed to be seen with Zach, but she had definitely been embarrassed about being tutored. "Oh, Zach. That's not what I meant. I was ashamed that I had to have extra help in English, not that I was at the Dairy Bar with you. Why didn't you say something instead of just leaving?"

"Even a brainy guy has a sliver of pride." His smile said he believed her, and relief flooded through her. "What a dope I was."

"Hmm. . .like I said earlier, Zachary Gaines, you've grown up." She knew she was flirting with disaster. Warm memories and childhood nicknames didn't change who he was—a very temperamental man. And definitely off-limits for her. She'd go crazy trying to deal with those mood swings. Nevertheless, when he leaned in toward her, she knew she was going to let him kiss her. It seemed inevitable, as if she'd been waiting for it all her life.

"Hey, Dad!" Jessa's voice jerked Beth back to reality, and she jumped as if she'd been burned. What had she almost done? Thank heaven for little girls.

Zach cleared his throat, but his eyes still held Beth's. "Yeah, I'm in here." Only when the kitchen door pushed open did he relinquish Beth's gaze and turn to face his daughter.

"Can we get pizza and a movie? Hannah says her aunt won't mind."

Beth leaned against the counter to supplement her trembling legs. Looking at the child who had saved her from a big mistake, she smiled. "Hannah's right. It sounds great to me, if it's okay with you, Zach."

"Sounds fine." He ruffled his daughter's wavy dark hair and tilted her face toward him in a tender manner that spoke volumes about his love for her. "Okay, Sport. How about we take Hannah and go pick it up while Miss Beth gets this mess cleaned up?" Turning back to her, he grinned. "If you don't mind me 'wigging' out on you again?"

"I'm starting to get used to it." She mustered a light tone. "Go on." Motioning toward the baby monitor on the counter, she said, "Drew should be up and ready to go full speed by the time you get back, though, so be forewarned."

❇

Zach handed the video clerk the money. As he waited for his change, he still couldn't believe he'd almost kissed Beth in the kitchen. For a few minutes, he'd forgotten she loved her career. . . had forgotten everything, in fact, except that she hadn't been ashamed to be seen with him fifteen years ago. It was amazing how distorted a young person's perception could be sometimes. Of course, if he hadn't had such a huge crush on her, it wouldn't have hit him so hard.

As he tucked the video under his arm and herded the kids out to the car, he allowed himself to remember how much he'd admired and respected her. It had always seemed mutual—they were the perfect complement to each other, the brainy newspaper reporter and the sociable but sweet beauty—until that day in the Dairy Bar. After that he'd gone out of his way to avoid her. It had seemed like the honorable thing to do, really, to keep her from having to violate her conscience by shunning him.

He pulled into the pizzeria and watched as the twins and Hannah unbuckled Cassidy. When they got out of the vehicle, they held her hands between them, being careful to hold tight. His gut wrenched as he realized that once again, only without misconceptions this time, it was up to him to do the honorable thing. He couldn't marry again unless it was to someone who would be a true mom to his kids. And someone with a busy career like Beth's definitely wouldn't have room in her life for motherhood. He'd learned that the hard way.

Chapter 4

Beth slumped against the comfy old couch in Lacey's den and for the tenth time looked across the room to the maddening man in the easy chair. Children dotted the floor and furniture between them like chocolate chips on a cookie. Maybe it was the kids' rambunctious presence that had made it so easy for Zach to ignore her while they'd eaten pizza. But every time she'd tried to share a grin with him during the comedy they were watching, she'd been confronted by his profile.

Here we go. Just like high school. The silly, redundant phrase she and Lacey used popped in her mind. Déjà vu all over again. Surely Zach Gaines wasn't the kind of man who would jerk her around for no good reason. At least in high school, he'd thought she was ashamed to be seen with him. Now he just seemed to have some kind of major aversion to her work.

"Time to go, kiddos." Zach's smooth baritone jarred her from her thoughts. As Zach's children scrambled to their feet, Beth stared blankly at the credits rolling on the TV screen.

She'd been so worried about Zach Gaines, she'd missed the end of a movie she'd been wanting to see for ages. Why did she even care what he thought? He was really doing her a favor. After all, he was the epitome of every man she'd avoided for years—a single father.

❇

"How come you quit talking to Miss Beth when we got back from the video store?" Jessa's casual question from the backseat pricked Zach's conscience.

"I didn't quit talking to her, Hon. I just had things on my mind."

"What kind of things?"

"Oh, I don't know. . .grown-up things." As he pulled into the drive, he adjusted the rearview mirror to look at his kids. Cassidy was asleep in her carseat, but both twins were staring back at him.

"Was she your girlfriend when you cut her hair?" Jeremy's voice cracked a little on the word girlfriend, and Zach smiled in spite of the uncomfortable turn the conversation was taking.

"We were friends, and she was a girl."

"I know that, but. . ." Even in the darkened interior of the vehicle, Zach could see his son's face turn red.

"What he means is, were you going out? Did Miss Beth used to be your girlfriend when you were a kid?"

"No, not really. Why?"

"We were just wondering." Jessa's vague answer was so reminiscent of his earlier "grown-up things" that he chuckled. He had a good relationship with his kids, and it wasn't like any of them to beat around the bush. But apparently that's what they were all doing tonight.

He started to pursue the conversation, but since he didn't

know if he'd have the answers they were looking for, he carried Cassidy to her bed in silence.

The twins, as if by unspoken agreement, rushed to check on the rabbits. Cassidy lay like a rag doll in his arms as Zach took her shoes and socks off and changed her into her pajamas. Long eyelashes swept her little red cheeks. The pert nose and tiny bow mouth topped off a face that was the picture of innocence. A fierce surge of protectiveness arose in Zach.

Lord, I know You can't want me to marry another career woman. If You would help me to resist the emotional and physical attraction I have for Beth, I sure would appreciate it. I know she can't be the woman for me, but my heart just doesn't want to admit it. Help me to be strong, for the children's sake, Lord.

To Zach's surprise, he felt no better about his resolve as he slipped out of Cassidy's room. He peeked in at the twins' empty beds, then headed down to the mudroom where they were, no doubt, cooking up some diabolical plan with their rabbits.

As he stepped into the semidark room, he heard their voices near the rabbits.

"Dumb old rabbit. Even if she wins a blue ribbon, it won't be as cool as the one Chelsea'll get for her quilt." The unfamiliar scorn in Jessa's tone caused his steps to falter. "Bet if I had a mom, she'd help me make one that could beat hers."

Even though Zach had mostly come to terms with his own grief over losing Claire, sorrow mingled with anger washed over him anew as the longing in his daughter's voice pierced his soul. Tears sprang to his eyes. His feet felt like lead weights, and he found himself unable to move.

"Just because she's entering a quilt doesn't mean she'll win a blue ribbon, Jess." Conflicting emotions were evident in Jeremy's voice, and the reason for them became apparent when Jessa spoke.

"Oh, admit it, Jeremy Rylan Gaines, you're hoping she will. You think if Freckles or Bugs wins a blue ribbon and her quilt does too, maybe she'll like you. Honestly." Disgust laced her words, and Zach started out of the shadows to defend his son.

But then Jessa's own voice softened. "I'm sorry she won't say she likes you, Jer. I just know she does."

"Aw. . .don't worry 'bout it. I shouldn't have ever written her that note asking her." Jeremy's misery was so close to Zach's own feelings tonight with Beth that he knew exactly how his son felt.

"I shouldn't have told you to."

Determined not to eavesdrop any further, Zach cleared his throat. "Y'all about ready for bed?"

Both twins jumped. "Sure, Dad," they chorused, but the look that flashed between them spoke volumes. Zach offered them an encouraging smile, but after giving him a quick hug, they bounded up the stairs to bed.

❋

Zach sank down into his recliner, relishing the peace that reigned over the house like a good-natured old king. He'd kissed the twins good night and listened to their prayers. When Jeremy had prayed for the rabbits again, he'd bit back a grin. But now that things were quiet and he was alone, he reflected on Jessa's words. She wanted to make a quilt for the fair. In this modern day, surely a father could be expected to help with something like that. Was he up to the challenge? A resounding no echoed in his head.

Why couldn't he have forced himself to be attracted to any

of the half-dozen unmarried women from church who had showered his children with attention and bombarded him with food for most of the last two years? He'd been thankful for the kindness, but eventually the benevolent women had realized friendship was as far as he would ever go, and they'd turned their eyes, not to mention their domestic skills, elsewhere.

Now he had no one to ask for help with Jessa's problem. He could have appealed to Lacey if she and Rob weren't gone. But he couldn't think of another seamstress he knew well enough to propose such a rush project to. Unless. . .

A bizarre idea seized his mind and refused to let go. He leaped from his chair and tore up the stairs to the attic. His hands flew over the dusty photo albums on the shelf. Finally locating the right one, he laid it gingerly on the old hardwood floor and knelt in front of it like a child on Christmas morning. He flipped the pages until. . .

There it was! A picture of the quilt division blue-ribbon winner from the Prairie County Fair, 1981. Her red hair was styled a little differently, but there was no mistaking Beth Whitrock's thousand-watt smile.

*

"I'll stir for awhile, Hon." Beth smiled at her niece. "I know you're tired."

"Not really." Hannah protested but passed over the wooden spoon. "This has been fun. Even though you and I both look like we have the measles."

Beth laughed as she carefully stirred the blackberry mixture. "Not to mention the kitchen. Your mom assured me with the berries already picked and frozen, making jelly would be a snap. Looks like she might have overestimated us."

"Oh, Aunt Beth. You worry too much." Hannah's mischievous grin reminded Beth of Lacey's. "Think you can handle it while I run upstairs for a sec and get a CD for us to listen to?"

"I'll do my very best," Beth teased. "But that might not be saying a lot, you know."

As Hannah ran up the stairs, the phone rang, and Beth grabbed it with her free hand. "Hello?"

"Beth, Bob here." Her boss's disgruntled voice resounded over the lines.

"Is something wrong?" Beth knew from experience that it could be something as small as his newspaper being late.

"Yes, there is. I tried to get you online and couldn't find you. That trip that you were planning for Wakasaki Corporation? Mr. Wakasaki wants you to finalize the arrangements with him in Instant Message on the Internet."

"That's really not a problem, Bob." Beth forced her tone to be soothing. "Just tell me a time. I've already got him on my Buddy list. All I have to do is boot up the computer."

"If only it were that simple. His wife is having gallbladder surgery, and he's not sure when he'll be able to talk to you."

"Well, then, just let me know. Or give me his number, and I'll set it up with him personally." She stopped stirring and reached in the drawer for the notepad and pen.

"No, I'll arrange it. But I'm warning you, Beth. I let you have this extended vacation because you've been with me a long time, and you promised you'd work some, but if you don't hold up your end of the deal. . ." The implied threat lingered in the air like smoke in a nonsmoking section.

"Mr. Wakasaki is a reasonable man, Bob." She bit back the urge to add, Unlike some people I know. "He and I will be able to work out a time to talk."

"Aunt Beth?" Hannah's urgent whisper and pointing drew Beth's attention to the stove, where liquid bubbled over the edge of the pot. Beth hurriedly turned off the burner.

". . .So you'd better make sure you're available no matter what—" The beeping timer punctuated his words, signaling that the jelly was ready.

"Listen, Bob, I've got to run. Just call me. You've got all my numbers. Bye." She hung up the phone and cringed when it started ringing again immediately. Giving Hannah a wink, she ignored the persistent ringing while she moved the jelly off the hot burner and mopped up the mess.

As she was rinsing out the rag, the phone rang again. "Should I or shouldn't I?" she asked Hannah, teasingly.

"Hey, I'm only twelve years old. What do I know?"

"What a cop-out." Beth grimaced at her niece and yanked up the phone. "Bob, I'm sorry—"

"This is Zach."

Heat rushed up her face as Beth stammered out a reply. "Zach! I'm sorry."

"Yeah, that's what you were telling Bob." Slight sarcasm edged Zach's voice.

"Bob is my boss, and we were having a small conflict. I just assumed you were him calling back." Remembering his hurried departure from her house Tuesday night, she inserted a professional note in her voice. "What can I do for you?"

"A lot, I hope. I have a big favor to ask you."

Chapter 5

Beth balanced the cordless phone on her shoulder as she rinsed the blackberry juice from the cloth and started wiping the counter. "Sure, Zach. What's up?"

"It's Jessa." The concern in his voice brought Beth's cleaning to a halt.

"What's wrong with Jessa?"

"It's not a big thing. Well, to her it is, I guess. . . ." His voice faded off.

Beth willed herself to keep her mouth shut until he got to the point.

"She'd like to do some kind of sewing to enter in the fair. But she thinks without a mom to help her, she doesn't have a chance."

Beth's already tender heart turned to mush over Jessa's plight. Casting a doubtful glance around the juice-splattered kitchen, she nodded, forgetting he couldn't see her. "I'll help her. Bring her over this afternoon. Hannah's riding with her friend Amy to ball practice, and Amy's mom is going to pick her up in just a few minutes. Drew is down for a nap. Jess and I can talk about what she wants to do while I attempt to restore Lacey's kitchen to some semblance of normalcy."

"More plumbing trouble?" Zach asked, his deep voice incredulous. "Why didn't you call me?"

"I'm afraid you couldn't have helped this time." Beth glanced at Hannah, who was quietly taking in the conversation and winked. "Unless you know how to get blackberry stain off of dishcloths."

"Uh. . .okay. I'm afraid you've got me there. I will bring Jessa over in a few minutes, though. If you're sure that's okay."

"Great."

"See you then."

As she hung up, Beth's gaze took in Hannah's beaming face. "What are you smiling about?" She regarded Hannah with suspicion, then carefully placed the small jelly jars on a cookie sheet to catch any accidental overflow.

"Oh, nothing." But the preteen's grin grew broader as they maneuvered the hot liquid into the jars.

"Nothing, huh? This wouldn't have anything to do with what you were whispering to your mom about last night on the phone, would it?" Beth was afraid she had a good idea of what the big secret was. She'd heard "Aunt Beth" and "Uncle Zach" mentioned several times in Hannah's hushed conversation with Lacey, punctuated with giggles. Just what Lacey needed in her matchmaking endeavors—a cohort.

"Aunt Beth, I think you're imagining things." Hannah carefully tightened the lids.

Beth could see Hannah wasn't going to admit anything. "I'm not imagining that blackberry juice on your face, Kiddo.

You might want to go wash up before your uncle Zach and the kids get here."

With another giggle, Hannah scampered out of the kitchen.

Beth hurried to the downstairs bathroom and rinsed her face. Back in the kitchen, alone with the blackberry mess, Beth sprang into action. She wiped the counter vigorously, then grimaced that her pulse raced at the thought of seeing Zach again.

When the doorbell rang a few minutes later, she peered at her reflection in the shiny door of the microwave and sighed. Her life was just one bad hair day after another.

With one more pat to the wild curls, she opened the door to Zach and the children. "Hey, Zach." She peered around him to see no children.

He grinned. "Yep, they're here. But when you're a kid, it's impossible to walk past a wooden swing fort without playing for a minute. I try to take that into consideration." He raised an eyebrow and the dimples in his cheeks made Beth's racing heart do a loop the loop. "Especially since you said Drew was napping. Outside seemed like the safest place for my bunch."

"In that case, come on in."

As soon as Zach got inside the door, Hannah came flying down the stairs, ball glove in hand. "Hi, Uncle Zach. Bye, Uncle Zach. Bye, Aunt Beth. I'm going to wait for Amy and her mom outside." Her last word barely drifted back to them as the door closed behind her.

"Was that Hurricane Hannah who just whipped through here? I thought she'd been downgraded to a tropical storm since she turned twelve." In spite of his teasing, Zach's affection for her niece was obvious.

"Sometimes she forgets she's almost a teenager. But not very often." Beth remembered Hannah's whispered conversation with Lacey and suddenly understood why the girl had exited the house so quickly, leaving her alone with Zach. The realization sent heat flaming up her cheeks. "We'd better call Jessa in and see what she has in mind for the fair, hadn't we?"

"Bethie, are you okay? You look like you may have a fever."

The concern in Zach's voice made her face grow hotter. Thank goodness he wasn't a mind reader. "I'm fine. Hannah and I have been making jelly. You know what a hot job that is."

The opening door saved Beth from further explanation. Jessa poked her head in. Her gaze traveled from her dad to Beth, then back to her dad. "Is it time?"

"Sure, Jess. Come on in. Beth, I'll go play with Jeremy and Cassidy while you two talk. Okay?"

Beth nodded and turned her attention to Jessa. "Sure. Come on in here, Hon, and let's talk while I clean up the rest of the mess Hannah and I made earlier." She didn't even glance at Zach as he eased out the door, but she felt his gaze on her face until he was gone.

Jessa followed Beth into the kitchen, where she perched on a bar stool as Beth grabbed a rag and began to wipe the already clean counter.

"Do you like my dad?"

Beth's hand paused in midswipe. "Sure, he's nice." Silence filled the short distance between them, and Beth remembered that she'd never been good with kids. "Even though we lost touch, we've been friends for a long time."

"I know. He told us. Jeremy asked him if you were his

girlfriend when y'all were kids, but he was evasive."

Beth grinned at the nine year old's proper use of the word evasive. "We were friends, and I'm a girl."

Jessa smiled. "That's exactly what he said."

"Your dad says you'd like to sew something for the fair."

"I want to make a quilt."

"Really?" Beth searched the girl's suddenly troubled face. "Why?"

"I don't know. I just thought if I made a quilt, I might win a blue ribbon." She played with a loose thread on her denim shirt and refused to meet Beth's eyes.

Beth struggled to understand the inner conflict Zach's daughter was going through, but she'd never felt more inadequate. "So you have no special interest in quilting, really?"

Jessa looked up from her thread inspection, her serious eyes begging Beth to understand. "I don't know much about it."

"What do you like to do?" Beth busied herself in the kitchen, hoping to make the child less self-conscious.

"I like to read and climb trees. Oh—and I like to draw." Jessa shrugged.

"What about Barbie dolls? Do you ever play with them?"

"Sometimes. I have a bunch. I sort of collect them." She wrinkled her nose. "I don't exactly play with them, though. I just dress them up in their different outfits."

"Hmm. . ." Beth pulled open the kitchen drawer and produced a pencil and a sheet of paper. She slid it across the counter. "Can you draw your favorite doll a new outfit?"

She moved over behind Jessa and watched in amazement as the girl's hand guided the pencil across the paper with confidence, swiftly rendering a likeness of a beautiful dress.

"Do you have that dress for your doll?"

"Not really. I sort of made it up. Is that okay?"

"Oh, yeah. Yeah." A relieved laugh bubbled from inside Beth. "That's perfectly okay. I think we just found your project for the fair."

❊

Zach paused in the doorway of the kitchen. Beth and Jessa were talking, motioning toward several sheets of paper spread out on the table. Jessa's face shone with an excitement Zach hadn't seen since her mother's death.

"I take it y'all have come up with an idea."

Beth's broad grin lit the room brighter than any lightbulb ever could. "Your daughter's very talented, Zach. She's designed a whole wardrobe for Barbie and her friends. Now all we have to do is sew them." She stacked up the papers and handed them to him.

Their hands brushed, but Zach didn't look at her. He couldn't bear to see whether she'd felt the electricity that jumped between them. Because it didn't matter. Staring down at Jessa's drawings, seeing the promise there, he was reminded again that his life was not his own.

"Dad?" He glanced up from the drawings in time to catch Jessa's worried expression back on her face. "Don't you like them?"

"Like them? Honey, I love them. I knew you could draw, but these are excellent." He reached over and enveloped his daughter in a hug. As he ruffled her hair, he avoided meeting Beth's gaze. "Is this it for today?"

"Yes, when Lacey calls tonight, I'll get permission to raid her scrap trunk, and tomorrow after school we can get started." She smiled softly. "Will that be okay, Zach?"

"Yes, but don't forget Cassidy and Drew have rehearsal tomorrow. So it'll have to be after that. Will that be good for you?"

"Sure. There's always a chance I might have to work, but we'll do what we can."

"Sounds good. Thanks, Beth. We really appreciate it." He gently propelled Jessa toward the door, but she suddenly broke lose from his hold, ran over to Beth, and threw her arms around her waist.

"Thanks, Miss Beth. You're the best!"

Zach's heart seconded his daughter's statement, but he kept his mouth shut and tried to push the errant thought from his mind.

Chapter 6

Come on, folks, bring your babies over and line up according to their number." Beth cringed as Mrs. Duncan's nasally voice screeched through the bright yellow megaphone.

"Looks like we're not late after all, Drew," Beth murmured. She dropped a kiss on the baby's head and headed toward the rapidly forming line.

"This is our last run-through before next Saturday afternoon." The loud voice resonated across the group.

"Yep. We'd better get it right this time, you little sweetie." Beth continued the one-way conversation with her nephew as her gaze scanned the small crowd for Zach.

A deep voice spoke in her ear. "That's right, and I've heard if the poor little things so much as drool the wrong way up on stage, they're out of here."

Beth swung around to face Zach. He rewarded her with a perfectly straight face, then wiggled one eyebrow outrageously. Just as she had a hundred times before when she was young, she dissolved into laughter.

"You don't believe me?" His incredulous tone made her laugh harder. He chucked Drew's chin. "Just watch and see, big guy. One wrong burp and out come the pageant police to take you away."

"Zach! Shame on you." She fought away the lingering traces of laughter and regarded him solemnly. "You'll scare him and Cassidy too. I can't believe you would say something like that." She waited for the first flash of uncertainty in his eyes, then she wiggled her eyebrow at him.

The surprise on his face was worth all the months she'd spent practicing back in junior high. She remembered how, after years of envying Zach's talented eyebrow, she'd finally perfected the technique right around the time he'd started ignoring her. Who would have believed she'd be using it on him fifteen years later?

"I'm impressed, Bethie. You've been trying since second grade to master that."

"I actually learned it in junior high. I just never had a chance to show it to you."

"Oh."

She watched his mind process her statement, then his eyes widened.

"That misunderstanding knocked us out of a lot, didn't it?"

Before she could answer, Mrs. Duncan spoke through her megaphone again. "Mr. Gaines! You're out of order. Cassidy's number is fifteen. You need to move three places back."

Zach half-saluted with a charming grin. He winked at Beth and took his rightful place.

As she waited for Drew's turn, Beth reflected on what Zach

had said about their youthful misunderstanding. They needed to talk. She thought she had a pretty good idea why he didn't want to get involved with her. Unfortunately there wasn't much she could do to relieve his apprehension. Zach needed a wife who would stay home and care for his children. Beth knew as well as he did she wasn't cut out to be a mother. She was married to her career in a way, and the last thing she needed were children who depended on her. As two grown adults, they would surely be able to salvage a friendship out of the attraction between them without jeopardizing their other commitments. Surely.

❋

"I'm going to drop you off while I run out to the hardware store, okay?" Zach asked Jessa as he pulled into Rob and Lacey's driveway.

"Sure. Want me to call your cell phone when we get done?"

"Yeah, oh, wait. . ." He looked down at the empty spot in the seat beside him. "I left it at the house. How about I just come back in a couple of hours?"

"Great. I'll tell Aunt Beth. Oops. I mean Miss Beth." Jessa tossed him an impish grin, opened her door, and scooted out, lugging her backpack full of who-knows-what behind her. Zach had never figured out why kids took those things everywhere. But he'd learned long ago not to question it.

"Be good."

"Always."

As he pulled out onto the street, Zach scolded himself for not facing Beth. Sometimes it was just too tiring. He'd lain awake last night wondering if there was some way to work it out. Could Beth move to a travel agency here? Could he uproot the children from Prairie Center and the house that had been in his family for generations and move to Atlanta? If he did, and he cringed at the thought of putting his children's needs behind his own, would it do any good? Could she provide the twins and Cass with any kind of motherly love? Hadn't she talked about how busy her work kept her?

The questions swirled around in his head as he drove to the hardware store and ambled aimlessly up and down the aisles. Strange as it might have seemed, this was where he'd come up with some of his best columns. The smell of lumber mingled with a slightly greasy, but not unpleasant odor usually kicked his brain into hyper drive. But not this evening. The only epiphany he'd had was a very unwelcome one. He was in love with Beth Whitrock.

❋

When Zach pulled into the driveway, Jessa was sitting in the swing. The forlorn tilt of her shoulders and the backpack dragging in the dirt with each half-hearted attempt to swing hinted all was not well. As soon as he could get parked, he jumped out and ran over to her.

"Jess?" He stopped short at the tears streaking down his daughter's red cheeks. "What happened?"

"Miss Beth didn't have time to work with me today. I tried to do it myself, but I messed it all up."

"Didn't have time? Why not?"

"She had to work."

"She left you here by yourself?" Puzzlement escalated to anger, not calming much when reason reminded him that Beth didn't have a workplace here.

"No, she had to work online. She said she tried to call, but we were already on our way here." Jessa wiped her tears with her sleeve, and Zach's heart constricted. Another wave of fury washed over him.

"Come on, Jess. Let's go straighten this out."

"I just want to go home. She's too busy to talk to us anyway."

Zach cast one more glance at the house as they made their way to the car. His fears had been right on target. He'd known better than to trust her with his children's hearts. "Fine. We have to pick up Cassidy and Jeremy from Aunt Leona's, then we'll all go to McDonalds. How about it?"

"I guess." She hid behind her curtain of brown hair so he couldn't read her expression, but the dejection in her voice kept the flames of anger burning inside him.

How could he have been so wrong? He'd known Beth would put her career before children. That's why he'd resolved to be no more than friends. But her sweet smile and soft beauty had caused him to think in terms of a future whether he'd intended to or not. And now Jessa was paying the price.

Somehow he made it through a Happy Meal supper. Jessa shook off her disappointment, and by the end of the meal, she was laughing and talking as if nothing had happened. Unfortunately, he wouldn't forget so soon.

Cassidy was asleep by the time he eased the vehicle into his own driveway. A little red car sat in his normal parking place, so he pulled over to the side and killed the engine. Beth jumped out of the red car and ran toward them.

"Jessa! I've been worried sick." Tears streaked down her face, and even in the moonlight, the black tracks of mascara made it obvious they weren't the first ones she'd shed. "I was about to call the police."

"The police?" Zach echoed her words.

"Yes, the police. She went out to sit in the swing, and I was checking on her every little bit. But when I looked and she was gone, I didn't know what had happened."

"This isn't Atlanta, Beth. Surely you knew I'd picked her up." Zach admired his own restraint for not mentioning that she'd deserted his daughter.

"You think bad things don't happen in small towns too?" she snapped. "You're living in a dream world. And apparently I was too, because I never dreamed you would pick her up and leave without coming in to tell me." Drawing in a deep shuddering breath, she turned to Jessa. "I'm just glad you're all right."

"Jeremy, you and Jessa run on in while I talk to Miss Beth." Zach strove for an even tone. The last thing he wanted was to cause his kids more distress. "I'll bring Cass in a little while. She's sleeping pretty soundly."

"So is Drew," Jeremy remarked as he passed the little red car.

"Yes, he went to sleep on the way over here," Beth explained. "With Hannah at her friend's house tonight, the backseat was boring, I guess."

Zach waited until the front door closed behind the twins before he spoke. "Beth, I don't understand you. I knew your career was important, but to break a little girl's heart over it. . ."

"Break her heart?" Beth's eyebrows knitted together under her curly bangs. "Jessa's? Zach, I told—"

"Told her what? That you were too busy for her? Let me tell you something, Beth." His voice automatically rose, and mindful of the children asleep in the cars beside them, he fought to bring it back down to conversational level. "She's had enough of that to last a lifetime. And I don't intend for it to ever happen again. Not on my watch."

Beth opened her mouth, but Zach wanted to get it all said before he lost his nerve, so he went on before she had a chance to speak. "You're just like Claire." He ran his hand through his hair and stared at the woman in front of him. "Her work always came first. . .and second. . .and third, for that matter. We were somewhere down the list pretty far, just like we are with you." He looked away as the anger that had flared in her gaze faded to hurt. Anxious to evade the pain evident in her eyes, he stared through the murky darkness at the bright windows of his house. "The difference is Claire had committed to us. You haven't."

As his own words sunk in, he saw their truth. "Don't feel bad, Bethie." He reached out and wiped away a tear that trickled down her cheek, but she pushed his hand away. "I allowed my feelings for you to cloud my good judgment. You never claimed to be anything different than what you are."

Her tears continued to fall as she stared at him as if disbelieving, and for a second, he had to physically restrain himself from taking her in his arms. "I'd better take Cassidy in and let you get Drew on home." His feet felt like they had taken root as he turned and walked to his car to get Cassidy.

He thought he heard a whispered "Good-bye, Zach," but when he'd retrieved the sleeping baby from her seat, Beth was in her car. He snuggled Cass in his arms, breathing comfort from her soft curls and drawing strength from her dependency on him.

Someday this night would be nothing more to him than the night he'd proved his love for his children by putting them ahead of his own needs. But looking up at the full moon as Beth's car shot down the driveway, he acknowledged that right now it felt like the night his heart had shattered into a million pieces.

Chapter 7

Beth swiped at her tears with the back of her hand and glared in the rearview mirror at the man silhouetted in the moonlight. How could she have thought she was falling in love with such a jerk?

She'd felt awful when Bob had insisted she close the Wakasaki deal this evening, but it wasn't like she hadn't warned Zach and Jessa that she might have to work. Zach had conveniently forgotten that, though, choosing to paint her as a heartless career-driven monster.

Beth gasped. At first she'd just been so angry at Zach's criticism, but as she maneuvered her car down the familiar road on automatic pilot, the impact of his words soaked into her heart. Had his wife really been like that? Had Claire cared more about her job than she did her children and husband?

Her anger waned some at the thought of what Zach must be going through if that were the case. Even though he'd hurt her feelings by being such a jerk, she couldn't keep from admiring a man who would choose his children's welfare over a woman he obviously cared about. Or were those feelings one-sided? Either way, Zach was right. They were better left unexplored.

Beth turned the vehicle into her sister's driveway and killed the motor. A quick glance at Drew showed the baby was still sleeping soundly. She rested her forehead on the steering wheel. Was it just this morning she had been thinking she might not make a bad mom? Hannah seemed to love and respect her, and even Drew had grown accustomed to having her around. She shared an easy rapport with Zach's kids, and the times they had all been together had been fun. But this episode with Jessa had caught her off guard. Was that what being a mom was about? Letting the child call the shots?

She raised her head and leaned back in her seat. Drew was probably down for the night, and the idea of going into that big empty house held no appeal. She had always enjoyed her solitary life, valuing the peace and quiet; but after a couple weeks in Prairie Center, she'd come to love the presence of active children.

What would it be like when she went back to Atlanta? Overwhelmed by the thought, she lowered her forehead to the steering wheel again and let the tears flow unchecked.

❋

As Zach stood in Rob's driveway watching the morning dew glisten on the freshly mowed grass, he thought of the tears sparkling in Beth's green eyes when she'd left his house the night before. Those eyes had haunted his dreams, culminating in a restless night. When he awoke, tired and guilt-ridden, he'd known where he was supposed to be.

When he'd gone into the house last night, after watching Beth drive away, Jessa had approached him.

"Are you mad at Miss Beth, Daddy?"

"Well, no, not mad, exactly, but a little disappointed that she hurt your feelings." He'd reached out and tweaked her hair, hoping to wipe the serious expression from her face.

Still solemn, she'd perched on his chair arm. "I guess it really wasn't her fault. Partly I was just mad because Hannah went to spend the night with Amy, and I didn't have anybody to play with. Then I tried to make the clothes by myself and messed them up." She put on her grown-up voice. "But you know, Dad, Miss Beth did tell us she might have to work. Remember?"

At his daughter's words he had suddenly remembered Beth saying, "I might have to work, but we'll do what we can." Then he recalled during his tirade, she'd said, "But, I told—" and he'd cut her off.

"Yes, Honey, I do remember. . .now. I owe Miss Beth an apology, don't I?"

Jessa had kissed him on the cheek and scurried off to bed, but unfortunately, Zach hadn't had a restful moment since.

He ambled up the stone path that led to the front door. It occurred to him suddenly that with Hannah sleeping over at a friend's house, Beth might have decided to sleep in. Or at least let Drew. He pecked tentatively on the bright red door. Realizing the chances of her hearing the light tap were minimal, he raised his fist to knock again. The door opened, and he pulled back his hand just in time to keep from hitting Beth in the face.

"Beth, I'm so sorry."

"That's okay. You didn't hit me."

The eyes from his dreams looked a little bleary and maybe slightly red, but they weren't staring at him with accusation like he'd expected. "No, I didn't mean that. I mean I'm sorry about last night. I can't believe how I treated you." He wiped his feet on the doormat as he struggled for the right words, then looked back up at her. "I wouldn't blame you if you didn't even let me in."

She smiled. "I guess I mishandled the situation with Jessa, Zach." She opened the door wider and motioned him in. "In one way you were right. I'm not mother material."

"How do you know?" He trailed behind her to the kitchen. When she slid onto a stool, he followed suit.

She raised her eyebrow, then shrugged. "You have to ask? Isn't it obvious?"

Suddenly, he wasn't so sure. "Humor me."

"Okay, I will." She poured him a cup of coffee to match the steaming one in front of her and slid it across the slick counter. She lifted her hand and began to name the reasons, counting them off on her fingers. "Number one, I've never been good with kids. Even when we were teenagers, Lacey was the babysitter, not me." She grimaced as if recalling a baby-sitting job gone bad. "Number two, I'm set in my ways. I've lived alone all these years, and my cream-colored sofa wouldn't last one day in your house." Her gaze burned into his, and he watched her eyes widen as she realized the implication of what she'd just said.

"We could always have it reupholstered." He wondered if she could see how flimsy her reasons were. Inching his stool toward her, he didn't stop until their hands were almost touching. Her hair, a wild array of curls, was brushing his shoulder. He reached out and loosely wrapped a ringlet around his finger.

"I hear vinyl is fairly durable."

"That's a definite possibility."

Her lips curved into a soft smile, and she didn't avert her gaze from his. Nor did she pull away when he lowered his mouth to hers. Sweet delight instantly swirled around him, an almost tangible presence. Kissing Beth was like coming home, only better. Every dream he'd ever had of what love could be culminated in those few precious moments.

A shrill beeping noise seemed to erupt in his ear, and he jerked back, staring at Beth in dismay. Had he set off her personal alarm? Had she pushed the panic button? Literally?

"That would be reason number three," she mumbled and jumped from the stool as the annoying noise continued. "Beeper," she breathed through gritted teeth, fumbling with the buttons on the little black box attached to the belt of her jeans. She wouldn't meet his gaze, and Zach watched her respond to the summons by automatically turning to pick up the phone. His heart sank.

You can take the girl out of the career, but you can't take the career out of the girl, he thought. As she stood with her back to him, speaking to Bob on the phone, Zach slipped out of the room and quietly left the house.

❇

"Bob, I'll call you back, okay?" Beth cringed as her boss went on with his latest tirade as if he hadn't heard her. Now that her heartbeat had returned to somewhat normal, she turned to face Zach, desperately hoping to find him wiggling his eyebrow at her. The empty room filled her with dismay.

She could have waited to respond to Bob's page. She'd only

called Bob back immediately to buy herself some time before acknowledging the earth-shaking kiss. Now her foolish action had bought her plenty of time. All the time in the world, as a matter of fact.

Suddenly, she couldn't take her boss another second. She interrupted him midsentence. "Sorry, Bob, I really have to go." She mashed the button without waiting for a reply.

Just in case, she rushed out the front door. Her spirits lifted some when she saw Zach's car still parked in the driveway, then took a nosedive when she saw him sitting in the swing, head bowed. The same coward who had turned away from him earlier wanted to slip back inside and close the door, but grateful for a second chance, Beth forged on. She eased onto the swing beside him and waited until he raised his head.

The hint of tears in his eyes tore her heart out, and all the old feelings of unworthiness came rushing back. "I guess you were praying."

"Yes." He stared out at the yard as if fascinated by the occasional dandelion. "I wanted to leave, but I think we've done enough running, Beth. Don't you?"

She nodded and silently offered a prayer of her own for strength. "It's not going to work, is it?"

He shook his head. "I don't see how it can." He stood and offered her a hand, then pulled her to her feet.

"As long as we agree, do you think we can be friends?" Her voice trembled. She looked down at the hand that was still holding hers and suddenly couldn't bear the thought of going back to the years of pretending each other didn't exist.

"I'll be honest. If you lived here, probably not, but you'll be going back to Atlanta soon." Zach smiled, but it didn't quite reach his eyes. "Who knows? Maybe our relationship will be much better long distance."

She cringed at his evaluation and gently removed her hand from his grasp. She started to turn toward the door, but he stopped her.

"Bethie. . ." His voice was husky, and she knew his emotions were running as strong as hers. "About the trip to the fair with the kids Friday night. . . We can still do that, can't we?" His green eyes, though dry, seemed filled with sorrow.

Her heart cringed at the realization that this was her last chance to really be with him before she went back to Atlanta. She nodded, not trusting her voice to come out around the lump in her throat.

"I'll bring Jess by later to work on her project. Okay?"

She nodded again and quickly slipped into the house before the tears began to fall.

Chapter 8

Jessa pulled the miniature evening gown from the sewing machine. With a broad grin, she held up the tiny dress for Beth to inspect.

"Oh, Jess! That's perfect. You've finished the last one, and they all look just like your sketches." Beth bent down and gave the girl a quick squeeze.

Over the last few days, there had been times both of them had thought they'd never get the clothes done in time. But with each sewing session, Jessa's skill had improved, and along with each victory had come an increase in her self-confidence.

"Thanks, Aunt Beth." Jessa rose from her chair and hugged Beth around the waist. "I couldn't have done it without you."

Beth held the child close and wondered for the tenth time if she was doing the right thing going back to Atlanta on Sunday. Maybe she should quit her job, give up her career, and beg Zach to marry her. Then do what? All she'd ever wanted was to be a travel agent. Without her career, who would she even be?

What about when the new wore off and she was left at home cooking and cleaning and wiping runny noses while Zach jetted off to accept awards for his brilliant syndicated column? Who would be happy then?

"Hey! Don't you be stealing all my hugs." Zach's deep voice boomed through the sewing room. Beth forced her feet to resist running into his open arms, then felt her face grow hot when Jessa released her and ran to hug her dad.

Beth did what she'd always done when flustered. She resorted to silliness. "I'll have you know I didn't steal that hug," she retorted. "It was given freely." The knowing look in Zach's gaze reminded her that he hadn't forgotten how she dealt with embarrassment.

"Jess, we'd better get out of Miss Beth's hair. Besides, we don't want to be late getting this project in at the fair. Jeremy and Cass are playing outside, but the rabbits are in the car." In spite of his words earlier on the porch about not running away anymore, Beth knew Zach too and recognized his evasion tactics.

"Aw. . . all right." Jessa came over for one more hug. "Bye, Aunt Beth, we'll see you Friday night at the fair." She looked at her dad. "I asked her if I could call her Aunt Beth, and she said yes."

Zach nodded, but under his scrutiny, Beth felt her face grow hotter. Surely he didn't think she was encouraging his daughter to grow close to her, knowing she'd be leaving. There was no denying the bond that had developed between her and Jessa the last few days. And when Jessa had asked to call her Aunt Beth, she hadn't felt she had a choice.

She tousled Jessa's hair and quickly helped her gather her things. As soon as everything was in the bag, Zach propelled the youngster to the door. "Thanks, Beth." He tossed the words over his shoulder as if afraid to linger.

Considering her wild thoughts a few moments before about begging him to marry her, maybe he was a wise man to beat a hasty retreat. Her growing relationship with Jessa had shown her one thing for sure. Jessa needed a full-time mom, and she was sure Jeremy and Cassidy did, as well. Determined to do the right thing, she paused in the foyer. *Dear God, please find those children a mother who can meet their needs and be a wonderful wife for Zach too.*

Resolutely ignoring the knife of jealousy twisting in her stomach, she sank down to the hardwood floor and continued to pray.

❈

"Dad, do you think Bugs and Freckles will win a blue ribbon?"

Startled, Zach looked up into Jeremy's solemn face. The conversation he'd overheard in the garage came back to him. "I don't know." Suddenly Zach remembered something his own father had told him when he was young. "Jess!" he called softly, being careful not to wake Cassidy, who was asleep on his lap. "Come in here for a minute."

Jessa bounded into the room, and he could see her grin hadn't dimmed since they'd left Beth. He motioned both twins to sit on the sofa. "Let's talk about blue ribbons." He ran his hand through his hair, and as always when he talked to his kids about something important, he breathed a silent prayer for guidance. "If you do win, what will that mean?"

The twins looked at each other, and finally Jessa answered slowly. "That my project is the best?"

"Okay. The best in whose eyes?"

"The judges." Jeremy piped in. He looked relieved to hear an easy question.

"That's right. Now, what happens if you get a different judge? One who thinks that rabbits with freckles are disgusting?"

Jeremy's face fell. "Then I'd lose."

Zach turned to his daughter. "Or what if you get one who thinks doll clothes are lame, no matter how well designed they are?"

Jessa squinted at him, and he could almost see her brain working. "My project wouldn't get a blue ribbon, either."

"Jer, do you like your rabbits? Do you think they're beautiful?"

"Sure." Jeremy narrowed his eyes. "Why? Don't you?"

"Oh, definitely. I do." He offered Jeremy a reassuring smile and addressed his daughter. "Jessa, what about your doll clothes? Do you like them?"

"Yes, Sir. I love them. They're the best thing I've ever made."

"I think so too, Honey." Zach shifted Cassidy's weight a little so he could lean toward the twins. "But what if the judges don't? Does that mean you and I are wrong?"

"No way! It just means that everything's not for everybody."

"Exactly. And any time we enter any kind of contest, unless God is the judge, we can't be sure of a perfect decision. Right?"

"Right!" the twins chorused.

"Now then, what if you don't win blue ribbons?"

Jeremy paused and twisted his lips in thought. "I'll be sad. But I'll still know Freckles and Bugs are great, with or without a ribbon."

"Yeah, and I'll know I did the best I could do on the doll clothes." Jessa grinned and the impish twinkle in her eyes warned

Zach right before she delivered the zinger. "And that the judges have no taste." She started laughing. "Just kidding, Dad."

"Come here, you two." He motioned them to him and hugged them, along with the sleeping Cassidy. "Just remember, everyone is different, and even the judges are individuals. You can't force someone to like something just because you do."

As the twins scurried up the stairs to bed, Zach reflected on his own words of wisdom. He loved staying home with the kids and writing his column from there. Had he been guilty of trying to force Beth into being what he wanted? Was that why he got so angry when her job took precedence?

God, am I wrong? Is my stubborn way of looking at things causing me to lose the woman I love? Or am I right to want someone who isn't like Claire? Please help me figure this out because I'm afraid I'm messing it up so badly on my own, Lord.

Zach slowly stood, cradling the sleeping baby in his arms, and carried her up to bed. In his own bed, he tossed and turned, spending every waking moment wrestling with hard decisions. Finally, as the morning sun streaked a sliver of light across the horizon, he dozed off, still uncertain of the future.

Chapter 9

The night sky glowed with swirling lights, and carousel music floated through the air, easily heard from one end of the fairgrounds to the other. The incredible aroma of cotton candy and corn dogs wafted to Beth on the crisp autumn breeze.

She paused at the beginning of the midway for a moment and closed her eyes. Though she still held tight to Drew's stroller and she knew Hannah was beside her, suddenly she was transported back in time to a simpler day.

Two kids, about twelve years old, stood side by side in this exact spot.

"C'mon, Bethie," the boy called. "Race you to the Ferris wheel."

"Last one there is a rotten egg," she replied, taking off before she finished speaking.

"Hey!" Behind her, Zach's voice was filled with indignation.

She stopped at the Ferris wheel line, out of breath, but giggling.

"You were supposed to wait until I said go," he complained

as he tugged on her braid.

She started to respond, but her glance caught the huge Ferris wheel. This one was twice as big as last year's. It looked like it touched the moon. Her knees felt like rubber. "Uh, Zach?"

"Yeah?" He too was staring at the humongous wheel, but instead of fear, she saw deep excitement shining in his eyes. "This is going to be great, isn't it?"

"I'm not so sure. . . ." She cringed. Would he make fun of her for being scared? Call her a baby? He never had, but they were almost teenagers now. They weren't kids anymore.

"You scared?"

With relief, she recognized his tone. Instead of teasing, it was the voice she'd heard him use last year with his dog Sugar, when Sugar'd gotten a bone caught in her tooth.

Beth nodded, unable to speak around the lump in her throat.

"Don't be scared." His soothing voice eased the knot in her stomach some, but she was still grateful she hadn't eaten yet. "You can squeeze my arm real tight if you need to. I won't let anything bad happen to you."

"Promise?" She peered under her sweaty bangs up to the top of the ride, then back into Zach's confident blue eyes.

"Promise. C'mon, Bethie, some stupid old Ferris wheel can't beat us. Together we can do anything." He took her hand and led her into the waiting seat.

"C'mon, Aunt Beth!" Hannah tugged on her arm, bringing her back to the present with a jolt. "Let's go find Jessa and them."

Beth nodded absently and pushed the stroller over the lumpy grass. Every step was another memory, but none as clear as the one with the Ferris wheel. Even as they walked, she remembered what a wonderful ride that had been.

At first she'd squeezed Zach's arm tight, but he'd only smiled and said, "It'll be fun." Zach had been right. With him beside her, she'd been able to relax and enjoy the amazing view and the spinning sensation. She'd only ridden a Ferris wheel two other times—the years she was thirteen and fourteen. Both times, Zach Gaines had ridden with her. After they drifted apart, the fear came back, and she hadn't braved it anymore.

❄

Zach stared up at the Ferris wheel and memories rushed over him like cool water. He felt, rather than saw, someone's gaze on him, and when he looked back at the crowd, Beth's face was the first thing he saw. She nodded across the way and offered a small bittersweet smile. Although no words were exchanged, he knew exactly what she was referring to. How simple life had been back then.

Before he could move, the twins had scampered across the midway. As he approached, pushing Cassidy's stroller, Jessa and Hannah were giggling and chattering. Jeremy had dropped down to his knees to play with Drew. All the noise and commotion receded, and it was like he and Beth were all alone in a long-ago memory. He opened his mouth to speak, but the kids swarmed in, effectively breaking the mood.

"What can we do first?"

"Can we ride the Octopus?"

"Can we go look at the animals?"

"I want to go see the exhibits."

"Whoa." He held up a hand. "One at a time." He raised his

eyebrows and in a mock pleading tone asked Beth, "Fair lady, can you come up with a plan for us?"

Though his "fair" lady pun went over the kids' heads, as usual Beth appreciated his attempt at humor and chuckled. "How about we do the rides first? Then we'll eat; after that we'll look at the exhibits and they'll be done with the judging."

"Great!"

"Sounds super, Aunt Beth!"

"Octopus first!"

The next two hours flew by as the children sprinted from ride to ride. Zach shepherded the older kids, while Beth stayed with Cassidy and Drew at the kiddie rides. When they all met back together, they finished with the carousel. Zach couldn't help but laugh when Beth ended up having to ride with Drew. Instead of looking bored, like the other adults on the ride, she waved and grinned with more excitement than the kids.

The happy group hurriedly ate barbecue sandwiches and ended up getting to the exhibit halls before the judging was complete. They made a quick run through to admire Jessa's doll clothes and Hannah's jelly.

When they approached the table with the fabric exhibits, a young woman in tattered clothing stood in front of them. She held the hand of a scrawny bedraggled little girl, who stared in apparent wonder at all the pretty things. Zach watched sadly as the little girl's eyes lit up when she saw the doll clothes Jessa had made.

"Oh, Mama!" Her thin voice resounded in the metal building. "Look. My Sarah would look so beautiful in these clothes, wouldn't she?"

Her mother nodded sadly but tugged the little girl on. "Yes, Marley, she would. But Sarah's going to have to be happy with her one dress until Mommy finds a job. Okay, Honey?"

Marley pulled away and walked the few feet back to the clothes. Her mother, impatient, hurried back to get her. "What are you doing now?"

"I'm remembering what they look like so I can tell Sarah about them."

Zach's hand went instinctively to his wallet, his desire to help overwhelming. But he paused in midmovement when Jessa burst forward.

"Wait!" she called to Marley and her mother.

Tears swelled at the corners of Zach's eyes as his daughter reached toward the doll clothes. She picked up one outfit, then two. Suddenly, she swooped them all up in her arms and stuffed them in the small box under the table. With the box in her arms, she walked forward to meet the surprised little girl and her equally astounded mother. "Here. These are for Sarah."

"Oh, Honey, you can't mean that," Marley's mom protested.

The little girl dropped down on her knees, the box in front of her, reverently examining the clothes. She gazed up at Jessa, her eyes shining brightly. "You must be an angel."

"Thank you." Marley's mom smiled at Jessa and nodded at Zach and Beth.

"You're welcome," Jessa said and walked back to meet the others. She picked up her sketchpad and handed it to Beth, then plucked Zach's pen from his shirt pocket.

With a grace and dignity that astonished him, the nine year old bent over the score sheet that had been placed beside each exhibit and marked a big X in the box that said "Exhibit withdrawn by artist."

He noticed Hannah and Jeremy both hugged her when she rejoined the group, and then the three older kids led the way to the animal barn.

"Wow." Beth's soft voice was meant for his ears only. "You must be one proud papa."

"Never been prouder."

"You've done a great job, Zach." The longing in her voice pulled at his heartstrings, and he wondered why God hadn't seen fit for Beth to marry and have children.

"God's been beside me every step of the way."

"Jessa's actions tonight make that obvious," Beth replied, then stopped. "Hey, can you go on, and I'll meet you at the rabbits? There's something I need to do."

"Sure."

As she returned to the exhibit building, he pushed Cassidy's stroller and caught up with the other kids.

"Want to go straight to the rabbits, Son?" he called to Jeremy.

"Nah, let's just look at all of them as we go. Maybe they'll be done with the judging by then."

Zach couldn't help but notice that Jeremy and Hannah flanked Jessa on either side as if to offer support in her great sacrifice. She didn't seem upset, though, and his heart expanded at the realization.

Beth and Drew reappeared just as the group reached Freckles and Bugs.

"All right!" Jeremy punched his fist in the air as he saw the blue ribbons adorning both cages. "Look, Jess, one for each of us."

"Thanks, Jer." Jessa grinned at her brother, then gave in to her teasing nature. "I guess I deserve one of them, considering I have to feed and water them half the time when you forget."

"She reminds me of you." Beth smiled at Zach.

"Hey! Tonight I'll take that as a compliment."

"Come on, y'all. Let's go see how Hannah's jelly did." Jessa grabbed Hannah's arm, and they skipped back to the exhibit hall.

Hannah's jelly had a blue ribbon too. "Guess I'll have to share mine with Aunt Beth since she helped me make it."

"You can keep the blue ribbon, Honey. Your aunt Beth and I'll just eat the jelly." As soon as the words were out of his mouth, Zach realized their implied intimacy. Thoughts of shared breakfasts—and lunches and suppers, for that matter—danced through his mind. He quickly glanced at Beth, and her blush said the remark hadn't gone unnoticed. Friendship was proving to be harder than he'd thought.

"Let's go look at the sewing projects," Jessa suggested, "and see who got lucky by me withdrawing."

Zach watched the twins share a secret look when Beth commented on a beautiful red-and-yellow quilt sporting a blue ribbon. So that was Chelsea's quilt. It wasn't any better than Jessa's doll clothes. He smothered a rueful grin. He'd better take a clue from his children. Winning wasn't everything.

"I was hoping we could look at the artwork," Beth mentioned as they started to leave the building. She led them over to the tables lined with sculptures, paintings, and drawings. "Look at this one, y'all."

Jessa gasped as she recognized her sketchpad. Draped across it were two blue ribbons. A handwritten note on the score pad asserted, "The clothes that went with these sketches deserved a ribbon too, so even though they are gone, their worth remains."

"How?" Jessa stared in astonishment from the ribbons back to Zach, Beth, and the kids.

"Ask her." Zach jerked a thumb toward Beth. He realized now where she'd disappeared to on the way to the animals. He should have noticed the sketchpad was missing.

Jessa hugged Beth tightly, and Hannah quickly joined the embrace. Even Jeremy tentatively leaned in with one arm around her waist. Zach wasn't surprised to see tears in his childhood friend's eyes. Only one more day and she'd be leaving this all behind. . .going back to her cream-colored sofa and quiet moments, void of children's hugs and sticky kisses. *Dear Lord, is that what she really wants?*

Chapter 10

Bob, you don't understand. I have a commitment tonight. One I can't break."

"More important than your commitment to me? To your job?" her boss growled.

Beth cringed, but she knew she had to hold firm. Bob was used to her not having a life, but just now that wasn't the case. "The kids are counting on me."

"Well, which is it going to be, Beth?" There was no mistaking the ultimatum in his voice. "Your job or the kids?"

"You're being unreasonable. This could easily wait until tomorrow. Or even Monday, when I'm back in the office."

"I want an answer, Beth. Either you're going to handle this request tonight, or you're fired. Do you hear me?"

Beth figured every person in the state of Kansas could probably hear him. But she didn't answer quickly, leaving the question hanging in the air while she silently prayed.

Lord, give me a soft answer, but let me be in accordance with Your will for my life.

"Beth! Give me your answer. Now!"

"I appreciate all you've done for me, Bob, but tonight I'll be keeping a prior commitment." She wanted so badly to yell back, but that she knew only God could have given her that calm voice.

"That does it! You're fired!" His breathing was so loud she could hear it over the phone. "And don't be expecting a good reference from me, either."

"Would you like for me to help you train someone?"

"I'd like for you to pack up your things and take your ungrateful self somewhere else. Maybe you can get a job flipping burgers."

Beth bit her lip, praying constantly she wouldn't allow herself to be goaded into losing her temper. "Either I'll pick up my things or arrange for it to be done. You take care of yourself. Good night." Her hands were trembling when she hung up, and she was surprised that a sense of relief warred with the sense of loss she'd expected to feel. Bob had been difficult at best, impossible at worst, and she knew she didn't have to put up with that in a job. Now that it was over, she wondered why she hadn't put her foot down long ago.

❊

Cassidy's lower lip trembled, and tears pooled in her blue eyes. She slipped her hand in Beth's. "You walk me?"

Zach stiffened as Beth cast him a helpless glance. Everyone who knew her was aware of Beth's stage fright. Hannah had just finished walking Drew across the stage.

Beth nodded. "Sure, Honey. I'll walk with you." She straightened her shoulders. "After all, there's not more than a couple of hundred people out there watching. That's nothing to be afraid of." Her face grew paler as she spoke. Remembering how she'd almost fainted while performing in the seventh-grade play, Zach wondered how she would make it across the stage.

"I'll do it, Cass. Miss Beth doesn't have to."

"Uh-huh." Cassidy nodded emphatically. "She said she would." The little girl tightened her grip on Beth's hand just as her number was called.

"Here goes nothing," Beth muttered to Zach and eased her way up the stairs, holding Cassidy's hand. Beth's red curls bounced, and for an instant, Zach could imagine her as a beauty pageant contestant, but her white face and tense smile proved she'd prefer to be behind the scenes rather than in the spotlight. An admirable trait for a mother. Zach looked around. Where had that thought come from?

As an obviously terrified Beth maneuvered across the stage with a beaming Cassidy in tow, Zach realized he was watching love in action. He'd seen the same thing numerous other times in the last few weeks, but he'd refused to acknowledge it. Had he been so wrapped up in the memory of Claire's selfish nature that he'd equated that with a woman having a career? He'd known Bethie most of her life, and there had never been a selfish bone in her body. Look what she'd put up with from him.

As Beth and Cassidy eased off the stage and joined Zach and the other children, Cassidy scampered in joyful circles. When Beth sank against him in relief, he instinctively put his arm around her. She looked up at him in surprise but didn't pull away. They stood in silence, the children milling around them, as the other contestants walked across the stage and the judges made their decision.

The three runners-up were called, and neither Drew nor Cassidy were mentioned. He started to let go of Beth so they could gather their things, but the announcer's voice rang out. "And the winner of this year's Prairie County Fair's Most Beautiful Baby Contest is. . .Cassidy Gaines!"

Zach laughed as Cass clapped her hands together in delight. Yes, his daughter was beautiful, but no more or less than all the other precious babies gathered there. He relinquished his hold on Beth when his toddler solemnly took her hand again and led her up on stage to collect the crown. He had a feeling this would be Cassidy's first and last crown. By next year, she'd be old enough to enter the preschool art category, so they wouldn't have to go through all of this in order for her to participate with the twins in the fair.

They—what an amazing word! A myriad of memories rushed through his mind. . .he and Beth as kids, always depending on each other; his broken teenaged heart when he thought she was ashamed of him; then all that he and the kids had been through since Claire's death; and like a soft answer from heaven, Beth once again entering his life. . .someone he could depend on. And fall in love with.

He desperately needed to talk to Beth alone, but as soon as she and Cassidy descended from the stage, the kids gathered around the triumphant toddler to see her crown. Zach edged closer to Beth and leaned to whisper in her ear, "That was a great thing you did—walking her across the stage. I know it was hard for you."

"Cassidy's very persuasive." Her green eyes sparkled.

"Hmm. . .hopefully it runs in the family." He smiled at the

puzzled expression on her face.

"Really?"

"Aw, Bethie. . ." Suddenly it was vitally important that he get this right. "I'm so sorry."

She opened her mouth as if to protest, but a plump blond woman came up to them with the kids close behind her. "Beth!"

"Jeanie! Great to see you!" She smiled at her sister's friend. "I've been meaning to call you, but the time has just flown by." They exchanged a quick hug.

"Hi, Zach. How does it feel to be the daddy of the most beautiful baby?" Jeanie grinned, and Beth remembered how much she'd always liked her.

Zach shrugged and smiled. "Ask any daddy around, and they can tell you."

They all laughed. Jeanie asked, "Rick and I were wondering if the kids could sit with us during the fireworks. Derek would have a great time with Jeremy there."

"Please, Dad. We'll watch Cassidy," Jessa pleaded.

"Please, Aunt Beth. I'll hold Drew." Hannah's eyes twinkled. "Since you're going back to Atlanta tomorrow, you and Uncle Zach could have some time to yourselves."

That little minx. She apparently still hadn't given up her matchmaking efforts, and from the looks of the grins on the twins' faces, she'd recruited them as well. As a matter of fact, even Jeanie looked a little too gleeful.

Beth took a deep breath. "I don't—"

"That sounds great," Zach interrupted.

"Great. Oh, rather than try to find y'all in the crowd, why don't you just pick the kids up at our house? Since we're just a block away, we'll walk on down when it's over." Without waiting for an answer, Jeanie quickly herded the children out to their seats.

Beth stared as Zach grabbed her hand and pulled her across the grassy midway. When he skidded to a stop, she looked up. The Ferris wheel. Some large things became smaller when one grew up. The Ferris wheel wasn't one of those things. Surely, he didn't. . . Surely, he wasn't. . .

She watched as Zach opened his wallet and handed the operator a green bill. When he returned, he took her hand. "C'mon, Bethie."

She pulled back. "I don't think so, Zach. Don't they close down the rides for the fireworks?"

"Yep. But he says, if we hurry, he'll get us up to a spectacular view before they begin." He gave her an appraising glance. "You scared?"

She nodded.

"You can even squeeze my arm if you need to." He leaned over, and his breath was warm against her ear as he whispered, "You're safe with me."

"Promise?"

"I promise. Together we can do anything." His blue eyes shone with confidence.

The Ferris wheel hadn't even started, and already her heart was doing flip-flops.

She allowed Zach to usher her onto the seat, but she closed her eyes tight and grabbed his arm as the operator started the big wheel, moving them slowly to the top of the world.

"Open your eyes."

Beth squeezed her eyes shut tighter and shook her head with a small giggle.

"I'm going to have to tickle you, if you don't."

Her eyes flew open. "You wouldn't dare!" The very idea of being tickled when she already felt so out of control was horrifying.

"Wouldn't I?" Zach held out his hands as if to tickle her, then smoothly slipped an arm around her shoulders.

Immediately her nerves settled. The crisp breeze was like a gentle caress on her face, and she reflected on how safe she really did feel with Zach. She relaxed against him, allowing the tension to seep from her body.

She looked over at Zach, expecting him to say something now that her eyes were open. He stared at the stars, perhaps searching for his own answers. She had to admit that in the back of her mind, ever since he'd taken her hand and pulled her to the Ferris wheel, she'd thought maybe he was going to ask her to stay in Prairie Center. If Zach asked her to be his wife and she accepted, that would be the end of her career. She couldn't have both. He'd made that clear.

She'd worked hard to get where she was in the business world, and there would always be a part of her that missed it, but weren't Zach and the children enough? How blessed could one person expect to be?

Her mind flitted to Proverbs, and she considered the virtuous woman described in chapter thirty-one. That woman had it all. . .children who blessed her, a husband who trusted her, and she bought and sold so that her family had plenty in the wintertime. Now, how could Beth convince Zach that she could keep her priorities straight if he would trust her to be a wife, mother, and career woman?

"Beth? The fireworks should start in a minute." Zach reached for her hand and lightly caressed it. "Like I started to say earlier, I'm really sorry for acting like a jerk."

"You didn't act like a jerk." Beth paused, then delivered one of Jessa's zingers. "At least not any more than usual." When Zach chuckled, she took his hand in both hers. "Seriously, Zach, you're just a man who puts the needs of his children first. There's absolutely nothing wrong with that."

"Since you brought that up, let me tell you a little bit about my children's needs."

Beth released his hand. She'd known he would have certain stipulations on her becoming the mother of his children—like her quitting work—but it had never occurred to her that he would have made a list. Now was as good a time as any to plead her case for having it all. She opened her mouth, but Zach silenced her with an upraised hand. She sighed and watched him count off on his fingers.

"First, they need supervision." A small explosion of red and blue lit up the sky, and Beth jumped, but Zach continued. "That's what is so great about me working at home. I'm there to keep an eye on them."

He held up another finger. "Secondly, they need nourishment, both physical and spiritual." His voice was very solemn as he continued. "I'm not a bad cook, if I do say so myself. We have a devotional almost every night. So with God's help, I've got that covered as well."

He reached out a hand to caress her face. She drew back

slightly, startled that he could go from such a businesslike listing of his children's needs to a look of such tenderness. A noisy outburst of color exploded in the sky, illuminating their faces. Was that a twinkle she saw in his eyes?

All thoughts left her mind as he leaned in and dropped a quick kiss on her mouth. She reached her hand up absently and touched where his lips had been a second before, then tried to concentrate on his words as he held up his finger.

"The third need is very important, Beth." He took her hand in his again. When he turned toward her, the Ferris wheel car shifted and rocked slightly. Beth gasped and grabbed his hand. When the movement stopped, he continued. "And it happens to be one that only you can handle. Jeremy, Jessa, and Cassidy. . .they need a mother's love." The twinkle in his eyes was unmistakable now. "And for that, you don't have to give up your career. All you have to do is be yourself."

"Oh, Zach. . ." Beth felt as if her heart would burst. "I quit my job today."

Zach tipped her chin and studied her face. "You didn't do that for me?"

She shook her head. "I would have, but in this case, Bob was just too demanding." She smiled at the man she'd grown to love so much. "I know there is a way to be a good wife and mother and at the same time have the career I love. It's just a matter of finding the right job."

He glanced out over the fairgrounds. "Prairie Center doesn't have a travel agency, you know."

She sighed. "I know." She would never uproot Zach and the children from Prairie Center, so maybe it just wasn't meant for her to be a travel agent.

Zach lifted her hand to his lips and kissed her fingertips. "My point is. . .we could use one."

She frowned in confusion. "What are you. . .?" Sudden clarity lit her mind. "Do you mean you think I should. . .? Her mouth dropped open, and she flung her arms around his neck, unmindful of the car swinging. She rested for a second there, then sat back and looked into Zach's eyes. "I know I can be there for you and the kids and still handle a business, but you have to know it too." She tenderly traced the outline of his precious face with her thumb. "Even though it would be hard for me, I could live without a career. But I'm not sure I could live without you and those wonderful kids of yours. I need you."

Zach captured her hand and pressed her thumb to his lips. "You also need your career. And how can I truly say I love you if I'm not willing to give you a chance to have it? Being a family is about fulfilling the needs of every member." Another blast of red, blue, green, and gold permeated the sky, adding color to his beautiful words.

"Oh, Zach, are you sure?"

He nodded. "God brought you back here for us, Bethie."

She smiled through tears. "And He brought me back for me too. He knew you were the only man for me."

With a sharp intake of breath, Zach pulled her close.

When Zach pulled away, Beth couldn't resist teasing him a little. "Can I take that as a proposal?"

"Well, I could always get down on one knee." He started forward, rocking the Ferris wheel car crazily.

Beth grabbed his arm and squeezed tightly. "Zach Gaines! Don't you dare!"

The mischievous glint left his eyes as he leaned toward her. He stopped when their lips were less than an inch apart. "Bethie, I'm so glad you came home."

"Me too—" Her last word was smothered as his mouth connected with hers in a kiss that put the magnificent firework finale to shame.

CHRISTINE LYNXWILER

Christine and her husband, Kevin, live in the foothills of the beautiful Ozark Mountains of their home state, Arkansas. They've been married for twenty years and have two daughters. In addition to writing, Christine runs their chiropractic office and homeschools their children.

She has always enjoyed writing and has written many skits for Ladies' Days and other church activities. Her first novella, "Beneath Heaven's Curtain, was included in *City Dreams*. She presently looks forward to the release of two **Heartsong Presents** in 2003.

Her hobbies include reading, kayaking, chatting with friends and family on the Internet, and spending time with both her and Kevin's close-knit families.

As far as Christine is concerned, autumn should always be accompanied by the tart taste of fresh-squeezed lemonade, the unforgettable aroma of corn dogs, and the dizzying spin of the Tilt-A-Whirl. *Prairie County Fair* rekindles many wonderful "fair" memories, and she hopes others enjoy the stroll down memory lane, as well.

She loves to hear from her readers. You may write her at Christine Lynxwiler, Author Relations, P.O. Box 719, Uhrichsville, OH 44683 or e-mail her at Christine_Writes@yahoo.com.

A Letter to Our Readers

Dear Readers:

In order that we might better contribute to your reading enjoyment, we would appreciate you taking a few minutes to respond to the following questions. When completed, please return to the following: Fiction Editor, Barbour Publishing, Inc., P.O. Box 719, Uhrichsville, OH 44683.

1. Did you enjoy reading *Prairie County Fair?*
   - ❑ Very much—I would like to see more books like this.
   - ❑ Moderately—I would have enjoyed it more if ________________

____

____

2. What influenced your decision to purchase this book? (Check those that apply.)
   - ❑ Cover ❑ Back cover copy ❑ Title ❑ Price
   - ❑ Friends ❑ Publicity ❑ Other

3. Which story was your favorite?
   - ❑ *After the Harvest* ❑ *Goodie Goodie*
   - ❑ *A Test of Faith* ❑ *A Change of Heart*

4. Please check your age range:
   - ❑ Under 18 ❑ 18–24 ❑ 25–34
   - ❑ 35–45 ❑ 46–55 ❑ Over 55

5. How many hours per week do you read? ________________

Name ________________________________

Occupation ________________________________

Address ________________________________

City ______________ State ________ Zip ________